S0-BZO-267

DISCARDED BY THE
URBANA FREE LIBRARY

URBANA FREE LIBRARY
(217-367-4057)

	DATE DUE	
DEC 14 2007		
MAY 2008		
JUL 2009		
AUG 11 2009		
NOV 2 0 2008		

OVER THE EDGE

By the same author

A Hunting We Will Go

OVER THE EDGE

Hal Friedman

URBANA FREE LIBRARY

HarperCollins*Publishers*

This is a work of fiction. The characters, incidents, and dialogues are products of the author's imagination and are not to be construed as real. Any resemblance to actual persons, living or dead, is entirely coincidental.

OVER THE EDGE. Copyright © 1998 by Hal Friedman. All rights reserved. Printed in the United States of America. No part of this book may be used or reproduced in any manner whatsoever without written permission except in the case of brief quotations embodied in critical articles and reviews. For information address HarperCollins Publishers, Inc., 10 East 53rd Street, New York, NY 10022.

HarperCollins books may be purchased for educational, business, or sales promotional use. For information please write: Special Markets Department, HarperCollins Publishers, Inc., 10 East 53rd Street, New York, NY 10022.

FIRST EDITION

Designed by Nancy Singer Olaguera

Library of Congress Cataloging-in-Publication Data
Friedman, Hal.
    Over the edge / Hal Friedman.—1st ed.
      p. cm.
    ISBN 0-06-018265-2
    I. Title.
  PS3556. R52094   1998
813'.54—dc21   98–8825
                                                       CIP

98 99 00 01 02 ❖RRD 10 9 8 7 6 5 4 3 2 1

For May and Manny, with love and gratitude

PROLOGUE

Mount Tammany,
The Delaware Water Gap
Elevation: 1,527 feet

Near the summit of the mountain, the students stood in a silent knot taking comfort in the proximity of each other's shoulders. Their teacher was higher up on the narrow trail, separated from the class by more than the physical distance between them. She could feel in her bones something was about to happen. For the first time in thirty years she was afraid of the children.

There was no doubt in her mind that she'd shown patience with the little girl during the climb, but when they'd arrived at the peak and she called for Jessie to step forward, Jessie refused.

The response came instead from the biggest of her boys, the self-appointed leader. As if he'd been waiting for the moment, he threaded his way through the group with a purposeful stride, his head cocked and his jaw thrust out at an impertinent angle. He carried a walking stick fashioned from a branch taken along the route. As he walked, he lifted it off the ground and it became something else.

Now, before it gets out of hand, she admonished herself. "Get back there. What do you think you're doing?" she shouted to him.

The young man stopped, but did not retreat. Emboldened by his example, two other boys swiftly left the group to join him. Tentative at first, their confidence increased as their own passage succeeded without incident. In a short time the three stood together with their eyes fixed intently on her.

A shiver of anxiousness spread down the teacher's rib cage. Her apprehension derived not only from the menacing challenge to her authority, but from the time and location chosen for it. Somewhere behind her, the trees opened up onto a thick granite ledge that jutted out into space to form the highest point in the state. Where it ended abruptly, the mountain plunged to a ravine of jagged rocks far below. Even the thought of the dizzying height gave her vertigo.

"You three get back with the others," she called out again, puffing herself up to full size. Again they didn't move. If anything, their expressions became more defiant.

In the gap between two of them she could see Jessie, the catalyst for the insurrection. Jessie stood rooted in place, her little melodrama calculated to keep her fellow revolutionaries incited. *Evil, disobedient child.*

"Jessie! You come up here right now, young lady."

"Leave her alone," the leader of the boys shouted back angrily. For emphasis, he lifted his walking stick in the air and pointed it in her direction.

Reflexively, she took a step backward, then another. It was a serious mistake. As soon as she retreated, the boys moved forward a greater amount. The choreography of fear, of advance and retreat, had been established.

Don't let them see it.

As imperceptibly as she could, the teacher craned for a glimpse of the returning park ranger. The ranger had remained at the last rest stop to attend to stragglers and was nowhere in view. The class mother, who'd come along as a proctor, was with him, her own daughter among the chief complainants. The only other adult had stayed near the bottom with those who didn't want to climb. The teacher was now completely alone.

In the confusion of the moment, she silently prayed for someone to help her, then quickly realized that she must have said it aloud. The three boys looked at one another with a sense of discovery and started forward again, their intention now confirmed.

"Stay back," she challenged them at the top of her voice. They did not stop. When she realized what was about to happen, she stepped off the path, turned away, and plunged ahead into the trees.

Hide. Wait for the ranger.

Deeper in, she fled over ground that was a tangle of roots and the tops of boulders. Behind her somewhere, they were chanting her name. *Wilkens. Wilkens. Wilkens.* Their taunting propelled her on faster. Her legs were growing weaker with each stride. She needed to rest but couldn't. Her throat constricted and she gagged on fear.

Run . . . run to live.

The trees thinned for a small space where the surface became a naked ledge. After a few steps she failed to spot the thick layer of moss that began to cover it, slippery from recent rains. The toe of one walking shoe skidded out from under her, and she spilled to the ground with a yelp of pain. In full panic, she scrambled to her feet and bounded headlong into another dense area of underbrush. By then she'd lost her sense of direction.

A hundred stiff thorns clawed at her sweater as she fled into a thicket of brambles. A few tore deeper, into the flesh on her arm. She shut out the pain and kept going. *So afraid. Worse than anything, ever.*

She had no idea how far she'd come when it suddenly became lighter and the vegetation gave way to solid rock. It was flat here and much easier to run. Something she remembered about this place skipped in and out of her mind, something dangerous she didn't have time to think about.

She looked over her shoulder as she continued to flee.

She couldn't see or hear them any longer but was certain they were still behind her, somewhere.

By the time she saw what was right in front of her it was too late to stop, and she let out a bloodcurdling scream that pierced the quiet at the edge of the earth.

PART ONE

1

Studio City, Los Angeles

The frenzied voice in Captain Dan Jarrett's earpiece belonged to Sergeant Ben Wasser, the normally unflappable stalwart of the Threat Management Unit. Wasser was in a chase car a mile away, keeping a measured distance from the subject of his surveillance in a white Camaro convertible.

The suspect was a thirty-year-old man who'd been dubbed "Lady" for his sick interest in certain female celebrities. In the past four months he'd stalked and attacked four of them in ways too perverse to print in the papers. With any luck at all, Lady was headed for the TV stage of Fahrenheit Studios, where Jarrett and half the TMU were waiting to take him out.

In theory he was headed there, Jarrett thought. To date, none of the guesses about where the degenerate psycho lowlife was supposed to have shown up had been worth a damn.

"This mother effer's a cool one," Ben Wasser said into the earpiece. Wasser never said the F word, though for some reason every other curse was permissible. "Top down, arm out the window. Taking in the goddamn scenery like he's got all the effing time in the world."

"Stay close," Jarrett chided. "You lose, you cruise." This was a playful reference to being dropped from the renowned antistalking team and put back on routine radio patrol. The TMU was considered a plum assignment. Its members interacted with some of Hollywood's most famous celebrities, as close to glamorous as you could get on the LAPD.

Jarrett was parked down the block from Fahrenheit Studios, on the opposite side of the street. Inside, on the ground floor, the Sally Grant afternoon TV show was produced live five days a week. The curtain on today's show was going up in fifteen minutes. Lady would have to hurry.

The inside men were Sergeant Steve Tobin and his partner Fred Thaler, who were backstage, nervously watching the audience gather. All the expected types were in the house, tourists and retired couples wanting cheap amusement, the temporarily unemployed, and a surprising number of young people who at two o'clock on a Wednesday afternoon evidently had nothing better to do.

Tobin was on edge. Lady's likely target was a female guest star who was only in town for the day to appear on the program. No one wasted time trying to figure out how Lady knew that.

According to the plan, Jarrett was to allow the creep to enter the building, then shadow him. Lady had a propensity for attacking his women in public places. This time, once he made a move, Jarrett would be on him like stink on a skunk.

"Turning off La Cienega onto Santa Monica," Wasser barked in the tiny speaker in Jarrett's ear. A minute later he said, "The son of a bitch is heading right for the studio."

Jarrett kept his eyes fastened on the end of the block. Lady had started his illustrious career with patience, harassing Jamie Macumber, an actress on a steamy soap. Eventually he visited her Laurel Canyon residence while she was away, and an arriving housekeeper saw him leaving with a few of her dresses. At the time there was speculation Lady got his rocks off by cross-dressing.

Three attacks followed in the next four months as Lady graduated to a dangerous creep. One actress was attacked in a makeup trailer during a break in filming, another in a rest room of the theater where her film was premiering. The third worked on a TV quiz program showing the prizes. Lady had found out what was behind doors number one and two in the studio parking lot.

"Coming right at you," Wasser said. His voice had become a whisper. "Give 'im a kiss for me."

Jarrett saw the Camaro turn into the block and slow as it approached the studio. Lady parked diagonally across from the entrance to Fahrenheit, the butt end of his car hanging impudently over an active driveway. Probably he didn't intend to stay long enough for that to be a problem. He stepped out of the car, stretched, and looked around.

Jarrett eased out of his Land Cruiser. Even from where he was, he could make out Lady's distinct features: a pinched nose that one of his victims reported to be like the carrot that kids put in a snowman's face, unkempt red hair worn long at the back, buzz-cut in front. He moved like a scarecrow stoned on downers. For this occasion Lady wore a loose-fitting corduroy sports jacket over a paisley Hawaiian shirt, the kind they still sold at used clothing stores in Santa Monica. "Nobody makes a move until I do," Jarrett said into the microphone under his shirt. Two voices in his earpiece said, "Check" at the same time. He pushed off the truck and started in Lady's direction. Lady was definitely going for the entrance.

Jarrett crossed the street, keeping his distance. Occasional passers-by coming toward him from in front of the building partially blocked his view. The first was a chesty young woman in her early twenties who showed a lot of wear. She had on a tight halter top and stared at Jarrett in a way that erased the twenty years that separated them. The next was an unkempt, stoop-shouldered man, an older techno-freak type who was carrying a copy of *Wired*.

The third was the last between Jarrett and Lady. He came at a swifter gait and with a swagger in his walk. He also had something wrong with one of his eyes.

Jarrett glanced at him, then looked past him to Lady. He walked a few more steps before a siren went off in his brain, and he clocked the face with the bad eye again. "Hey you," he yelled at him all at once, blowing all decorum. Lady heard it and froze in his tracks.

The man Jarrett had called looked at him suspiciously and slowed. Jarrett worked hard to fit the face against an old mental template. The bulbous nose, bent in the middle from an earlier unset break, the full-lipped mouth set in a perpetual leering grin, the same partially closed left eye— from a desperate last second punch Jarrett had thrown at him!

A name to go with the face: *Julio Vasquez.*

The large muscles in Jarrett's body went to full alert. His hair bristled. Every part of him was a receptor. There is a God, he thought. Vasquez locked his eyes onto Jarrett's and froze in mutual recognition.

"Don't move, police," Jarrett shouted. His hand went to his shoulder holster under his jacket and his six-shot Smith & Wesson Medusa, named after the snake-haired Gorgon.

Vasquez made a quick sweep of the street and the building in front of him. He chose the building and abruptly sprang to his left and pounded the glass door open.

Holding his Medusa shoulder high, Jarrett raced toward the door after him.

In a heartbeat, Wasser, Thaler, Tobin, the whole goddamn TMU, and Lady were out of his mind.

2

"The bastard is going back to his effing car," Dan Wasser shouted in Jarrett's ear.

No one answered him.

Jarrett reached the door before it closed all the way behind Vasquez. He was too busy running to respond.

"What the hell is going on?" Tobin screamed from behind the stage.

"Something's come up," Jarrett finally answered.

Vasquez was past the pretty young thing at the reception desk, running full speed down a hall that led to the TV studio. A bewildered toy security guard just stood at the hall entrance watching him.

Jarrett charged ahead without breaking stride as Vasquez turned a corner and disappeared. His mind raced back in time to the face he'd seen for only a few fleeting seconds seven years earlier, and then only through a grimy warehouse window. It was a night that turned out to be as shattering in its own way as the one when he'd lost his wife, Beth Ellen.

He and his partner Frank Foley had gone to a deserted building in Pico to surprise a violent gang leader in a drug sting. The man was Domingo Vasquez, known to his friends as "Loco." At the last minute, something went wrong and the suspects took off, except for Domingo's brother. The assassin sprung from the shadows with a knife, and, in one unspeakable moment, Frank's neck was wide open and his life flowed out in a torrent. He died in Jarrett's arms a few minutes later, choking on his own blood and begging Jarrett to watch over his daughter. Jarrett had blamed himself. At the last minute Frank had told him to switch places, and he'd agreed.

Later, he'd spotted Julio on the other side of a storeroom window and sent his fist flying through the glass at him. A piece of the glass sliced into the killer's left eye before he took off. For seven years Julio Vasquez had eluded one of the most intense manhunts in L.A.'s history—until now.

"What about Lady?" Wasser screamed again.

"Another time," Jarrett said coolly. He tightened his grip on his pistol. *One shot*, he prayed. *Just give me one shot.*

Jarrett reached the final corridor in time to see Vasquez go through the double doors past a distracted usher. "No, don't do that," Jarrett moaned when he realized where he'd gone. He got to the usher with his badge out, and was looking at a good two hundred people.

Inside, there was no sign of a disturbance. A voice from a control booth announced Sally Grant, and curtains opened to Grant, her first two guests, and wild applause.

One guest was a teenager with red shock hair and more earrings than there were at Tiffany's piercing her body. The woman next to her, ostensibly her mother, was crying and the show hadn't even started yet. Grant said something about "children who sue their parents for neglect." Two cameramen at each side of the set were locked in place, their blinking cameras pointed at the threesome.

An ear-piercing shriek brought Grant's sermon to a halt. Near the bottom of the steps that led to the stage, Vasquez had risen and hauled an obese woman out of her seat by her hair. His other arm was around her neck with a knife to her throat. Screams from around the room raised the volume.

"Let her go," Jarrett boomed from the back. He brought

his Medusa head high and pointed it at the ceiling, initiating a second round of screams.

"I'll cut her," Vasquez shouted back.

The place quieted eerily and Jarrett lowered his weapon.

"Me and her are leaving together," Vasquez announced, looking around.

"I don't think so," Jarrett snapped back. He took a step down the aisle.

"Not any closer."

"Can't we talk this out," Sally Grant blurted from the right side of the stage. "That way we might—"

"Shut the fuck up," Vasquez interrupted her.

Grant shut the fuck up.

"You're coming with me," Jarrett shouted, creeping down the aisle to the stage. "Walking or deceased. Your choice."

Vasquez backed down the stairs with his hostage, who'd stopped shrieking and was flirting with the idea of passing out. Vasquez stepped up onto the stage with her, between Grant and her guests, and searched for a way out through the wings.

The studio was as quiet as a mausoleum, but no one tried to leave. With new actors on the stage, the line between terror and entertainment had blurred for the audience.

"What'll it be?" Jarrett stepped onto the stage and pointed his Medusa at the man's head. There was no way he'd risk a shot, but Frank's killer couldn't know that.

"Bullshit," Vasquez snarled. He drew the knife lightly across the sagging woman's throat, leaving a thin wet red line. She closed her eyes and squeaked like a new shoe.

"All right, we'll try it this way," Jarrett said. He put the gun down on the floor and started to walk toward him.

Vasquez's eyes darted stage left. He was desperate for a way to go. "Okay, no problem," he said finally. "You can have her." He hoisted the woman as high as he could, then shoved her hard at Jarrett, and she crumpled to the floor. He took off to the left side of the stage.

Jarrett was already in motion. In high school he'd run the hundred in under ten seconds, and he still had some of his speed. With a furious burst he hurled himself at the fleeing man and brought him down with a perfect ankle tackle. Vasquez let out a loud grunt as he fell. He twisted to one side and came off the ground knife-first, slashing wildly.

Jarrett dodged the first two thrusts and parried with an accurately placed blow that struck Vasquez's below his bad eye and cracked a bone. Blood flowed freely down that side of his face. Jarrett's body was a single coiled muscle of infinite rage. "That was for Frank," he cried.

Vasquez launched a feeble punch, but Jarrett thrust a knee into his chest and the attempt fell short. Jarrett's fury found its way to his fists again as the man wriggled beneath him. He tried to hold himself back, but Frank's pitiful dying face filled his vision, and he was unaware of where he was. The next few unreasoning moments went by in a blur, and when it was over Vasquez law motionless beneath him.

Jarrett got to his feet clumsily and took a few steps backward. In time he heard a new sound, like popcorn exploding. He looked around and remembered where he was.

The mother-daughter act was long gone, as was Sally Grant. Her microphone was on the floor where she'd dropped it when she fled. Most of the audience was still there. The noise that he was hearing was their applause.

One of the cameramen had taken off, but the other was still at his post. Sometime earlier he'd swung his camera in Jarrett's direction and kept it running.

The remaining cameraman had held it on him while Jarrett punched the face of Frank's killer.

Again and again and again and again and again.

3

"Are you all going to sit there like statues, or is someone going to risk the wrath of Foley?"

From her spot in front of the blackboard, Meg Foley scanned her new crop of freshly scrubbed students. They were a world away from the undernourished and inattentive faces that had stared back at her in the Clayton-Trent Public School in Washington Heights, New York. More like a galaxy away.

The hand that poked impudently into the air belonged to Timothy Sullivan, the self-anointed leader of the boys' group. He was the biggest kid in the class, and his impish Irish face, partially hidden by a shock of copper blond hair, belied a cool and calculating mind. She'd seen him in the lunchroom negotiating table assignments. At thirteen he was a skilled power broker.

"We don't get it. It doesn't make any sense," Timothy said. His sentiment was echoed by several others. Anything Timothy said was totally cool.

"Okay, let's give this a try." Meg moved to the blackboard. "A literal equation is one that has no numbers, only symbols." She wrote a problem as she said it. "I just want you to know the general rule that lets you solve it."

There was a sea of blank faces until Sullivan waved his hand again. As bright as he was, he often said the first thing that came to his mind and didn't take kindly to being wrong in front of his friends. The class had been edgy all week about math, for many weeks about her. Now she needed Timothy to be right.

"Move the rest of the numbers to one side until you end up with the one you want by itself," Timothy volunteered. He looked around, beaming to his buddies.

He had the mechanics down, but it wasn't the answer she was looking for. "Yes, that's very good. But I was looking for the overall rule."

Timothy's smile died abruptly. The other students sensed his discomfort and started to squirm. *Damn it.*

"Okay, no problem. Remember we said an equation is like a seesaw? So whatever you do to one side you have to do to the other? That's the rule Timothy was trying to express."

"I knew how to do it, didn't I?" Timothy shot back angrily. "Who cares about a stupid rule?"

The class braced.

"This isn't the way we were taught," Doogie McMillan quickly complained on behalf of his friend. Doogie was the Mutt of the Mutt and Jeff combo, a head shorter than Timothy, and not as bright a bulb.

The caution light that blinked in Meg's brain went from yellow to red. The conversation had zigged to the place she didn't want to go, the topic she'd been warned not to approach, even remotely. It had been months since her predecessor's fatal accident, and the kids had been in grief counseling for much of it. But Mrs. Wilkens, and the different way she did things, was at the heart of Meg's inability to get through to the children. "How were you taught, then?" she said guardedly. "If there's a better way, I'm all for it."

Her response cast a spell over the class, and the room fell still. The kids knew they were close to transgressing on the rule of rules: No Reference to the Past.

Augie Templeton, Timothy's other best friend, shot a

glance at Sullivan, and the latter's head moved from side to side. Augie settled back in his chair.

"Never mind," Sullivan said.

His easy capitulation was disheartening and brought on the same rush of frustration Meg had experienced since the day she came to Knollwood Middle School five weeks earlier. The students' enduring depression over what happened to Elaine Wilkens was a stone wall between them and their new teacher.

"It's not just math, Ms. Foley," the pretty blond peacemaker, Katie Hathaway, volunteered. "It's . . . everything. Nothing's the same."

Many of the other kids echoed her, and there was no doubt about what was really bothering them. Meg had her own ideas on ways to deal with it, and they were in conflict with those of the school administration. She made a quick decision.

"All right," she said. "Close your books. I think we all know that there's something more important that we have to talk about."

Taken off guard, the children complied slowly. Meg put the chalk down and came forward to the front of her desk and leaned against it. She was nervous. High-stakes stuff.

"First of all, I know I've only been here a short time, but it doesn't take long to see you're a very smart bunch of kids. The smartest by far of any I've had." She stared directly at Doreen Drew, the leading brain, and added, "Not to mention totally cool dressers."

A few titters filtered into the silence, but the air had a strange feel.

"But there's something keeping you from being the excited and brilliant bunch that you were before. And I'm guessing it's because you've all been through something very painful . . . that you still haven't gotten over." Her broaching of the sacrosanct topic sent a shock wave around the room. Chins swiveled, eyes met in hushed uncertainty, heads hunkered down nearer to the desks.

"I know that it's still a bit upsetting, but I think it would be good if we could share some of our feelings . . . about Mrs. Wilkens."

Nobody moved, not even a bit. The kids looked lost, not what she'd thought would happen. She suddenly had strong misgivings about having ventured into no-man's-land.

"Who'd like to say something about Mrs. Wilkens? I'll bet you're still very sad about it and wish she were still here with you. I know I would be if I were you."

Meg looked around the class for the first glimmer of release.

"Maybe you feel that you could have done something to prevent what happened to her. That's perfectly normal. But the main thing to remember is it was something that will probably never happen to you again."

She searched the vacant faces individually. *Something. Someone. Anything to get it going.*

One by one, the reclusive heads began to lift. In twos and threes the students turned in the same direction. In a short time, almost all of the them were staring at the left side of the room, to the first seat in the front row near the wall. In that chair, a frail but pretty little twelve-year-old girl named Jessie Lerner sat staring straight ahead, as if in a trance.

Meg stared at her intently and didn't like what she saw. Jessie's normally rosy face had gone ash white, and her lips were pressed together so tightly they were bloodless. Her frail body trembled from some private emotional upheaval.

She looked as if she was about to be sick.

4

"It was an incredibly reckless and ill-advised thing to do. I couldn't admire you more for trying." The sharp Dickensesque features of Errol Volpe peered slyly at Meg from across the coffee table in the teachers' lounge.

"Well, you're in the minority," Meg said, "but I appreciate it."

The fifty-three-year-old earth sciences teacher, her first new friend at the Knollwood Middle School, had sat down next to her at the cafeteria on her first day and struck up a conversation. She'd been impressed by his openness.

"It doesn't take a genius to see there's something wrong with these kids," she continued. "They're still spooked by Mrs. Wilkens's death, after all this time. Do you see it in your classes?"

Volpe nodded. "I have to admit I haven't gotten over it myself. Elaine and I became close over the years. Has anyone in administration paid you a visit yet? Arno?"

Meg raised an eyebrow. Lester Arno was a name that elicited fear response among students and faculty alike. As vice-principal, he was in the Gestapo part of the education matrix. "No, why, think he will?"

"He and the principal were frantic after the *accident*. That was understandable, I guess, but it lasted for a long time."

Meg heard the emphasis he placed on the word *accident*.

Volpe went on before she could ask why. "I went to the inquest and raised questions no one wanted to answer. I was, shall we say, *talked to* by Arno and Melacore. In effect, they told me to keep my mouth shut, which, as you may have noticed, I have a difficult time doing."

"What made them so unhappy with you?"

"The death of a respected teacher can be hell for an administration like ours, especially the way this one happened. In theory Knollwood has the perfect school system, number two in the state and all that. It's the kind of place where bad news or scandal is swept under the rug so fast it makes your head spin. Anything that blemishes the holy record shakes everyone to their core. And not just for the administration," he added pointedly. "We have some really manic parents here, and they have power."

Meg shook her head. The politics of death were getting thicker.

"The best thing that could have happened was for the whole thing to go away as fast as possible, and that's where I transgressed. I thought the investigation ended too soon and said so."

"I thought it was still open, officially."

"Officially, yes. It's bogged down in red tape and juridictional matters. Practically, it's a done deal."

"Mrs. Wilkens was a legend," Meg said. "Maybe it *was* better to get it over with."

Volpe narrowed his eyes. "Contrary to what you may have heard, not everyone was a fan of hers."

Meg sat up straight. "I thought everyone idolized her. Wasn't she the president of the State Board of Ed once? Wasn't her whole career here?"

"All of it's true, or was. She was on her third generation of students and universally popular, until this year." Volpe stopped when the passing chimes that signaled the end of the present period interrupted him.

"Well, you sure got my attention." Meg rose with him

from their chairs. Their schedules matched for six of the eight daily periods, and this was one of them.

"To shorten the story, Elaine had been having a rough go of it," Volpe continued. "I don't know what happened exactly, but this year a few of her students came home with stories of mistreatment by her. Complaints were lodged with the Board of Ed, but she was exonerated in every case. She didn't talk about it and I didn't ask."

"I had no idea."

"Not a good place to leave off," Volpe said. He looked at his watch, then checked his slacks and brushed a few wrinkles out of the herringbone worsted weave. Even at sixth period, his crease was nearly perfect.

"The point is, for the first time she made a few enemies in town. That was very painful to her."

"Two minutes," a husky voice from the door cut Volpe off.

Leaning into the lounge, barrel-chested assistant principal Lester Arno raised an accusing brow. Meg had the distinct feeling he'd been listening before he announced himself, and she and Volpe exchanged poker-faced glances. Arno ducked back out, and his footsteps echoed in the hall.

"Creepy the way he did that," Meg pondered.

"Creepy does as creepy is."

Meg stepped to the door, disconcerted. Their talk had given her a queasy stomach, and Arno's sudden appearance chilled her. She turned back to Volpe before leaving. "Why do I get the feeling you think there was more to the accident than anyone found out?"

Volpe made a tent out of his hands and poked the sharp point of his nose into it. "Why do I get the feeling Elaine must have had a hell of a good reason to have gotten so far from the path?"

5

Los Angeles Police Headquarters

"A hundred calls an hour, including the mayor and every member of his council. Who are you anyway, the anti-Christ of law enforcement?"

Chief of Detectives Elliot Stryker lifted a gnarly chin and struggled to loosen his hundred-dollar designer tie. When he yanked on it, the silk ripped, and his commentary ended with "Son of a bitch."

Jarrett stared at his boss's pristine bald spot, which looked comical in the midst of an otherwise thick tangle of gray curls. It unnerved Stryker when he stared at his bald spot, which was precisely why he did it. "What the hell was I suppose to do?" Jarrett said. "The guy ran into the studio. How was I supposed to know they'd keep the cameras running?"

"You beat the shit out of a Hispanic kid," Stryker shouted back. He shook a fist in the air and was breathing fire. "In Los Angeles. On live TV, for Christ's sake!"

Stryker turned his attention back to a Sony video monitor. The tape playing on it was the latest episode of jeopardy—not the game show, what Stryker's chances to win a mayoralty election someday were now in. Jarrett saw himself pummeling Vasquez and winced.

"I got hundreds of detectives, thousands of uniforms. Why is it always you?" Stryker bellowed.

Jarrett had the answer, but Stryker wouldn't like it. It was him because he was the third generation of law enforcers, and because he was the most pissed off of any of them by far.

"Don't fucking believe it," Stryker shouted. He stared in incomprehension at the monitor. "Don't fucking believe it!" he sang again, up the octave.

If Jarrett remembered correctly, the current record for *don't fucking believe it*s was five in one visit.

Jarrett watched himself hold Vasquez's head by his hair and slam it into the stage floor. It was hard to see the punk's original features, but there was still some fight in him. After a few more punches, Vasquez lay motionless. The sound man had fled but left the boom on. It recorded Jarrett's final curse at the unconscious figure. On the tape, Jarrett stood, then turned to discover the camera.

"You beat the crap out of a youth half your age," Stryker said, pointing to the screen.

"I guess I lost it. I don't feel good about it."

"You know what's gonna happen if Julio wakes up dead in the morning? He'll be the goddamn Spanish fuckin' Rodney King, that's what." Stryker paused to swallow some saliva that had built up in his diatribe. He glared at Jarrett with malice dripping from his jowls.

"All I could think about was that he killed Frank."

"We haven't proved that."

"We will. I saw him do it from ten feet away."

"Only if he lives to stand trial."

Jarrett was frustrated. Any sane person had to admit that justice had been served. "I know you felt the same way about Frank as I did. I figured maybe you'd understand."

"Don't you dare goddamn lecture me about that." Stryker clicked off the monitor and dragged himself wearily to his desk. "Frank and I went back a long way. I cried like a baby at his funeral. It would have been different if you'd been defending yourself—" He stopped abruptly and looked up to see if Jarrett understood the code.

"If he'd gotten away, you would've felt a lot worse," Jarrett tried, as an afterthought.

Stryker put his head between two surprisingly delicate hands. He pressed his eyes with his palms and kept them there. "Maybe he should have. I wouldn't want to be either of us if the scumbag dies."

6

The shouts carried the length of the corridor and invaded her classroom through a closed door. It was lunch hour, and the tumult had an ominous feel. Meg put down the next day's lesson plan and bolted for the hall.

At the end of the corridor a growing cluster of faculty and students jammed the entrance to the earth sciences lab. They were being held back physically by Lester Arno, who was using his body as a bulwark to plug the entrance. A female student from a lower grade turned away from the lab with her hand over her mouth and tears in her eyes. The sounds of sirens outside somewhere added a layer of menace.

"What happened?" Meg asked the girl, stopping her with a hand on her shoulder.

"There was an accident. Mr. Volpe's hurt really bad."

Meg stiffened. She'd spoken with Errol briefly that morning and he'd been atypically upbeat. With rising fear, she pushed her way through the students to the gatekeeper.

"What's going on?" she shouted to Arno over the din. "Is he all right? Is there anything I can do?"

"Just keep the area clear," Arno said without emotion, as if he were a traffic cop. "The ambulance will be right here."

"Is Errol hurt?"

Arno looked annoyed, but took the time. "Something exploded in the lab. He's been burned on his hands and face."

"How badly?"

A male and female paramedic rushed into the corridor behind them before Arno could answer and arrived at the lab in a trot. The woman held a collapsed stretcher under her arm, the man an emergency medical satchel. Arno made a space for them to enter but cut off Meg when she tried to follow.

Meg remained outside while the medics worked. There was no word on Volpe's condition or what they were doing. Fifteen minutes later, Arno gave way to the medical team, and they backed out with Volpe on the stretcher between them. Errol was conscious and recognized her as he passed by.

Meg was appalled at what had happened to his face. The skin on one side was blistered, as was a major part of his neck. His arms were taped to the sides of the stretcher so his hands, which were a dark angry color, could hang free. There were no bandages. She tried not to look at the charred flesh, only at his eyes.

Volpe was bewildered. "I couldn't have made a mistake," he said weakly. "I've done it a hundred times." He looked up at Meg for an explanation, but he was whisked away too quickly for her to answer. "Is there anyone you want me to call?" she shouted after him, not able to keep up with the stretcher.

"A hundred times," he repeated, scarcely loud enough to be heard.

He was out of range before she could think of anything else to say.

Inside the lab, Arno stared at the damage without acknowledging Meg's presence. It looked as if there had been a fire, not an explosion as she was told. There was a blackened area on the lab counter where Volpe must have been at work, but little harm done on either side of his work space. The accident had been confined and seemingly focused on Volpe.

"They think the chemicals he mixed together must have caused it," Arno said, more with contempt than sympathy. "The paramedics were concerned that he'd inhaled fumes and damaged his lungs, but he was breathing normally. Poor man, he should have been more careful."

"It's not like him to be that careless," Meg said. "No one's more cautious than he is."

Arno didn't respond. He didn't seem to think he had to.

7

On the way back to her classroom, Meg's own words about Volpe stayed with her. *Not like him.*

She recalled their conversation in the teachers' lounge. He said he'd asked too many questions about Wilkens's accident and had become a pariah. He'd been discussing Wilkens again with her when Arno interrupted, and she thought Arno had been eavesdropping before that. Now Errol had had his own accident. The timing made her shiver.

She entered her classroom and glanced up at the clock. It was only a few minutes until the next period started. She hadn't eaten and didn't want to. More than anything she wished she could follow the ambulance and be at the hospital to comfort Errol. He'd looked so scared and confused. She wondered if he had family in the area and realized how little she still knew about him. She'd call the hospital right after school, she decided, and try to go there that night.

The blackboard behind her desk caught her eye as she went to her desk. She was taken aback by a large chalk drawing on it that hadn't been there before she'd left for the lab. Her first thought was that one of her students had gotten playful with the chalk, a creative practical joke at a badly chosen time.

Actually, it was a fairly accomplished rendering, advanced for the average eighth grader. The only figure in the scene was a woman, but she'd been rendered with skill.

It took only a split second more for the dark subject matter of the drawing to register fully. The subject was a woman suspended in air. Her body was pitched forward with arms outstretched. The artist had more trouble with the face, but the expression was effective at portraying terror. The woman had obviously fallen from the edge of a precipice that loomed above her. Below, a long way down in the rough perspective, was the suggestion of the jagged ground she was headed for.

The clear reference to Wilkens's death was as tasteless as anything Meg had ever seen. In a flash of anger, she shaped the beginning of the outraged speech she was going to make to the children, no matter how taboo the topic was.

Then she focused on the face in the drawing, and when she realized what she was staring at she gasped aloud.

The woman in the drawing wasn't Wilkens at all.

8

Some people dreamed of running from phantoms that kept gaining on them. Some became lost in a hopeless maze. Jarrett's recurrent nightmare was trying to warn people who would not listen about imminent disaster.

This night's variation on a theme was earthquake. Jarrett was a boy again in Rochester, New York, the home of Eastman Kodak. He was far from his house when the ground started to shake. All around him, the street was buckling and buildings were coming apart at the seams. He raced up and down the streets shouting his warnings. In time he came to the looming tower of the Kodak building, an indelible icon from childhood.

The tower was rocking violently, and when he looked up at the top he saw Elliot Stryker standing at an open window, gesturing and making a speech like the Pope. Jarrett called to warn him, but Stryker was lost in his own rhetoric. As Jarrett watched, the building snapped in two, and millions of pounds of cement and steel came down at him. He could still see Stryker in the window, hurtling down to crush him in Kodak's final moment.

The ringing of the phone roused Jarrett from the dream just before he was buried. The green numbers on the digital clock read 12:02, and his chest was bathed in perspiration.

"Oh Jesus, Jarrett, I'm sorry," the embarrassed voice said at the other end of the phone when she heard his inelegant greeting. "I thought you'd still be up. I'll call back in the morning."

"No, it's okay," Jarrett lied nicely, then realized another reason he would have been better left unconscious. The memory of the bad news that had preceded his restless sleep returned with a vengeance. "How are things out there in Jersey?"

He forced his eyes to stay open.

"Well, let's put it this way, this isn't just a catch-up call. It's three in the morning and you may have noticed I'm not sleeping."

"Oh joy." He pushed the earlier news out of his mind and concentrated on the face that belonged to the youthful voice. She had to be closing in on thirty by now, he estimated, but he could still see wisps of reddish brown hair dancing on a lightly freckled early twenties forehead, large sea green eyes rife with disillusionment. Seven years earlier she'd been a deeply wounded young lady, Meg Foley, Frank Foley's daughter.

"Yeah, not exactly a walk in the park," she elaborated, letting out a sigh. "Well, maybe Central Park." When he didn't respond, she added, "Hey, that's a joke."

"I'm laughing on the inside."

He'd only seen Meg in person twice since her father's funeral, and they hadn't spoken in a few months, a long time for them. He reminded himself why: She'd been busy with her new teaching job in some ritzy-titzy little town on the other side of the planet in New Jersey, and he'd been busy prosecuting justice in L.A., with his fists, as usual. "Well, how's the teaching going at least?"

"That's the topic. There's something weird going on here. Actually, I'm feeling a wee bit . . . threatened by it."

The T word did wonders for Jarrett's state of wakefulness. He sat up and rested his shoulders against the wall that served as a headboard; hot back, cold plaster. Her voice had started the warehouse scene replaying again: Frank giving up the ghost and making him promise to watch over his daughter, Jarrett imploring his partner to hang on, knowing it was a useless plea.

Meg had been adrift then, with more than her share of hard knocks. After her father had gotten into trouble with Internal Affairs, her mother had walked out on him. Their eventual divorce devastated her, and the joint custody didn't help. She considered it the capper to a life that had been marked by bad luck and disappointment.

Jarrett never forgot the epigram she'd used to sum up her first twenty-three years: *Gypped again.* "I'm listening," he said, the haze of time lifting. His head was suddenly clear, too clear.

"I was hired in midterm to replace a teacher who was killed in an accident, on a class trip of all things," she said. "Her name was Elaine Wilkens."

In the next few minutes she recounted the highlights of the past few weeks, ending with what had just happened to her teacher friend, Errol Volpe.

After listening without comment, Jarrett was up to date on the perversity and politics of a death in a public school. "And all this time I thought you'd found a job in Camelot."

"It gets worse," Meg continued. "Tonight someone called me at home and told me I'd be sorry if I kept asking questions about Mrs. Wilkens. A couple of lewd remarks were thrown in for good measure."

The number of incidents, if not their seriousness, started to make Jarrett uneasy. "What did the caller sound like?"

"Male, but I couldn't tell how old. He was hard to hear, like he was talking near some loud machinery."

"Did you call the police?"

"Of course. They thought it was a crackpot and suggested I get Caller ID and let them know if it happens again."

"What did the school say about the drawing?"

"I made a mistake. I didn't want the kids to see it, so I erased it right away. I should have showed it to the principal first."

"Did you tell him about it at least?"

"The principal is a she, and yes. I made an appointment to go over it again, but I'm not expecting much. The vice-principal is an ornery S.O.B. He gives me the evil eye every time I talk to him. I think he's identified me as a trouble-maker, and I know he speaks for his boss."

Jarrett shook his head sadly for her. "If I remember correctly, didn't we have a conversation like this about a year ago, at your school in New York City?"

"So okay, maybe I have a gift for being politically incor-rect," she said. "From what Dad told me you're familiar with the phenomenon."

He grunted his acknowledgment.

"He meant it as a compliment. He was your biggest fan."

Her reference threw him back in time again. Jarrett had been a cheerleader for her father in a big way, too. He remembered the scenario again, in more detail this time. Before they'd become partners, Frank had been accused of taking money from a big-time hoodlum. The charges were never proved, but he suffered the double loss of rank and his blue-blood wife, who was less forgiving than the P.D. Frank said his wife had been looking for a reason, and the scandal was made to order. He was trying to pull his life back together when he and Jarrett were partnered and Jarrett took Frank under his wing.

"Want to hear something else totally weird?" Meg said. She sounded as if she were fifteen. "A few times I caught some of my rougher boys whispering when they didn't think I was looking. They were definitely scheming about some-thing. Once one of them pretended to fall out of his desk and crash on the floor. I'm sure it was a pantomime of Mrs. Wilkens's death."

"Maybe they were swooning over a pretty new school-teacher."

"Uh-uh. Some of them look at me that way, but this is dif-ferent. I get the feeling they think I'm a threat to them, and they're trying to figure out what to do about it. They give me the creeps."

"Have you tried corporal punishment?"

"Not funny. It's all got to do with Wilkens, I know it does. And it's not just in the classroom. A lot of adults around here are unhappy about my questions, too. I don't know how I did it so fast, but I think I'm in trouble again."

Jarrett could identify with her situation, in spades. At that very moment certain people in L.A. were anxious to put his head on a spike, and a lot faster than anyone wanted Meg's. Julio Vasquez had died less than six hours before. That was the news he got before trying to sleep. The call from Stryker was the reason for the Kodak nightmare.

"I'll be damned if I'm gonna run again, Jarrett," she rallied when he didn't answer right away. "But I don't know what I'm supposed to do."

Jarrett had known the answer to that the moment he heard she was in trouble. And he knew exactly how he'd respond. Stryker screaming on the phone about Vasquez and how he, Dan Jarrett, should make himself invisible for a while just made it easier.

"You might start by giving me your address," he said. "And a day or two."

9

The Board of Ed building was an austere brick structure that left no room for taxpayers to claim that money had been wasted on frills. In her short journey from the middle school, Meg developed a severe case of nerves that started with the feeling she was being watched.

Inside, the main hallway was blocked by a desk, its occupant an officious, overly tan receptionist who looked as if she'd just gotten off the plane from Boca. In a town like Knollwood, some women worked only to occupy their time. Meg could feel the receptionist's eyes on her even after she was directed to the records room.

Could you possibly be more paranoid?

One long wall-to-wall countertop spanned the room. The back walls were shelves at the bottom, fiberboard bins compacted neatly with files above them to the ceiling. Behind the only desk, an orthopedic-style swivel chair was draped with a fuzzy pink sweater for protection against air conditioning that was cold in that part of the building. The chill fed into Meg's sense of peril.

The thin, sixty-something clerk wore ruffled sleeves on an elegant spring blouse, half glasses on a chain around her neck, and the requisite brooch. Claire Davies took the request from her visitor without an inquisition, and in a few minutes placed copies of the B of E's minutes for the two months prior to Wilkens's death on the countertop.

Meg slid the reports to the wall and skimmed through them standing. The bulk of the proceedings dealt with appropriations and use of funds. One interesting meeting centered around a motion to censure the board based on their decision to tear down an unneeded school. Only three years after the building was razed, the school-age population burgeoned unexpectedly. A bond issue was then floated to provide the outrageous sum it took to build another school, on exactly the same spot. *Wasn't there a course somewhere called city planning?*

Disappointingly, there were no specific accounts of any complaints lodged against teachers, but in a dramatic turn there was a reference to the result of one such hearing in the indexed reports, without the name of the accused.

Meg turned the book upside down so Claire Davies could read it and asked about the proceeding.

Claire reeled in her reading glasses and looked it over. "A wonderful woman, Mrs. Wilkens," she volunteered.

Meg lit up.

"The talk about her behavior with the children was nonsense." Claire looked at Meg over the rims of her glasses and whispered confidentially, "The problem is, some parents can't stand the idea of their children being disciplined, no matter what they do."

"I'm sure," Meg said, taking the easy way out. "If you don't mind, though, I'd like to get an idea of what it was about." Claire mumbled something unintelligible at the bad idea, then went dutifully to the shelves.

The proceedings against Elaine Wilkens were in a thin folder entitled "Staff Inquiries." Meg tingled as Claire placed it in front of her. Once she opened the folder she knew she would be committed to the same course that Errol Volpe had taken. She wondered what he would say about it. So far he wasn't taking any calls at the hospital.

Meg squeezed close to the end of the wall and shielded

the papers with her back. There were four complaint docu-
ments in the jacket, two pages each. The first was dated
October 6, and accused Elaine Wilkens of using derisive language toward the student in question on a number of occasions. Meg vaguely remembered the student's name, Marco
Cuesta, from attendance sheets she'd found in Wilkens's
files. She'd also seen an old memo informing Wilkens that
the Cuestas had moved. The page the complaint was
clipped to specified in handwriting that insufficient cause
had been shown to carry the issue forward.

The next was dated October 12, and Meg braced at the
name. Phillip and Carolyn Lerner were the parents of
Jessie, the pretty little girl who'd begun to shake uncontrollably in class. She'd met them twice and recalled how they'd
scrutinized her closely. They'd asked if she was used to
dealing with special ed students. Now she saw their questions in a whole new context.

In a lengthy list of grievances, the Lerners accused
Wilkens of singling out their daughter for unwarranted pun-
ishments, undermining her self-confidence, and inflicting
extreme psychological trauma. There was also a grievance
about Wilkens's ability to deal with their daughter's learning
disability, attention deficit disorder. The language here was
technical enough to have been written with the help of a
psychologist. These charges were not dismissed, as the
Cuestas' had been. The results of the board's hearing were
held in abeyance pending further inquiry.

The next complaint also had the Lerners' names on it,
and the one after that.

"Doing some extracurricular research, are we?"

The voice at Meg's back was frighteningly familiar. Vice-
Principal Lester Arno stood there glowering. Meg could feel
the hairs on the back of her neck stand on end. She closed
the file so quickly and awkwardly that she was sure Arno
suspected the worst. "Yes . . . actually, I was," she blurted
out. "A person can learn a lot by getting familiar with Board
of Education issues."

She took a step toward Mrs. Davies, who had been enjoying the seemingly pleasant exchange between two friendly educators. Meg handed her the folder. "Thank you. You can put this back now."

Arno's gray eyes darkened. He reached for the file before Davies could take it and perused it. He handed it back to the older woman with a courteous nod. "Not exactly the routine business of the board, is it, Ms. Foley?"

Arno expected an answer. He stood close to her, blocking any way around him in the narrow space.

A surge of anger overrode Meg's initial apprehension. She looked Arno in the eye and said, "One of my students is frightened about something that had to do with Mrs. Wilkens. I thought I'd better find out why."

Arno was a study in the slow burn. "I thought we discussed your not getting involved in this area. You had clear instructions on that."

"Why don't we talk about this somewhere else," Meg said, referencing Davies, who by then was clearly uncomfortable.

"No need for that, I'll be down the hall if you need me," Mrs. Davies volunteered. She left the room with an accommodating smile at Arno, and Meg felt deserted.

When they were alone, the vice-principal walked over to her and grabbed hold of her elbow roughly. "This has to end, do you understand?"

"Hey, you're hurting me," Meg said. She took a step back, trying to wrestle her arm free, but Arno's grip was like a vise, and there was fury in his eyes. She had the distinct impression that he was about to hit her.

"You're not from around here. What happened to Mrs. Wilkens was painful. People here were grateful when the matter was put to rest. I will not have you trying to stir it up again."

Using her arm for leverage, Arno forced her upper body closer to him until their faces were almost touching. "Do you hear me?"

"Let go of me. What are you doing?"

"Do you understand?" Arno continued, grasping her hard enough to bring a tear to her eye. He was losing it more every second, going out of control.

"The lady told you to let her go," a new voice said suddenly from behind them.

Arno looked down at his right shoulder where a compact but powerful hand was applying an incredible amount of pressure and producing an amazing amount of pain for its size. When he didn't release Meg right away the pressure increased, and he had to move away from her in the direction the hand pulled him.

He turned and studied the intruder. The man was sturdily built and around forty, several inches shorter than himself. There were no bulges under his clothing to suggest large muscles, but he was incredibly powerful. His face was complex, a solid, hard-boned strength softened by a scattering of wrinkles and deep creases in the forehead. The rugged symmetry was accentuated by a few thin scars that placed him in past battles. His stance was aggressive, not a man used to being pushed around, not remotely like the people Arno usually dealt with.

The grip tightened again and Arno's knees sagged. He let go of Meg and reached for the pincer on his shoulder, but it was like trying to open the Jaws of Life. A current of fire traveled down along a nerve that reached the base of his arm. With a last excruciating increase in pressure, the hand came off him abruptly.

Without looking at Meg, Arno adjusted his jacket and said, "At your earliest convenience, in my office."

His eyes never left the stranger's as he squeezed by him, allowing as wide a berth as possible in the narrow space. He left the room in a quiet rage.

Meg stared at her rescuer. She remembered the long black hair swept back in waves, the careful, intensely blue eyes, the little-boy grin under the rough exterior. But the hair had a light dusting of silver now, and he looked more tired than when she'd last seen him in L.A. years earlier.

"That line was like something out of a Bogart movie," Meg said when Arno was out of sight. She rose on her toes to kiss Dan Jarrett softly on the cheek. "Welcome to New Jersey," she said admiringly.

10

"What are you, psychic? How'd you know where to find me?" Meg asked after they got out of their separate cars at her place.

"I went to the school to check on how you were doing, and got there in time to see you leaving. When I started to follow, I saw I wasn't the only one, so I waited to see what would happen."

"Good call."

Jarrett took off his worn leather jacket and swung it over his shoulder. Meg stared at the holster strapped under his left arm. "You wear that thing everywhere you go?"

He look at the Medusa revolver the holster housed. "Joined at the hip."

She made a face. "Whatever turns you on. How long can you stay?"

"That depends on how much trouble you have."

"That long, huh?"

She led him up the steps to the back porch of a white clapboard two-family house. The rented residence, in the worker-bee part of town, was modest compared to the opulent estates Jarrett had passed on the way there. Meg's property was large, though, compared to her immediate neighbors, a double lot ending in a fringe of spiky-leafed trees with no particular pedigree. By habit, Jarrett's eyes darted around the property, appraising its security.

"Who owns all the mansions in this town?"

"Old money, and new. Lots of Wall Street types and lawyers. But I'm comfortable on the other side of the tracks, and I like the backyard."

Jarrett heard a few shrieks of laughter that came from children playing somewhere beyond the trees. All the place needed was "two cats in the yard," Jarrett thought, remembering the old Crosby, Stills, Nash, and Young song. He tapped his foot from unspent nervous energy. Seven hours earlier he'd been on the perpetually uneasy streets of L.A. He felt like a fish out of water.

Inside the three-room apartment, he eased himself into a crinkly pretend-leather sofa that made a noise like milk drenching shredded wheat. He examined Meg's face more closely. The years had given her more confidence and focus, he noticed right away. She'd also blossomed physically. Her angular girlish features had found a soft, blended balance, and the promise of womanly beauty had been fulfilled, really fulfilled. He hadn't noticed until then how perfectly formed her mouth was, with soft, full lips and nearly perfect teeth that had probably cost Frank a bundle. He imagined that when she freed her hair from the barrette it would cascade over her shoulders. Her hair smelled of jasmine.

"What?" she said, uncomfortable under his scrutiny.

"Nothin'. How are you doing since we talked? How's your lab teacher friend?"

"Recovering, but bitter. I don't think he's coming back to school."

"What about the kids?"

"Nothing specific, but there's still something weird going on."

"Like what?

"Subtle things, innuendoes whenever the past comes up. Of course, no one mentions Wilkens anymore. But situations arise that automatically call her to mind. Yesterday, for instance, when we were discussing another class trip a few weeks from now. Mainly it's the same three boys. One, named Tim Sullivan, is the initiator, the other two take their leads from him."

"Whose bright idea was another class trip?" Jarrett shot back incredulously. He hadn't believed she'd said it.

"The administration's, but for once I'm on their side. I know it'll be good for the kids. The counselors agree, too."

"It's not the kids I'm worried about." He leaned back in the sofa, lacing his hands together behind his neck. "I wish this had been easier for you. The odds were in your favor of latching on to something more normal."

"What's strange is, I usually have a pretty good instinct about people. I can pick up on the evil ones right away, and I'm getting that signal about this little thirteen-year-old boy, Timothy. He's still a baby." Her right hand worked its way into her hair and twisted a lock tightly around a finger. Jarrett recalled that same nervous habit from the last time he'd seen her. "Not that I know what to do about it," she added a moment later, releasing her hair. A tight curl remained where her finger had played.

"Hang in there, we'll figure it out."

She reached for Jarrett's hand and held it tightly. "Thanks for coming so fast."

Jarrett wasn't prepared for the warmth or softness of her skin. For some reason his face grew hot and he slipped his hand out from under hers, searching for a topic. Mercifully, the phone rang in the kitchen, and Meg got up and excused herself.

Alone, Jarrett felt like a schoolboy. He berated himself over the discomfort that such a simple act as touching could cause.

To distract himself he examined the room. Only a few furnishings looked like they'd been added by Meg: an old bronze and glass lantern that she'd turned into a planter for ivy; a silver tray, elaborately etched, which might have been her mother's; a surprisingly racy sculpture of a naked couple touching at more places than he thought possible, definitely not provided by the landlord.

"What are you talking about?" Meg shouted from the kitchen. "You've made a mistake. Nothing like that happened here." She quieted to listen, then started again. "I told you I don't know anything about it. How did you get my number?"

Holding the phone to her ear she leaned back from the partition that separated the two rooms and beamed an annoyed look at Jarrett, then went back to the call. "If you do this again I'll notify the police," she shouted angrily and slammed down the receiver.

She came back into the living room, her face stony. "I don't believe it. That was a funeral home, one of their drivers. He was given my number and told to find out what time he should pick up a corpse, for embalming," she added with a shiver. "When I told him it was a mistake he read me my own address, Longview Road."

"Is there another Longview? Street or lane or something?"

"It doesn't matter, this wasn't any mix-up. He said the name of the deceased was Meg Katherine Foley." She looked at him with a mix of dread and bewilderment. "I haven't used my middle name in years. I have no idea how he knew it." She reconsidered. "I guess I did put it on my employment forms for the school."

Jarrett considered it. He had two feelings at the same time. One was the urgent desire to find the prankster and beat on his head, using his fists as drumsticks. The other was something he knew he'd find a lot harder to do: take Meg in his arms and comfort her.

In the end he settled for a hand on her shoulder. "It was a tasteless thing to do, but I'm sure it was only a joke."

"Yeah, I know," she answered immediately. "Like something a kid would do."

11

Dr. Frances Mae Melacore, the principal, left the main entrance of the Knollwood Middle School with an air of ownership and did not slow her pace when Vice-Principal Lester Arno joined her. Their most private conversations generally took place outside and on the move, where there was no risk of being overheard.

"I don't understand why you're having such a problem with her, Lester," Melacore said with measured nonchalance. "You made it clear what the penalties are?"

"Yes, but what she's doing isn't exactly illegal. And there's a union to deal with, potentially."

The subservience in his voice was never heard by anyone other than his present companion. Melacore had the power to fire him, without consulting the board.

"The discussion she had in class about Wilkens was against my specific instructions."

"She knew that. I've called a meeting with her first thing tomorrow to read her the riot act, about that and her sneaking around at the board." He neglected to mention that he was still working on exactly how to handle a situation that was much more delicate than Melacore acknowledged.

In a classroom on the third floor a young girl in a yellow

dress held a watering can over a window plant and looked down at the two most powerful personages in the school. Melacore glanced up at her at the same time, and the girl darted quickly away.

"Have you found out who her friend is yet?" Melacore wanted to know.

"Of course. After our encounter I stayed around to check the license plate of the car he was driving, and the name of the dealer he rented it from was on it. I went there and it took a lot of persuading, but I finally got a look at the copy of the driver's license he used. His name is Dan Jarrett. He's with the Los Angeles police. That's why I wanted to talk to you right away."

Melacore stopped walking and turned to him. Her authoritarian aura was suddenly diminished. "Lester, you're scaring the shit out of me. Why is he here?" She glared at him as if Jarrett's arrival were his fault.

"I have no idea, maybe he's a relative or a friend. He's not too old to be a boyfriend."

"I suggest you give Hudson a call about him."

Hudson Perry was a personal friend of Melacore's, Arno knew. He was also the Knollwood chief of police.

"I want to find out more about Foley, so we know what to expect. See if you can find out about anything improper in her background that doesn't appear on the résumé. We were in so much of a rush to get a replacement for Wilkens it's possible we weren't thorough enough, if you know what I mean."

Arno nodded dutifully.

She put a lilac-scented hand on his shoulder. The smell was so potent he wanted to gag. "Dig deep, Lester."

Privately, Arno cursed the luck that had put him in such an unfavorable position with his superior. How many teachers could he have recommended who would have had the balls to disobey him so blatantly, and who had such an insufferably combative friend, a cop no less, to help fight her battles?

"We can't let a couple of outsiders open up a wound that

took so much to close, can we, Lester? There are too many people that could get hurt."

He shook his head in agreement.

She flicked a piece of dust off his shoulder with a fingernail shaped like a talon.

The symbolism was not lost on Arno.

12

From the outdoor basketball court, the biggest kid in the eighth grade was able to spot his teacher as soon as she left the building. She'd come out of the side entrance, as she always did, cocky, full of herself, sexy, as she always was.

Timothy Sullivan launched his basketball in the air a few feet with a reverse spin, caught it on one bounce, and initiated his mock drill, charging forward, bobbing and weaving, dribbling through his legs, taking the fake pump and driving to the basket for an easy lay-up.

Other than her generalized fleeting glance at the schoolyard, he didn't think that Ms. Foley noticed him as she walked briskly to her car. When she passed he held the ball to his chest and peered over it, noticing her a lot.

The first thing he observed was that Ms. Foley was wearing the same light green silk blouse she'd had on in class that morning, no jacket. The blouse was thin and clung to her upper body when she moved. If you looked closely at the way the fabric moved you could see the outline of everything underneath. Foley had a whole lot more than Debra Caruso, who'd let him feel her up twice at parties in her basement. The shortness of her skirt caught his attention, and he wondered how he could find a way to see everything inside without being caught. So far the ways he'd conjured were too dangerous. On the other hand, the danger excited him.

For a moment he was diverted, thinking about the feelings he got around girls and what they made him want to do. He suspected that it had to do with what his doctor called "poor impulse control." The doctor told his mom that he was born with it. *Poor impulse control* was the reason he got into so much trouble at school and spent so much time chilling in the detention room. He'd been given little blue pills for *poor impulse control*, but they didn't do squat. That's why he'd stopped taking them without telling anyone.

Timothy angled his body so that he appeared to have his back to Ms. Foley when she reached her car, which was in the second row from the court. He was confident that there was nothing suspicious about a thirteen-year-old shooting hoops after school with his bike spilled on the lawn nearby. Good thing she couldn't read his mind.

At exactly the right moment, Timothy aimed another shot left of the rim so he could catch the rebound facing her when she opened the door and had to wriggle in. He was watching when her skirt hitched up and showed a major part of her upper thigh. When he saw it his heart pounded in his chest. The hell he had *poor impulse control*. If he did he'd be all over her by now.

When she started the engine of the red Cherokee and pulled out of the lot, Timothy took a last shot from half court. It was a mighty heave, but the ball fell short of the backboard. But by then, he was in no position to take notice of it. He was already on his seven-hundred-dollar Cannondale twenty-speed racing bike, heading after the Jeep.

There was no doubt in his mind that, with all the traffic lights and stop signs ahead, and some luck, he could keep up with her all the way to her home.

For his first actual look at it.

13

By the time they returned to Meg's place from dinner, a legion of New Jersey crickets were celebrating the demise of the day. Meg went into a desk drawer and produced an envelope that contained copies of old newspaper clippings on Wilkens's accident.

"The local paper did a big piece on her," she said, unfolding the front page of a newspaper for Jarrett's inspection. "I got a copy at the library."

Jarrett sat forward on the sofa and read the headline from the *Standard:*

REVERED MIDDLE SCHOOL EDUCATOR
KILLED IN WATER GAP ACCIDENT

The editor had chosen a winsome head-and-shoulders shot of Wilkens that looked as if it had been taken fifteen years earlier. In the photo she looked nothing like the ferocious and deeply disturbed disciplinarian Jarrett imagined from Meg's accounts. Her expression was open and serene, her head held high with a engaging smile, as though she were reacting to the punch line of a joke. She was confident, with a touch of the prima donna. It was the way the community wanted to remember her, more than the way she was near the end, Jarrett assumed.

The *Standard* had devoted two of the six front-page columns to the story, which was dated October 29.

A freak accident during a middle school class trip has claimed the life of Mrs. Elaine Wilkens, a respected teacher in the Knollwood school system for the past thirty-six years.

When Wilkens did not return to a group of students she was with near the summit of a mountain in western New Jersey, a search party was sent out and her body was discovered in a rock-strewn section of the ravine that lies just to the north of the Delaware River. The preliminary cause of death was listed as a broken neck.

According to accounts given by State Forest Service rangers, Wilkens fell to her death from a steep precipice in a part of the Delaware Water Gap that lies in Knowlton, New Jersey, in the Worthington State Forest. The time of death was listed at approximately 11:45 on Wednesday morning. The reason that Wilkens had wandered so close to the edge of the summit is not known at this time.

The fatal mishap took place on Mount Tammany, a popular visitor site at the Delaware Water Gap, and the highest point in the area at 1,527 feet. The accident was discovered after a parent, Hilary Schlag, a trip chaperone, could not locate the fifty-seven-year-old teacher and called the Forest Service for help.

The twenty-three eighth-grade students at the scene were not informed what had happened until they returned to school, where they were told in a spe cial meeting called by middle school principal, Dr.

Frances Melacore. By then a number of the students' parents had been notified of the incident and arrived at the school in time to meet the returning bus.

Jarrett looked up from the page, his mind working. "Someone must have interviewed the children to find out what they saw. Ever hear anything about that?"

Meg shook her head. "Just what it says in the newspaper, that they were told about Wilkens *after* they got back to school, which implies they didn't see anything happen." She poked her head forward to look for that place in the story. "Errol Volpe said there was an inquest into Wilkens's death. Is that unusual?"

"No. It would probably be treated as a death under suspicious circumstances, just because of the unusual nature of it, and only until the authorities were sure it wasn't a homicide. Did the inquest commission publish any findings?"

"Not that I know of. I don't think they ever came out with a public position. Even though it's effectively over, Errol said the investigation was never officially closed," she added. "Evidently, it got complex because of where she died. There were state police and park rangers involved at one end, and the local police at this end. It must have gotten very bureaucratic."

"Still, the police had to have talked to the kids. They were the last ones to see her." Meg shrugged and Jarrett continued reading.

A graduate of Trenton State Teacher's College, Elaine Wilkens began her career in the Knollwood school system in 1963. Starting in the Knollwood High School, Wilkens spent time in two other community primary schools before coming to the middle school in 1986, where she remained until last Wednesday. In the current year she had begun to teach members of the third generation of the same family in town.

During her service to the educational community, she had held posts as president of the Knollwood PTA on three different occasions, as well as serving for two years as president of the New Jersey Special Conference on Education. The then governor praised her as "a consummate educator, valued not only for her teaching skills, but her compassionate approach with her students."

There was no word at the time of this printing about any surviving family members. Mrs. Wilkens's husband was a town landscaper who died in 1978. Her only child, a daughter, succumbed to a rare blood disease two years later.

On Thursday, at a special memorial service held for Elaine Wilkens on the middle school lawn and attended by an estimated two hundred people, Mayor Mary Rosario described her as a "town treasure."

A few more paragraphs of personal information were followed by a section devoted to tributes by local residents, which included the school superintendent, president of the town council, and various tradespersons, all of whom had been her students at one time. "How long after it happened did you come to the school?" Jarrett asked.

"Five months or so."

"What did they do for a teacher in the meantime?"

"They tried a series of substitutes, which wasn't a good idea. The kids needed continuity more than anything. I took a chance and told them that in my interview, and I think they were impressed."

"It must have been rough the first time you stepped into that classroom."

Meg sighed deeply. "That's an understatement. It was very emotional, for me and the students. I remember how bewildered the children looked. The grief counseling could do just so much, I guess. Aside from what happened to their teacher, the death of an authority figure that close to them had to make them afraid personally. I also had a sense they resented me being there."

"Like being forced to accept a new parent?" Jarrett suggested.

"Maybe not that traumatic, but, yes, that's very perceptive."

Other newspaper clippings, which Meg had garnered from neighboring town libraries, contained abbreviated versions of the story. Jarrett skimmed through them before stopping at an article from the *Monroe Times Dispatch.* After the list of the notable posts Wilkens had held, this journalist had added what at the time was a startling piece of news for most people. It hadn't been mentioned in the local paper.

According to an unnamed source, the Knollwood Board of Education had met on at least two occasions that year to examine complaints lodged against Mrs. Wilkens. The complaints alleged "untoward and desultory" behavior in her classroom, but resulted in Wilkens's exoneration. These were the only incidents that blemished an otherwise stellar career of thirty-six years.

Jarrett showed the statement to Meg.

"Yeah, I saw that, too," she said, "and it's not completely true. I found four complaints and she wasn't actually cleared on any of them. Most of the decisions were postponed for further investigation."

"Which never had a chance to happen."

"There was hardly any point after she died. Actually, I was surprised to see that the paper chose to discuss it at all. It wasn't very tasteful in what was essentially a eulogy. I also wondered who their source was."

"Someone who still held a grudge," Jarrett offered. "The parents who'd complained, maybe."

"They'd have to be pretty angry to do it by then." She straightened up and stretched. "You see what I mean? The more you get into what happened to Wilkens, the worse it gets. And God knows what you being here is going to do."

She wrestled with a difficult decision, then pressed her

hands together in an unconsciously prayerful position. "I know this is going to sound completely out there. After all, we're talking about a group of eighth graders here, kids with everything going for them. They're some of the smartest in the state, parents involved in their education, every support system in the book, all that good stuff. A teacher's dream."

She looked up at Jarrett, who was attentive. "So what would you say if I told you it's possible the children in my class . . ." She stopped herself. She was having difficulty going on. "That the children murdered Mrs. Wilkens?" she finally uttered. "And that some of them may be planning to get rid of me?"

When she finished she didn't move a muscle. She studied Jarrett's expression, expecting either an amused grin or a fatherly rebuke for having reached such a ridiculous conclusion.

Jarrett stared back at her for a few long seconds before his scowl deepened perceptibly, and he nodded. "The thought had occurred to me," he said in all seriousness.

14

At 8:15 A.M., Meg Foley stood outside Frances Melacore's door with the same feeling she used to have as a primary school student when she was sent to the principal's office for punishment. This time, however, the stakes were a good deal higher.

When she was finally summoned inside, Melacore flashed the vague smile that Meg remembered on her first employment interview with her. Melacore sat ramrod straight and looked self-assured. If she'd worn a black robe she could have passed for a Supreme Court Justice.

Lester Arno was seated on a sofa opposite the desk. His one concession to congeniality was a pained look of welcome that lasted for about a millisecond. When Meg was seated, Arno cued his boss with a tilt of the head.

"I thought it would be better if we all did this together, and Lester agreed," Melacore said, taking control.

The tension in the room was palpable, not only between Meg and Arno, but between Arno and Melacore.

"Lester told me about your encounter at the Board of Education yesterday. Both of us regret what happened. We try to work together here, and frankly, that's why we've been concerned about some of the things you've been doing."

Meg noticed that the faint smile had vanished from her face as easily as it had been worn. "I wasn't trying to set up sides," she said. "As I told Mr. Arno, I was trying to find out what my students experienced with Mrs. Wilkens so I could help them. And to be frank," she echoed Melacore's word, "I didn't expect to be berated for it—or manhandled, for that matter."

Her gutsy rejoinder took them by surprise, and they exchanged uneasy glances that for some reason reminded Meg of those between Timothy Sullivan and his pals.

"Mrs. Wilkens's death had a huge emotional effect on all of us here," Melacore said smoothly, as though she'd made the remark a hundred times. "We're all extremely sensitive about that, and perhaps that's why Lester may have . . . over-reacted." She stared at Arno expectantly.

Nod like a good little boy, Lester, Meg said to herself.

He did, but almost imperceptibly. "I was disappointed by the secretive way you were going about your inquiry," he replied with an unctuous edge. "Besides, the complaints against Mrs. Wilkens were exceptional, the only ones in three and a half decades of teaching."

"But all within the past school year," Meg pointed out.

"And I didn't appreciate being accosted by your friend. He's a bit rough around the edges, for my taste."

Meg was wondering how long it would take for that topic to be raised. "He only tried to help me when he saw you grabbing my arm. He had no way of knowing who you were." *From the way you were acting*, she added silently.

"Would you mind telling us who he is and why he's here?"

"His name is Dan Jarrett, a friend from Los Angeles. He and my father were partners, before my father died. He's looked after me since then. He's a police officer," she added after hesitating.

She waited for the shock to register. Instead, both of them took it in stride. They must have already known.

"Is he here in the capacity of a friend, or a law enforce-ment officer?" Melacore stated too casually.

"A friend. Obviously, he has no jurisdiction here."

Arno started to say something but Melacore stopped him with a slight shake of her head. On the surface she remained a portrait of serenity, but she'd begun to fray around the edges. "Let's cut to the chase, Meg," she said. "You've shown a lot of interest in your predecessor since you arrived, more than we think is in the interest of the students and the school. Why are you going to all this trouble?"

For a moment Meg wondered if Melacore was open to an honest dialogue. That remote possibility required a conciliatory response.

"Look, I'm not insensitive to how painful Mrs. Wilkens's death must have been, but she's still such a strong presence in my class that it interferes with everything I try to do. I thought something might have happened between her and them that I could work on. When I heard about the complaints I thought it was a good place to start."

"Why didn't you come to me for help? That's why I'm here."

"There were some incidents in class, and at my home, that were very personal. There was a drawing of me on my blackboard that was a clear reference to Wilkens's death, and I took it as a threat. Unfortunately, as you know, I erased it before showing it to you. I also received a threatening call at home and wasn't sure it was a school matter. I had to find out why these things were happening."

"But we did advise you not get involved," Arno scolded again. He caught a castigating look from Melacore and retreated into the depths of his chair.

"I assumed it was just one or two of my students acting out, and that I could fix it myself. I didn't want to get any of my kids in trouble."

"Just so you know, I don't tolerate any harassment of my teachers, in school or anywhere else. I considered everything you said a school matter, and I'll personally look into all of the incidents." After her show of concern, real or otherwise, she sat back and changed direction. "In any case, Mrs. Wilkens was an exemplary teacher. If you had come to us we would have put to rest any concerns about that. The complaints leveled against her were inaccurate."

The board didn't say that. "The reports said the charges were still being considered when Mrs. Wilkens died."

Melacore braced. "Let's not fight about technicalities. The children's welfare is what we're all talking about. I'm concerned that rooting around in the past is the wrong thing to do, so I'm afraid I'll have to insist that you just stick to teaching in the best way you can. Sooner or later your students will come around, I'm sure. This is also the opinion of the counselors who've been working with your students."

Meg considered that the counselors might not take that stand if they knew how poorly their work had succeeded. "I live in that classroom every day. I see what the kids are going through, and I'm telling you something is still disturbing them a lot. Something is wrong with them."

Melacore was not happy. Her good cop routine hadn't gotten her what she wanted, and her politeness was at an end. "Are you aware that one of your students has become so upset that his parents called me to find out what's going on in your class? And that they've had to send their child to a therapist?"

Meg was stunned by the declaration. Other than the secretive looks between a few of her students, there'd been nothing to suggest anything that serious was bothering them. Then she remembered Jessie Lerner, shaking and turning pale at the mention of Wilkens's name. "Which one?"

"Augie Templeton. His parents said he's so afraid of you he's become phobic about school."

Again she was surprised. Templeton was one of the three boys who appeared contemptuous of her, one of the *co-conspirators*. She thought about that knee-jerk frame of reference and suddenly felt silly. The Watergate crowd were co-conspirators. These were eighth graders. Maybe she had gone off the deep end.

"His parents think your discussion about Wilkens was inexcusable," Arno offered bluntly.

"I hardly think anything I said could have caused that kind of problem, unless it was there to begin with," Meg answered quickly, but with apprehension. There was always the chance that Templeton's emotionality had been border-line about Wilkens, and that her discussion had pushed him too far.

She looked past Melacore to the window. The tops of playground climbing constructions were visible outside, empty because the kids were in class. Templeton was one of those kids, and perhaps he was still suffering more than she'd known.

Jessie Lerner is suffering more.

She shifted her attention back to Melacore. "I admit I'm not a therapist, but I think it's possible that—*am I really doing this?*—the children have a sense of . . . responsibility about what happened to Mrs. Wilkens."

The word reverberated in the room and Melacore and Arno went stiff in their seats. Meg estimated the reading at a ten on the Richter scale.

It would have been worse, she knew, if at the last moment she hadn't stopped herself from using the phrase she'd wanted to.

A sense of *guilt*!

15

A flurry of rustling noises somewhere outside the house defeated Meg's latest attempt to read the mystery novel and piqued her curiosity. The unusual sounds, plus the darkness, underscored her sense of self-imposed isolation.

The thought had occurred to her—Jarrett's favorite expression, she remembered—that after all this time she was still caught in the same repetitive, self-destructive pattern as always. For reasons she'd been unable to discover, she'd again positioned herself in a new community without friends and was unconnected to any society outside school. She was running before she could walk, immersed in a bizarre controversy that had swiftly made her an outcast and threatened to end her latest attempt at establishing roots. It was the same pattern of attack and retreat. She fervently wished history wouldn't repeat itself this time, but she knew it would.

Her reverie was interrupted this time by a rustling sound outside that seeped in through the window. She suddenly wished Jarrett were there, for safety, and maybe another reason she didn't want to deal with at the moment.

The disturbance on the lawn could have been an animal. It was unusual for area youngsters to be out after dark. The conservative couple that owned her two-family house didn't have kids, either, and so far had shown no inclination to entertain friends who might have brought some along.

A sudden hooting sound spread a thin layer of frost down the sides of her back. Clearly, she'd deceived herself by believing she had a greater tolerance for solitude than most people. A normal woman her age would have had a husband or lover at home, someone to help chase away the things that went bump in the night.

What's wrong with me?

Her mind filled up with Jarrett again. With him came a confusion of issues: safety, connection, trust, morality, all jumbled together. Her long stretch of celibacy confounded the issue further.

When the noise came again she slid over to the table lamp and switched it off. It was the only light on in the apartment, and she felt like it put her on display. As soon as it was dark inside she realized that the light on the deck had gone out—or had been put out. She was certain she'd left it on.

With heightened concern, she left the sofa and tiptoed into the kitchen to the window that faced the landlord's quarters. By the time she got there the sound stopped. In daytime, the sheer cotton curtains offered privacy from any peering eyes, but at night, with no light behind them, they turned opaque. She pulled them back all at once and looked out.

The ghastly creature that poked its head into the screen close to hers took her breath away. The face was bloodied and horrible, with deep gashes that had carved its flesh, as if slashed repeatedly by an axe. One eye was rendered sightless by an oozing gash that extended from a cleaved forehead down through one cheek.

Meg went rigid with fright and couldn't move. The cadaverous thing pressed harder into the window and made a wet, rasping sound that she recognized as *foleeeeeeee*.

Nearly frozen with terror, Meg backed away. She turned and tried to flee to the living room but stumbled and lost her balance. Scrambling to get up, she raced toward the front door with a single idea: escape. Her hand went to the knob and started turning it before she willed herself to stop and consider what was out there. She pressed her ear to the door, trying not to breathe so she could hear.

Someone playing a trick. But the face looked so real!

No matter what, she had to be safer inside, she quickly decided.

She let go of the door and crept back to the living room. There were two windows there, the shades pulled down on both, but one window was open at the bottom to let in fresh air.

Just a bad joke, like the drawing.

She tugged on the bottom of the shade gently, but it wasn't enough to engage the spring. She pulled harder, and this time it caught and shot all the way up to the top with a bang. Instantly, a hand on the other side tore at the screen, trying to claw its way through it. She let out a howl.

Not a child's hand. Not close to human.

She wondered why the couple next door hadn't heard her cries and come to investigate. Then, with a sinking feeling, she remembered that they were away visiting relatives. She ran to the phone, started to dial 911, then changed her mind and punched in Jarrett's phone number when pounding on the back door ruined her concentration. Slowly, in a building rhythmic cadence, it built in intensity until the noise sounded like feet stomping on benches in a stadium. Her hand shook so much she had a hard time holding the phone.

She felt trapped inside a cage.

The house was racked by a series of concussions. Now the thunderous sound came from along the entire back of the house, moving closer to where she was, heading for her. Many of them!

They see me, know where I am.

Above her, the ceiling shook with a synchronized assault on the roof, uncountable fists, or clubs, maybe hammers. The noise was deafening. The house vibrated violently, as if it were about to come off its foundation.

She pressed the telephone buttons more carefully this time, unable even to hear if there was a dial tone. She waited long enough for Jarrett to answer if he was there, then shouted for him to help her. She didn't know how long she'd been pleading when the pounding stopped all at once. By then there was static in the receiver.

Her power to reason returned slowly. It had to be kids. The face in the window was a mask. No one who looked like that could have still been alive.

The realization generated a sudden flurry of anger. It had been partly her fault. She'd allowed it to go on too long and should have confronted them. Kids run.

She turned and moved deliberately to the front door, her heart thumping heavily. On the way she thought she heard the sound of feet scurrying down the steps of the deck. She'd figured it right. They knew she was coming after them and were taking off. In the end, the risk that she'd recognize who they were was too great for them to take.

The light didn't work when she tried it, and she flung the door wide open all at once. The deck was empty. A few child-size figures scampered into the trees and disappeared.

In the darkness she could see something lying on the deck. It took shape slowly as her eyes became accustomed to the lack of light. The object was red and gray, the size of a small cat. The creature's eyes were closed. It was wet on the bottom where the insides of the animal's belly lay exposed from where it had been . . . *slashed?*

In pity, she stooped, wanting to stroke and comfort it, but she was afraid at the same time. When she was very close to it she suddenly made out what it was, and gagged. *A rat!*

She fell back in total revulsion, but was unable to look away. When she could stand again she reached for the door.

Before she was able to slam it shut, the rat opened its eyes and looked right at her.

16

There was no way the prearranged visit to police headquarters was going to be the high point of the day, either for him or for Hudson Perry. The best he could hope for was a modicum of professional cooperation, for as long as it lasted.

The Knollwood Police Headquarters on Mercer Street was a combination police station and volunteer fire department. It had been that way ever since Knollwood had been incorporated in 1873. Hudson was an ox of a man with endlessly broad shoulders needed to support a gut that required its own zip code. His face was round and pudgy, his eyes moist. The swollen end of an aquiline nose had been eroded by years of drinking. There was a faint smell of cigars in the room, cheap domestic ones at that.

"Thanks for taking the time," Jarrett said, remaining standing.

"Don't worry about formalities around here," Perry said agreeably.

The chief was soft-spoken, maybe to compensate for his size. Jarrett wondered how long the good times were going to last.

"This is about the Foley woman?" Perry recapped.

"Yeah. But it's gone beyond the incidents I told you about.

Someone came to her house last night and terrorized the hell out of her. A bunch of kids, she thinks."

Perry showed part surprise, part suspicion. In a moment suspicion won out, and he asked if she recognized any of them.

"No, she didn't. They wore fright masks and beat on the walls. She guesses there were at least a half dozen of them. It lasted until she finally chased them away." Jarrett fixed the big man with a steady stare. "We've got one frightened woman here. It's gotten to the point where something's gotta be done."

Perry kicked back in his chair and clasped two pasty, liver-spotted hands behind his neck. "Just for the record," he said, studying the new face, "what's your connection to Foley. She a relative?" he said with a supercilious glare.

"Her father and I were partners in L.A. We were close. He was killed on a raid with me seven years ago, and I promised to watch out for her. When she called me for help I came to see what I could do."

"And that's all there is between you?"

The question was inappropriate, which is what Jarrett's look of disdain conveyed.

"And what is it you want me to do?"

"It's a good bet that her harassment has been by kids, probably from the middle school. One or two of your men hanging around there asking questions would send a message. It could be as easy as that."

Perry leaned forward and put his palms on the desk. "It would have been better if Foley called herself."

"I offered to handle it for her."

"Even so, I don't know anything about it being kids, let alone from which school. I'll send someone to her house, but without any evidence I can't just start rousting children. Their parents would throw a shit fit, and I wouldn't blame them."

"Everything that's happened makes you suspect that it's her students. The drawing on the blackboard, maybe even that science teacher getting hurt. They're trying to scare

Meg for some reason, and it's escalating fast. You have to try to stop it."

His imperious tone didn't sit well with Perry. "Those were both school matters. We investigated the accident at the lab, and there was no reason to suspect it was anything else. As far as a drawing on a blackboard, hell, I can't send an officer to a classroom every time some kid throws a spitball."

"People bashing someone's house at night isn't exactly a spitball. It's part of a pattern I see all the time in stalking cases. It needs to be stopped now, before it gets worse."

"Gimme a break, Captain," Perry said with a condescending smile. "Even if it was a bunch of little boys pounding on their teacher's house, that hardly constitutes stalking in my book."

Perry's confident appraisal forced Jarrett to a place he didn't want to go. "For what it's worth, I'm not convinced it is her kids."

"Now you're really reaching."

"I hope I am, I really do."

Perry reached into a desk drawer and plucked out a fat cigar with a pointed tip. He squeezed it to see if it was fresh, then used a cutter to snip its end. "I want to tell you something," he said when he was done. "This is a quiet little town, and it's my town. I'll give you the courtesy a fellow officer deserves, so long as you don't interfere in local matters. But I have my limit. Go over it and I'll personally escort you out, you got that?"

Jarrett understood. He'd heard the speech before, in about a hundred iterations. The best response, he'd found, was to agree unconditionally, then go do what he had to do anyway. "I got it," he said.

"That's good," Perry added with less agitation. "And since you're cooperating with me, I'll send a man to Foley's house to see what we can find."

"I know Ms. Foley will appreciate that," Jarrett said. *Like you had a choice*, he thought.

Outside of headquarters, Jarrett drifted toward his rented

Explorer with serious misgivings. For an unknown reason he'd had to badger Perry into doing the right thing. The sense of a nonevent was still eating at him when he felt a tap on his right shoulder and spun around quickly with his fists formed.

"Take it easy," said a man who put his hands up protectively. He looked strangely familiar, and Jarrett realized why. He was the same height and build as Jarrett, with a strikingly similar face. The stranger noticed it, too, and was squinting to make sure of what he saw.

"What are you, my long-lost twin?" Jarrett said.

"Weird, isn't it," the officer said, extending a hand. He had shining black hair fringed with silver, and, on closer inspection, was probably a few years Jarrett's senior. He also had the wan look of an obsessive long-distance runner, or a macrobiotic freak.

"Paul Haucklin."

"Dan Jarrett, LAPD."

Still pumping Jarrett's hand, Haucklin said, "I have a kid brother in L.A. who told me a lot about you. He's not with enforcement, just a social services lawyer, but he likes to keep up with everything that's going on."

"I get a lot of press lately."

"It's an honor."

The handshake was getting embarrassingly long.

"What can I do for you?" Jarrett said, wedging his hand free. It had been a long time since he'd received anything approaching praise for his activities, especially from someone in L.A.

Haucklin indicated that there was a better place to talk, and guided him to part of the parking lot lost in shadow. "Speaking for some of us on the force, we're glad you're here. We're behind you one hundred percent."

"I'd appreciate it more if I knew what the hell you were talking about."

Haucklin was surprised by his reaction. "You're here about the Wilkens case?"

"Maybe, maybe not. I'm here to help a friend."

Haucklin winked. "Well, me and some of the other guys wouldn't mind one little bit if the Wilkens investigation was reopened, I mean for real. And the more private the better."

"For what reason?"

"I never bought into the idea that the old lady just happened to fall off a mountain. And that the kids who were there had nothing to say about it. Can we talk?"

The blatant appeal for his confidence was unnerving. On the other hand, Haucklin had an ingenuous quality that Jarrett liked immediately—or else the man was a good actor. It also occurred to him that Haucklin might have been sent by Perry, to tail him.

"What the hell," Jarrett said at length. "Tell me some more about that damn fine brother of yours."

17

For the second time that day, Jarrett observed the group convene away from the other students and take turns looking around in fear of being overheard. Maybe they were just shooting the bull about sports or school or girls. Maybe because they were on the fateful class trip, there was more to it than that.

Timothy Sullivan, Doogie McMillan, and Augie Templeton held court on the fringe of the schoolyard near a wooded area donated to the town as an arboretum. Because conformity was not a liability in the late nineties, all of the boys wore oversized T-shirts and loose-fitting pants that hung halfway down their butts, the official uniform of the skaters. Where he came from, skateboarders were usually part of the less scholarly crowd, the asphalt surfers.

Sullivan and Templeton talked nose to nose. At one point Sullivan stuck a finger in Templeton's chest and appeared to be lecturing. Templeton left a short time after that, looking upset. After he was gone the other two said something to each other, knocked their fists together, and separated.

Jarrett caught up to Sullivan a block from school. The boy turned when he called his name and looked belligerent. "My name is Jarrett. I'm a friend of your teacher, Ms. Foley."

Sullivan's reaction told him it wasn't the best credential he could have used.

"How do I know that?" he said confrontationally.

"You sit in the fourth row, third seat, and you're gonna get a B minus in math this marking period 'cause you think you know all the answers but you don't. I hear you're a pretty good athlete. Football, baseball?"

"Soccer, lacrosse," Sullivan said, making Jarrett feel like he was from the Middle Ages. "How do I know you're not a kidnapper? Or some psycho child molester?"

The question was absolutely appropriate, and its bluntness reminded Jarrett of someone else as a kid. "If I was a molester I'd pick someone a lot less ugly."

The rejoinder forced a limp smile out of the scowl, but it didn't last for long. "Whaddaya want? I gotta get home."

"I was just wondering how you are at drawing?" Jarrett watched Sullivan's eyes, but they held steady. "Ms. Foley told me about a drawing on her blackboard the day Mr. Volpe had an accident in the lab."

"So?"

"It was a pretty good drawing. A woman who looked just like Ms. Foley falling off a mountain. You wouldn't happen to know anything about that?"

Sullivan replied with a quick shake of his head, too quick. He looked as if he'd rather be anyplace else in the universe.

"Actually, she's had a couple of problems lately, not all at school. Some weirdo called her house and said he was an undertaker. Ring a bell?"

"Why was that so weird?"

Jarrett leaned closer and whispered, "Nobody died."

Timothy shrugged.

"Also, a bunch of people came to her house the other night and started playing it like a drum."

"I don't play drums. Soccer and lacrosse, remember?"

Cool customer, Jarrett thought. "Well, if you know anyone who gets his kicks doing stuff like that, tell them the bogeyman will get them if they don't watch out."

Sullivan smirked.

"What's so funny?"

"I didn't know that's what you guys were calling your-selves these days. Bogeymen."

Jarrett had no idea what he was talking about.

"Cops. Isn't that what you are, a cop?"

The kid was a lot spunkier than he'd given him credit for.

"Just a lucky guess," Sullivan chirped, reading Jarrett's mind. His expression was victorious. "See ya around, Officer Jarrett." He turned away and headed for a path through the trees.

Jarrett had the urge to take the kid down a peg, but thought better of it and let him walk away.

Before he was out of earshot, Sullivan revealed another one of his many talents, whistling.

The tune sounded a lot like "Who's Afraid of the Big Bad Wolf?"

18

Meg hurried from the middle school and met Jarrett in the parking lot. Her face telegraphed major concern, and the paper she clutched in her hand appeared to be the cause of it.

"Take a look at this" she said, slipping into his Explorer. The paper was a computer printout that read simply, *I know what happened to Mrs. Wilkens*. The note had no signature, and the bottom was torn above the normal perforation line, suggesting the writer might have signed it and then changed his or her mind.

The envelope it came in was addressed to Meg. Her name appeared to be cut out from an official school form and pasted on.

"It was on my desk," she said. "Could have come from any computer in school. They all use the same paper."

"Was anyone around when you found it?"

Meg shook her head impatiently. "Why would someone go this far and then not sign his name?"

"Why not talk to you in private?"

"There is no real privacy in school. Any student talking to me would have risked being seen by others."

Jarrett reached for the envelope and turned it over. It had been sealed with clear tape and the job was sloppy. "I'm glad you ripped it open from the side and not the back," he declared.

"Why does that matter?"

"You might have spoiled the tape."

Meg let the thought sink in, then got it. "You're not really thinking of taking fingerprints?"

Jarrett's solemn stare answered her question. "I'll need something each of your kids has touched."

She mulled it over disagreeably. "I guess I could pass out an assignment, say on acetates with their names on it."

"First thing tomorrow?"

"I guess so, yes." She nodded, but was still in a mild state of disbelief. "Isn't this against the law or something—fingerprinting minors without them knowing?"

"Your point being?" Jarrett said without looking at her.

Careful not to touch the tape, he folded the envelope in half and put it in his pocket with the note.

19

At twenty after six on Wednesday afternoon, the students and most of the faculty had cleared the building, but the ground-floor doors were still unlocked, allowing young athletes to leave after their various practices. The custodial staff hadn't begun their daily sweep of the lower level. They worked from the top down, and not every day.

The boys' lockers at Knollwood Middle School were located to the rear of the main gymnasium on the bottom floor, one stairway below street level. Jarrett walked with a determined air of authority through the side entrance to the gym to blunt the challenge of anyone who might question him. Most people, he'd found, would opt for a judicious dereliction of duty rather than risk a confrontation with someone who appeared empowered.

An encounter with Arno, on the other hand, would present a different problem. In that case Jarrett was prepared to say that he'd come to meet Meg and gotten lost; weak but plausible. If Arno caught him during the commission of his proposed crime he was prepared to be totally screwed. He'd calculated the odds and decided to go ahead.

A day earlier, Timothy Sullivan had not observed the man who'd passed behind him as he packed up for home.

But Jarrett had noticed Sullivan, and the number on his locker. Now, as he approached the area, he was quickly able to locate 316.

The combination lock was low-grade with a cheaply made spin dial. The rounded top jiggled loosely in its engaging mechanism, allowing it to move up and down a quarter inch or so. It might be effective against adolescent pilferage, but it was not the greatest challenge of his career.

Looking around to make sure he was alone, he retrieved the tire iron he'd gotten from his Explorer and inserted it into the open space between the pieces of metal. With one quick jerk the lock popped open. The sharp sound it made resounded in the space, but no one came running.

The metal door opened onto a scene from *Tales from the Crypt*. A fraction of the cubicle was used for books and clothing, all heaped together at the bottom. The rest was a montage of bizarre posters on all available surfaces, the front pages of female superhero comic books and pages from explicit porno magazines. All had flagrantly sexual imagery, women with jutting breasts and chains, female vampires in an orgy of blood, alien females who could have come from the pen of Vargas.

As another common thread, each picture had a violent component. Several had mutilation themes. Our little pervert has a very sick side, Jarrett thought.

On the top shelf, there was an assortment of grimy items in a clump. Some were sticky to the touch, and Jarrett wished he'd worn gloves for the job. Taking care not to start an avalanche, he removed several half-eaten candy bars and an open bag of chips with a greenish mold growing there since before penicillin. The foodstuffs were flanked by a small stash of cosmetics, an acne cream, aftershave and mirror, and a package of condoms. The condom package had been opened, but none of its contents was missing. There was a half-smoked joint inside.

The last two items were visible only after all the others had been pushed to one side. These articles had been wrapped in lunch bag paper, probably to preserve them amid the trash.

The first was a swatch of folded fabric. Jarrett spread it open and stared at the cloth, which was a woman's handkerchief, lacy on one side, with the initials E.W. embroidered on it in old fashioned script. With a shiver, Jarrett wondered how the little thief had gotten hold of one of Wilkens's personal articles. *Why* he'd wanted it was a matter for a therapist—or a grand jury one day.

The second item was a pair of pantyhose.

A sudden sound behind him gave Jarrett a start. He turned in time to see the back of a head and an arm vanish up a stairway to the first floor. After that he heard the soft padding of sneakers.

Quickly he rewrapped the handkerchief and pantyhose and put them back in the locker. He did his human best to recreate the original mess, then pressed the door shut and fit the rounded section of the lock back into the solid base.

In the morning, Sullivan would find his locker as he left it, except, for a mysterious reason, his lock would be totally useless.

Not a problem. In a school like this he'd have his choice of new ones before he hit homeroom, no questions asked.

20

Aerosmith was so hot in the Cherokee's rear speakers that it took a few extra seconds for Meg to notice the flashing lights at the crossing. When she finally brought the vehicle to a swift but late stop on the gravel apron, she was nearly up to the gates.

To her right, the freight train was still a good half mile away, pulled by twin locomotives facing opposite directions. The locomotives' arrangement was a good metaphor for herself, she mused, never sure which way to go, often going both ways at once.

The train had about twenty cars and was traveling fast. With her proximity to the tracks, she felt a giddy tingle of excitement, like she used to get as a kid before going on a roller coaster ride. Danger was definitely part of the feeling. Every year she read a story about some poor soul who'd gotten struck on the tracks only a few feet from where she now was.

The thought of one kind of wreck begat another, more familiar: her latest career move that appeared to be bound for disaster. It wasn't the first. After bouncing from college to college and finally getting her teaching certificate, she'd had two stints at private schools and the post in New York, the total time of which was less than three years.

The job at Knollwood had been a welcome bolt from the blue. One of her professors had recommended her to Melacore, who, in the middle of a term, was anxious to find a replacement teacher for Wilkens. But the successful and cordial interviews were history. Meg was in trouble again, back on the wrong side of the tracks.

A light tap on her rear bumper diverted her from the unsettling thought. In the rearview mirror she saw a sports utility truck much larger than hers, which had evidently stopped a little too late. A group of boys were inside, a few of high school age, maybe some younger.

She turned down the radio and debated getting out to look for damage, but the bump had been gentle. She checked the train again. It was a few hundred yards away and closing fast. The shrill warning of its horn convinced her that this was not a good time to abandon her Jeep.

A second impact from behind was strong enough to push her car forward a few inches before she stomped down on the brake and stopped moving. This time it was obvious that the collision was deliberate, and forceful enough to have done some damage. Meg was fuming mad. The kids in the truck were playing a very dangerous game, considering where her truck was.

She lowered her electric window and stuck her head out to look back at them. "What the hell are you doing?"

The youth on the passenger side of the truck leaned out of his own window and yelled something back, but the roar of the approaching train made it hard to hear. The lewd expression on the boy's face, and the way the others laughed, told her it was probably better that she didn't understand him.

His unintelligible remark was followed by another moderate jolt, and the boys in the truck became more animated. A smaller impact followed, then another and another, until it felt as if the two vehicles ended up touching.

A respite lasted for only a few seconds, when her car started to slide forward again. Shocked, she held her foot down on the brake as tightly as she could, but her effort failed to overcome the power of the larger truck. In panic, Meg felt the brake fighting her. Without waiting she threw the shift forward until it locked into park, and held her breath.

Even with its wheels locked the car continued to move forward. The locomotives were less than a football field away.

The hood of the Jeep contacted the crossing gate and kept going, bending it back until it looked as if it were about to snap. Her front bumper was now only an arm's length from the tracks themselves, and she didn't know how far out the locomotive's carriage extended.

Behind her she could feel the vibration of the larger engine straining. In a last-ditch effort she pulled the emergency brake up as far as it would go, but it didn't help.

The train's engineer was leaning out of the cab window, waving his hands furiously and operating his blaring horn in rapid bursts to get her attention. At the relatively short distance, and the speed he was traveling, there was no way he could stop in time. It was up to her to get the Jeep out of the way, or get out.

Her hand went to the door handle as she started to count. It was locked. In confusion she kept yanking on it instead of lifting the pin that would release it. The train was on her and she was still being pushed into its path. She screamed and closed her eyes.

Mercifully, she felt the force acting on her from behind stop. The racing locomotive engine sounded its horn continuously as it passed within a few inches of her hood. The Cherokee shook as if it were going to come apart, but there was no collision. In seconds, the sound faded away with the passage of the locomotives. Meg put her head down on the steering wheel and shook uncontrollably.

The world was eerily still after the last car passed. Meg's head was still down on the steering wheel when the young man from the truck appeared at her window. She made sure the doors were still locked as soon as she saw him. The youth stopped at the front window and signaled for her to lower it.

His face was fresh-scrubbed and surprisingly gentle. His gaze was conciliatory, probably with the awareness that he and his friends had gone too far. They had come to their senses, she guessed, and he'd come forward as their emissary to apologize. Their prank had put her through living hell, but the gesture was better than nothing.

She lowered the window a little, just enough to talk.

The young man bent down to the level of the opening with a choirboy face.

He said it without the slightest hint of reluctance.

"Hey, teacher. Why don't you get the fuck out of our town."

21

Jarrett's second scheduled meeting with Hudson Perry in two days never came off. At the last minute, the Knollwood chief of police was called away on unspecified personal matters, this according to the precinct sergeant. Perry had left his assurances, however, that he'd personally follow up on the train incident when he returned.

At the station house, a young officer conducted a perfunctory question-and-answer session with Meg that produced only enough data to fill out his accident report. Following that, a run-through of local high school yearbooks did nothing to help identify the young man who had left the truck to threaten her. That dashed the theory that he might have been an older brother of one of her eighth graders. Her description of the SUV was so general as to be useless.

The ride to her place was somber, and Meg was still resentful when they settled on two high kitchen chairs. "Perry didn't want to deal with me, it's as simple as that."

"He doesn't strike me as the kind to run from a confrontation."

"But he did. It feels like I'm trying to dig up something about Wilkens, and his job is to keep it buried."

"We don't know that."

"Thanks for your support." Meg shot him a disparaging glance. "I especially enjoyed the detective calling the whole thing a prank. I mean, is it me, or did someone try to push me into a speeding train? What ever happened to assault with intent to kill?"

"It looks like those kids only intended to scare you. From what you told me they could have done anything they wanted to."

"Small comfort."

Jarrett looked at her with sympathy. At that moment she reminded him of her father, staunch on the outside but with a center as soft as brie. Meg was a powerful presence, too, but her intensity came from contradictory qualities, innocence fused with cynicism, a searcher with a gift for black humor. She was also a beauty, albeit a restless one. Her contrasts distracted him—captivated was a better word.

Making matters more confusing, he'd started to feel the boy-girl thing at work, the last thing he intended. The admission generated a flashback to a time two years earlier, a hospital bed, his wife Beth Ellen lying unconscious, and a pang of guilt for what he was feeling now.

The dumbest line in sexist history passed in and out of his mind. *You're beautiful when you're angry.*

"I know what you're thinking," she was saying. "It's that paranoid lunatic streak again."

He was relieved to see that she misread his sudden silence as censure. "Don't be so hard on yourself."

"Who, me?" She sprang from the chair, bristling with unspent energy, and went to a cupboard for two glasses. In a short time they were filled with cabernet. Jarrett wished it were scotch and remembered his fledgling ulcer, a thirty-eighth birthday present from the cop fairy.

Feeling the warmth of the wine, Meg retreated to the living room and the sofa's pillows. He followed.

"What is it with this town, anyway?" she said. "It was supposed to be the best place in the world."

Jarrett ruminated thoughtfully. "I think it's the garbage and the lawns."

She stared at him in amusement.

"No, really. I never saw a place where the trash is tied up so nice and neat. Yellow bins for this, green bins for that. And the grass—it's like someone runs a comb over it every morning. People here want everything to be like their well-ordered lives, everything in its place, right down to their garbage. It probably reassures them."

Meg speared a lock of her hair and twisted it until it knotted. "I think it's all about winning. You got a lot of kids here who are the sons and daughters of amazingly successful parents. Some of my students' parents get multimillion-dollar bonuses every year."

"God bless America."

"God bless *some* Americans. But it does have its advantages. The schools' curriculum here is twice as thick as other places. And a number of parents spend some of their big bucks on extras for their kids, like special tutors and counselors. Some of the athletes have personal trainers, and when they find a good one they don't tell anyone about it, just so their kids have an edge. And that's no big surprise—not in a place where Little League is bigger than religion."

Jarrett tilted his head incredulously. "Where I come from, a good day for a kid is when he doesn't get beaten up. Your students have it pretty cushy."

"Some of them, not all. But this need for your kid to win at all costs is totally out of control. I heard about one thing I still can't believe. A kid was competing with another for the last spot on the All-Stars baseball team, and it looked like he was out of the running. But it turned out his father employed the father of the one who was going to beat him out, and the father was suddenly transferred out of town with his family. Of course, no one could prove it was because of the All-Stars, but it certainly took care of that problem."

"Did the other kid make the team at least?"

"Uh-uh. He was knocked off at the last minute by another one who was secretly taking pitching lessons from an ex-Yankee. The pitcher moved in with his family for two weeks, for cryin' out loud."

"Gotta love it."

"Makes you wonder about the expectations the affluent children grow up with. I think they're headed for a dose of reality they might not be able to handle in the real world. And the normal ones tend to get lost in the cracks. Imagine what a culture like this does to a regular kid's self-image."

"Maybe it toughens them up more than you think. In the end, maybe it's an advantage."

Meg thought about it and nodded at the new perspective. "I had a chance to look into Timothy Sullivan's locker," Jarrett said, suddenly off on a new tangent.

Meg looked askance at him. "Had a chance? What, did it just fly open when you were passing by?"

"Something like that. There was a lot of weird stuff in there, and I'm not just talking about the condoms and marijuana." He stopped, feeling awkward. "Would you mind if I asked what kind of pantyhose you wear?"

Meg turned a rich shade of lavender. "That's what you found in his locker?"

"You got a pair for me to see?"

She hesitated, then got up and left for the bedroom. She returned with an unopened package of L'eggs, dark brown.

"Do you ever wear black?"

"Most women have a few pair of black. I can't believe the little creep had these in his locker? Was it this brand?"

"I don't know, there wasn't any package. They all look the same to me."

"Not if you look close." Meg churned for a moment, then leaped to a fearful thought. "How do you think he got them? Did he go into my trash? Were the ones you found ripped?"

"I didn't notice. I also found a handkerchief with the initials E.W. on it."

Meg's eyes were enormous. "He's collecting articles of clothing from his teachers?"

"Looks like it."

"My God." She settled back into the sofa and quieted. "The more we talk about the school and my students, the more depressing it is. Sometimes I wonder why I just don't pack up and forget the whole thing." She leaned to her side and her shoulder touched Jarrett's. The contact was warm and reassuring. She felt safe with him. "So, you enjoy this breaking-and-entering fetish of yours?" she asked provocatively.

Jarrett grinned. "I like to think of it as bending and entering."

"But it's okay to do, so long as you get what you need?"

"If the circumstances call for it."

"Which circumstances this time?"

"Watching over somebody you care about, someone who's part of my family," he said tenderly.

His choice of words triggered a troubled reaction in her. She fashioned an insecure smile and put her hand on his chest. Up close his rugged features seemed softer. His hair was tousled, and he smelled faintly of old leather. He was more handsome than she'd noticed, and his crinkly eyes cast a curious spell.

A new thought took shape and surprised her with its intensity.

I'm not sure I want you to think of me as family anymore.

22

Tim Sullivan snapped his new lock shut and spun the dial. There was no accounting for how his old lock had broken. No one he knew would have had the guts to tamper with it. They knew the price they'd pay if they got caught.

It was still a few minutes before Foley's math class, enough to slide over to where Maria Mandis was and get something going with her. He'd noticed that Maria had become totally hot since last year. And he could tell by the way she looked at him that she liked him, too, that and the way her friends giggled when he walked by.

Instead, he cast a glance to his left where Augie Templeton was at his locker, moving in slow motion. Augie wasn't the same kid as before, when they used to hang out and have sleepovers. In fact, he didn't like the way Augie was acting at all lately, not showing up for practices, avoiding him like the plague, taking little blue pills when he thought no one was looking.

Also, Augie didn't look so good. He had dark shadows under his eyes, like he was allergic or something, only he wasn't. The worst part was the scared expression he'd get in class whenever something reminded him of Mrs. Wilkens. The look was there all the time now, even in other classes they shared. From the day the accident happened he'd feared that Augie was weak and couldn't be trusted. Now he knew he was right and that something had to be done about it.

Maria Mandis shot a disappointed look at him when he ignored her and went up to Templeton. Augie saw him coming and became immersed in his locker, like he didn't want to talk.

"What are ya doin'?" Sullivan said. "You're gonna be late."

"I don't feel so good," Augie croaked, like he was about to cry.

"You're all messed up. What's going on with you?"

"Nothing. I don't know."

"I think I do." Timothy put a hand on his shoulder.

Augie ducked out from under the contact. Hurriedly, he pulled his math book from the bottom of a pile in his locker. As it came out, a loose envelope came with it and landed on the floor face up.

Sullivan got to his knees before Augie did and speared it. The principal's name was written on it in pen, good writing like an adult's, probably Augie's mother. The word "Important" was under Melacore's name and underlined.

"Gimme that," Augie said

"Looks serious."

"Give it back," Templeton made a grab for it, but Sullivan turned his back, tore it open, and read aloud: "'Dear Mrs. Melacore. Since my son is still having the problems we spoke about, I'd appreciate it if you would ask his teachers to monitor him and give me their feedback. Please allow him to visit the nurse if he requests it, and call me.'" It was signed Barbara Templeton. Sullivan wheeled around. "What the hell is this about? What are you seeing a therapist for?"

The color drained from Templeton's face. "It's personal. I'm not supposed to talk about it."

"You don't see a therapist because you have a virus or anything."

There was no answer from Templeton. He was stonewalling

him, Sullivan guessed. "Whaddaya going mental or something?"

"None of your business." Templeton grabbed the note back, stuffed it in his jeans pocket, and closed his locker. He clicked the lock shut just as the tone sounded for the new class to begin.

Sullivan looked around at the few remaining students rushing from the area. He took a step closer to the smaller boy, effectively blocking his exit. In a few seconds they were alone. "It's about Mrs. Wilkens, isn't it?"

Templeton sized up the bigger boy. Sullivan was pissed off, and when he got that way he could do anything. He had once shoved a sixth grader down a flight of stairs because the kid made fun of his Nikes. "Maybe it is, I don't know."

Sullivan's thin lips pressed together tightly, and his shadow fell across Augie's face. "You didn't tell your parents about it, or your therapist? About what happened?"

"Uh-uh. I haven't told anyone."

"But that's what this is about. You *want* to tell."

"I don't know. I don't feel right anymore."

"We took an oath, you, me, and Doogie," Sullivan admonished loudly. "You know what happens if you tell?"

Templeton nodded. He looked as if he was going to throw up.

"They'll kick you out of school. They'll send you to one of those prisons for kids. Not even your mother could stop them."

With effort, Templeton fought back tears. He made an effort to shove the heavier boy aside. "Leave me alone, I gotta go see the nurse." He moved defiantly around Sullivan, but only because Sullivan let him. He took a few steps down the hall, then looked back to see if Sullivan was going to try to stop him.

Sullivan glared at him. Augie had been his best friend once, now he'd become an enemy who could get them into trouble, real trouble, all three of them.

"Hey, I didn't get a chance to tell you," he shouted to the retreating boy, thinking fast. "I just learned about this cool new karate move on the Internet. A way you can snap some-one's neck in a second. Wanna see how it works?"

Templeton stood like a statue for a moment but didn't answer. Eventually, he turned and walked away. He was praying there was nobody between him and the nurse's office. No one to see him crying.

23

"It was no accident. It was sabotage, pure and simple."

They were on the patio behind Errol Volpe's quaint Victorian residence. Angry purple blotches on Volpe's face and neck showed the healing process still had a long way to go. He now had a permanent wounded look that had aged him considerably.

"I wanted to perform an experiment for my students to try to stimulate their interest in chemistry. It was dramatic, but completely innocuous. Even though I prepared the chemicals the day before, to be safe, I did a test before my students arrived."

"Is it possible you made a mistake when you set it up?" Meg asked.

"Not a chance in hell. Someone tampered with the materials *after* I prepared them. They must have added a combustible that I didn't detect. That's one reason I'm not going back."

"I hope you don't mean that," Meg said swiftly. "You're too good a teacher. It would be a big loss for the school. And for me."

"I said that was one reason. There are others."

"The police couldn't find any evidence of tampering," Jarrett volunteered.

Volpe's expression was sardonic. "Has the lab been used since the explosion?"

"No, but it was cleaned," Meg said.

"So it's the word of the police against mine." He shrugged. The verdict was in and he'd lost. "The other reason I'm not going back is that I know it won't end here if I do."

Jarrett could see how frightened he was. "Any idea who might have wanted to hurt you? Do you think it was a student?"

"Possibly. I've even considered that it could be Lester Arno."

"You must be kidding," Meg said.

"The explosion happened the day after he overheard us talking about Wilkens in the teachers' lounge. You said you thought he'd been listening to us before he ordered us to class. That was about the time you found the drawing on your blackboard. Maybe each of us got our warning."

"I can't believe it," Meg said, even though she'd had the same thought. "He could go to jail. Why would he take a risk like that?"

Volpe just stared at her, and Meg felt a shiver.

After they left Volpe, the ride home took them within a few blocks of the high school. Jarrett was driving and ruminated over the incident at the railroad tracks. He wished that Meg had had the presence of mind to get the license plate number of the truck, but that was asking a lot considering the approaching danger.

Meg could almost hear the clicking of Jarrett's mind, like the sound her laptop computer made when it was thinking. She noticed the way he held the wheel of the Explorer with two fingers, a very capable hand. He was strong and in control in most areas—but not all, she recalled. His reaction when she touched his hand, quickly withdrawing it, was a clear indication of his shyness.

"Where does Jessie Lerner live?" Jarrett asked abruptly.

"I don't know. I can look it up, why?"

"The fingerprints on the note matched hers, on the

acetates you passed out. I just got them back and didn't want to tell you just before we talked to Volpe."

"Are you sure?" Meg said, not completely shocked.

"I had them FedExed to L.A., to a friend who's very thorough."

She stared out the windshield blankly. "I think she lives in the local district. She's such a fearful kid. I'm impressed she had the courage to send it."

"Weren't Jessie's parents one of the ones who complained about Wilkens?"

"One of two families, yes."

"Dum da dum dum," Jarrett hummed the old *Dragnet* music.

"There's something I've been meaning to tell you, too," Meg said abruptly. "You know how Wilkens had started to teach the third generation of students?"

Jarrett nodded but kept his eyes on the road.

"One of them is Timothy Sullivan."

"Really?" he responded with mild interest.

"I also thought you'd want to know about the first member of his family to have her as a teacher. He was Hudson Perry, our illustrious police chief. Turns out that Perry is Timothy Sullivan's grandfather."

That got more of a reaction from Jarrett.

24

William Wesley Gomes drew a deep breath and pushed a stack of ten one-thousand-dollar chips into the exact center of the betting circle. A moment later he did the same with another stack, fussing with the two columns until they were perfectly symmetrical. Everything had to be perfect. It was time to win. Winning was absolutely necessary.

Gomes's expression was impenetrable behind round wire-rimmed glasses. He reminded himself again that the stakes were a lot higher than the bet. If he won he would have his reprieve. A loss would start a process that could send him to jail for the rest of his natural life.

In another dim precinct of his mind he had begun to fear that the game itself was becoming as important as its purpose. There was a serious question whether he would be able to stop playing, even if he won the absurdly high figure he needed to put his accounts right.

He swallowed and cursed the run of bad luck that had driven him to his current excessive level of risk. Not all of it had been at the blackjack tables in Atlantic City. Had everything gone right, by now he could have tossed his entire bet to the dealer as a tip.

Gomes folded his hands and waited for the dealer to finish gathering the spent cards from the previous hand. A bead of perspiration dripped from his underarm and slid down the already sticky skin on his ribs. He'd been waiting all night, biding his time with fifty-dollar bets, the minimum at the high-stakes table.

And counting. Always counting.

He studied the dealer's fingers with manic focus, alert to any departure from his established rhythm. A change in rhythm might signal an irregularity brought to bear against a player making a huge wager. Dealers did not have to cheat to win, but some did anyway, he knew, especially on big bets. The chance for the house trying to cheat him had been minimized by his taking the first player position. That afforded the best angle from which to watch for double dealing.

Each hand was dealt from a wooden shoe using four decks, more than enough to frustrate most card counters. But Gomes was not like most counters. His memory was photographic. His eyes were a camera, his mind as fast as a Casio.

On the previous deal he'd counted two tens, eight pictures, and sixteen cards from ace to nine. With his new calculation, the running total had gone to an amazing plus nine, the highest he'd ever seen. The more positive the number, the heavier the required bet. The counting system, performed correctly, gave him an edge of exactly 1.5 percent over the house, a huge advantage.

Gomes watched the other players place their bets, aware of every nuance of their movements. He took comfort in his choice of the Domino Hotel and Casino. It was the most heavily supervised gambling house in Atlantic City. He admired the way in which the game was managed down to its smallest component, how the nearby pit boss folded his hands across his chest the same way before each new deal started, how his eyes visited the dealer's hands frequently. Cheating could work both ways.

When the dealer was ready, Gomes checked his bet again visually and recounted twenty thousand dollars with his fingertips just to make sure. He had trained himself to ignore the amount of the bet as an irrelevancy. Still, the size of it gave him pause.

The dealer passed by him leaving a card face up and continuing until he dealt himself his down card. Gomes registered his card without change of expression, a six, the worst possible first card. The second card he turned over for Gomes was the nine of diamonds. Gomes's heart thudded heavily in his chest.

After servicing the other players the dealer dealt his second card face up, a queen. He slipped it under the down card and used the edge to peek at his bottom card, then he looked up directly at Gomes. The dealer was Hispanic, late twenties, with a trim dark mustache. For a fraction of a second, Gomes thought he could read a minuscule flicker of acknowledgment in a half-formed smile.

Gomes made the only assumption he could, that his under card was a ten, for a total of twenty. If it was an ace, nothing mattered. He'd already lost.

The taste of bile built at the back of Gomes's throat. The dealer was restless, waiting for a decision from the biggest bettor. The pit boss looked on with more than average interest. Gomes squirmed on his stool. The other players had gone quiet and were also waiting on him. They'd been impressed with his bet, but now they were ready for a vicarious thrill, one way or the other.

The odds of taking another card and staying under twenty-one were low. Also, the running count made the deck ten-rich, the last thing he needed now. His internal calculator was useless. It was only a matter of having the discipline to stand pat and force the dealer to take the chance he himself did not have to. The hardest thing of all to do with a bad hand was nothing.

But a conflicting thought came from what he thought he saw in the dealer's expression. Perhaps his grin had been a warning that he had him beat, an inexplicable kindness that his pit boss could not see. Or perhaps it was a lapse in protocol that allowed him to enjoy a personal victory over a wealthy bettor who didn't have to work the late shift in a casino. If that were true, Gomes had to take control.

The impulse came swiftly. It was the undisciplined act of

bravado that he had sworn to guard against. Before he could stop himself, Gomes lifted his head and said "Hit."

A murmur of surprise made its way around the table. No one's eyes left the bottom of the shoe where the supple fingers were poised to strike.

"Are you sure?" the dealer asked unexpectedly.

The courtesy broke Gomes's concentration. The dealer had given him a chance to change his mind, possibly telling him he'd made an incredibly bad decision. Or was it a continuation of his mind games?

Out of the corner of his eye, Gomes saw the pit boss drop his arms to his sides and lean forward to observe the game more closely.

The dealer's hand went to the bottom of the shoe and flipped over the card, a five for a total of twenty. A black curtain lifted and Gomes relaxed. He'd been on a fool's mission, but it had paid off. He now had twenty, and an excellent chance of winning.

Gomes glanced to his left and barely recorded the insignificant hands that followed. The two next players went over right away. A stout, chain-smoking woman, who had waited for a long time for her moment, produced a blackjack, and won three hundred dollars. Two more men stood pat. The last man took four low cards before staying with eighteen.

The dealer showed the table his under card, a six, like Gomes's first, to go with his queen. Gomes breathed a sigh of relief. He had gone to the brink, trusted his instinct, and survived. The odds had now shifted overwhelmingly in his favor. One more card, a six or higher, and the dealer would bust. Gomes was infused with energy.

The dealer reached for the shoe and slapped it down onto the table.

The first thing that registered was that it had too much white space. The number at the corner swam in Gomes's vision and he felt dizzy. Incredibly, the dealer had drawn a five for a total of twenty-one.

Gomes put his hands on the table and slowly pushed

away. He felt as if his chest had been opened and everything inside scooped out. He had trouble standing.

Slowly, he pivoted away from the table and walked past rows of one-armed bandits. A young couple in front of him shrieked with joy over a paltry jackpot they'd just won.

Gomes cursed the cards and his string of bad luck which had defied all the odds. He cursed the dealer who had tempted him to change the course of the cards. He cursed the impulse that he'd acted on and that had defeated him.

When he was outside the casino, he shifted his attention to the latest reason that he had been forced to hurry his schedule, and been compelled to endure a final and costly humiliation at the gaming table.

A single image swam in his vision. A picture of a young woman who had unexpectedly blundered into his tidy world and suddenly threatened to destroy a timetable that was crucial to his survival.

In a moment he made the decision that his bad luck had decreed.

Now there was no other way.

PART TWO

25

Jarrett's decision to accompany Meg marked his first intrusion into the sanctity of the teacher-parent relationship. The Lerners said they looked forward to a home meeting with Jessie's new teacher, but the added presence of an out-of-town policeman, even though Meg had cleared it, was a wild card that might prove unsettling.

"Just show them how charming you can be," Meg said when they arrived in her Cherokee.

"I've been described in a lot of ways. Charming hasn't worked its way onto the list yet." Jarrett grinned nicely.

Once inside, Jarrett explained that he was there to help Meg with problems that were traced to the school and possibly Wilkens. Meg braced at his directness, but from that point on, the Lerners were accepting of him.

The worst moment came when Meg produced the note sent to her anonymously, and the Lerners were stunned to learn that it was their daughter who had sent it. For obvious reasons, it had been wiser to tell them that Meg had seen Jessie leaving the message on Meg's desk.

Carolyn seemed to be a very intelligent, thorough woman who would be equally at home in a playroom or a board room, Jarrett thought. She passed the note to her husband, who was a well-built, good-looking man with a full head of blond hair and penny loafers. He read it with a scowl, then excused himself and left for Jessie's room. He came back a few minutes later nodding to his wife.

"You won't find a more honest or empathetic kid than Jessie," her mother said. "She's uncomfortable with subterfuge. She was probably trying to help, and didn't know how else to do it."

"I'm more concerned about why she didn't want anyone to know. She's very open with us at home," Phillip added. He looked at Jarrett, inviting his insight.

Meg was about to speak when she felt Jarrett's hand on her arm. "Just how bad did it get between Jessie and Mrs. Wilkens?"

"Bad enough for us to complain to the board of ed, more than once," Carolyn said.

"Not that it did any good," Phillip added.

"I read the minutes of the meetings you came to," Meg said. "I didn't expect to see them there."

"Normally you wouldn't have," Phillip explained. "Criticism of teachers is usually done in private between parents and the school principal, or the superintendent of schools. That's where we started before we finally had to go higher. We demanded the complaint be read into the public record, but that was about all we accomplished."

"Dr. Melacore was interested," Carolyn went on, "but she wanted time to evaluate our complaint. She said she'd discuss it with Wilkens directly. When nothing happened after a few weeks, and the abuse continued, we went to the superintendent. He referred us to his assistant, and that was a dead end."

"The superintendent hires the principal," Jarrett guessed.

Carolyn nodded tellingly. "We didn't want to go to any more board meetings because were afraid Jessie would become identified as a troublemaker, but we had to do something. Every day was a torment for her."

Torment was a strong word, Jarrett thought, and the Lerners didn't seem like the hysterical type. "What did Wilkens do, exactly?"

"Ridicule Jessie, inflict inappropriate levels of criticism for the slightest infraction, like if Jessie didn't understand her homework, or asked Wilkens to explain a lesson again. It didn't help that math wasn't Jessie's best subject."

"Jessie would come home almost every day with a new story about how angry Wilkens was toward her," Phillip said. "The woman isolated her from the other kids, and they ended up treating her like an outcast."

Meg remembered how the other students had looked at Jessie when she asked the question about Wilkens. She shot Jarrett an ominous look.

"Middle school is a rough place for a lot of kids," Carolyn said. "Ask anyone how cruel some kids are to anyone who isn't in the mold. I don't know what kind of homes they must come from to be that way. Or what kind of values they teach."

"I assume you're talking about verbal attacks by Wilkens, nothing physical?" Jarrett said.

"Trust me," Phillip snapped back with enmity. "If it had been physical I'd have pulled that woman out of the classroom myself." He looked capable at the moment of throwing Hulk Hogan out of the ring.

"It was psychological punishment, and it wasn't only directed at Jessie," Carolyn said. "There was a nice boy named Marco Cuesta who was also her target, at least at first. Don't know why. Other children felt the atmosphere change in the class, too. For some reason Wilkens became enraged easily and had no patience, not her usual style. Some kids told their parents about it, but Wilkens had a great reputation so everyone took a wait-and-see attitude."

"Was it as bad for the Cuesta boy as Jessie?" Meg asked.

"We don't really know. We persuaded his parents to come with us to the board, once, but their complaint wasn't taken seriously. They'd been transferred here from overseas and didn't know anyone, so they felt uncomfortable when it happened and dropped out. They left town just as we were getting going."

"For business reasons, they said," Phillip added, "but I'm still wondering if it was because of Wilkens."

"Marco moved without saying goodbye to Jessie, and she was hurt by that." Carolyn shrugged her shoulders sadly. "They'd become friends."

"Have you been in touch since?"

"No, no one's heard from them. They didn't leave with very fond memories, or any real bonds."

"What happened in class after that?"

"When Marco left, Wilkens focused on Jessie," Carolyn said, "so the problem went away for the rest of the kids. In a way, that was bad for us. This is a town where parents usually become hysterical if anything threatens their kids, but when it was only Jessie . . ." She hesitated. "Not my kid, not my problem, I guess."

Phillip said, "There wasn't much we could do. We're not part of the influential group of parents here, so we just kept hoping it would change."

"We also didn't want to send Jessie the message that she could solve her problems by running away, like the Cuestas," Carolyn went on. "But she became phobic about school, and it affected our whole family. Jessie's older brother had a hard time coping with it, and he didn't need any more to worry about."

She stopped after a cautionary glance from her husband, but Jarrett's antennae had already gone up. A younger sister in trouble, and a brother who had something else going on. He made a mental note to check on it.

As he listened to the Lerners' account, Jarrett became caught up in Jessie's plight. As a rule, he stepped back from personal empathy for victims, but he'd never learned to distance himself from the mistreatment of children.

"She went to school anyway," Carolyn said in a diminished way. "Jessie is a very brave kid. I don't think I could have dealt with it at her age."

"Frankly, we were getting to the point where none of us could," Phillip said. "We didn't know what to do—and then the accident happened."

"Do you have any idea what made Wilkens act this way?"

"Not sure," Phillip said swiftly. "She taught for thirty-five years or so. Maybe she was burned out. It's possible that Jessie was just the wrong person at the wrong time. She's not the easiest child to teach."

Carolyn took her cue. "Jessie has ADD, attention deficit disorder. She has trouble focusing, and doesn't always get lessons the first time. A teacher has to take the extra time to explain things to her, and almost all of her other teachers have been great about it. Very patient and compassionate. But maybe Wilkens found her problem too much to deal with, even though we'd just gotten her an in-class aide." She turned to Meg. "But as you know, the aide wasn't always there."

Meg understood. In-class support could be spotty. She herself had only seen Jessie's aide a few times.

Jarrett braced for a second time. "There was another adult in the class with Wilkens? Did you speak to her about Jessie's problem?"

"Of course," Carolyn said. "The woman's name was Janet Elder. She said Wilkens was strict but didn't notice any special bias against Jessie. Then again, she wasn't around all the time, and I doubt Wilkens would have acted the same way with another grown-up present."

Phillip leaned forward in his chair with his hands clasped. "Look, we appreciate why you have to ask these questions, but this isn't that hard. There was something really sick going on in that classroom, and most of it was directed at my daughter. Wilkens may have had a great reputation, and a principal and her tenure to protect her, but the woman wasn't right upstairs. I'm sorry about what happened to her, but she didn't belong in the school system anymore."

Jarrett let Jessie's father calm down. There was still something he had to ask, and he had been carefully trying to frame the question. "Would it be all right if I spoke with Jessie myself?" he said finally, as gently as he could. "We have to find out more about the note."

The request galvanized a fear reaction in the Lerners.

"You can be with her if you want," Meg said quickly. She signaled her alarm to Jarrett.

The couple exchanged tense glances, each waiting for the other to speak.

"No, I'm sorry," Phillip finally said forcefully. "Jessie's had enough to remind her of Mrs. Wilkens. It's over now. It's enough."

26

The phone company had no listing for Roberto or Maria Cuesta in any of the nearby towns. A laborious check of public and private school eighth grades for Marco likewise produced no result. So far the Cuestas had disappeared without a trace.

Taffy Eldridge was the agent the family had contacted to sell their house. She struck Jarrett as the quintessential Social Register real estate lady, elegantly tailored, preppie background, a genuine honey blond with straight-angled Tudor features. Her family had probably arrived in America in time to receive the *Mayflower*'s passengers.

After Jarrett had spent five minutes in her car, however, Taffy proved to be nothing like the way she looked. "You don't go Platinum for Century Real Estate just by having connections," she said while driving. "You do it by busting buns and digging up leads, even if it means leftover suppers and a cold bed for hubby."

The trip to their first destination took them through the heart of the older section of town. The homes there were as opulent as advertised, and included soaring Tudors, picturesque Queen Anne Victorians, and stone mansions that were billboards for the rich, if not the famous. Taffy described

one of the more unusual houses as a half-timbered English
manor house with a brick-walled courtyard. It looked as if it
had been transplanted out of medieval England, and some of
it was: the stone foundation, piece by piece. A "For Sale" sign
staked to the lawn had Taffy's name on it.

"The part that's timber was cut from a stand of chestnut
trees on the original property a year before the blight that
wiped out the species on the East Coast."

At over eight hundred thousand an acre, the going price
he'd heard for land in town, Jarrett estimated the grounds
alone were worth a million.

"Turn three or four of these a year and you're home
free," Taffy said cheerily.

"Must have taken a helluva mortgage from the bank,"
Jarrett said.

"Honey, they are the bank."

After they left the affluent section she drove a few blocks
to an older clapboard building, a modest house by local
standards, on a much smaller piece of land. There were six
trucks and a backhoe on the premises. Workmen were all
over it like ants on a crumb cake.

"This was the Cuestas'," Taffy informed him, pulling off
the road. "I could have gotten them another forty thousand
easy."

"They used another agent?"

"I never saw people in such a hurry to lose money. They
came to me because they heard I was good, but they wanted
me to sell their house overnight. I told them they wouldn't
get the best price that way. Then they went ahead and sold it
on their own and never even told me."

"What was their big rush?"

"The word was trouble at school. Their son wasn't cutting
it. He's an only child, so I guess it made it easier to pull up
stakes and leave."

"Not making it how?"

"The Cuestas didn't get into it, but you could see they
were bitter about something." She faced Jarrett with an effi-
cient grin. "Naturally, I have my own opinions."

He knew she would.

"Knollwood isn't the easiest place to fit into. Not big on welcome mats, snooty. Hell, the darn place was set up that way, as a privileged little enclave for rich business people from New York. The Wall Street crowd is still the backbone of the community—great for the price of houses, but not so great for a working-class family like the Cuestas." She shot him a knowing glance and added, "It's not easy for a normal kid to compete with the sons and daughters of Goldman Sachs, if you catch my drift."

"I've heard their son had trouble with a teacher named Wilkens," Jarrett tried as a test, "the one who had the accident." He waited for a strong reaction, to either part of the query.

For once Taffy's knowledge gave out. "I wouldn't know about that. Wilkens had been teaching here for years. If the Cuesta boy had trouble it might have been the group he found himself in."

"In what way?"

"From what I know, this particular eighth grade is reputed to be the kind that comes along once a decade. An unusual amount of super brains and athletes, plus a bunch of world-class obsessive parents pushing them. Really tough on the average all-American kid."

"Norman Rockwell's gotta be turning over in his grave," Jarrett mused. "And it must make it a harder sell to some prospective buyers," he added, allowing himself a pseudo-professional speculation.

"Are you kidding? The Type A's love a place like this. Want to take a look at Wilkens's house?"

Elaine Wilkens's residence was back toward the big homes, but not all the way. The three-story ramshackle affair in white clapboard and flat-cut fieldstone was set on a modest-sized piece of ground, half of which was littered with dead trees. The house itself was large but run down enough to be an eyesore to neighboring owners.

"Built in 1888. Six bedrooms, three baths. Original cherry paneling and built-ins from the Arts and Crafts period. Used to be a running brook behind it till it went dry."

"Needs what you people call TLC."

"MLC," Taffy corrected. "*Major* loving care. Wilkens's husband bought it for her when it was on the outskirts of the rich section. He was a landscaper for the big estates in the area, and busted a gut to pay the place off before he died. He left her with a nice property, but one which she couldn't afford to maintain on a teacher's salary. He was a pretty good man in my book," Taffy said, and meant it.

"What's a place like this worth these days?"

"Six-fifty, six-seventy." She raised an eyebrow. "But it would take another four or so to bring it up to code. Interested?"

"We could work something out."

"Love to flip it myself, but it's been padlocked for months, ever since the investigation into Wilkens's death. It was supposed to come on the market as soon as the executor got the okay from the Superior Court, but that was months ago." She shrugged at what appeared to be a lost opportunity.

"I'm sure when it does you'll be first in line," Jarrett said.

Taffy didn't crack a smile. It was assumed. "Had enough?"

"Yeah, unless you have an idea where the Cuestas ended up."

"Sorry. Out of town, out of mind."

"Any way you could find them through multiple listings?"

"I could try. If they bought or rented another place in the county it would be on the computer." She slowed the car, her face suddenly solemn. "I don't think you'd get a very warm reception, even if you found them. I remembered something Mrs. Cuesta told me."

Jarrett was listening.

"I remember her saying she didn't want anyone to know where they were going because she was afraid someone might bother them. She used a Spanish phrase I'd never heard before, *monos con navajas.* It stuck with me for some reason."

Jarrett shrugged in incomprehension.

"I was curious, so I asked my Colombian housekeeper

about it. She said it's a South American expression that literally translates into 'monkeys with knives.'"

When Jarrett didn't know what to make of it she added, "Actually, it means something like 'troublemakers who can reach out from far away.'"

"What could they be afraid of, once they left, I mean?"

Taffy shrugged. "Maybe that the record of their trouble with the school would hurt their son in the next town. Or maybe they were just plain paranoid. This place can do that to you."

27

"You picked a good time to skip town," Willy Dunellen said from three thousand miles away. "That animal you beat to death had a lot of friends. They've been calling for Stryker's testicles in a glass ever since you left."

"The lowlife killed Frank," Jarrett snapped. He took a moment to imagine what his reception would be like when he returned home. His status as everyone's favorite outcast had risen to new heights.

One of his few remaining friends was Willy "Guano" Dunellen, chief of forensics at the L.A. Crime Lab. People who knew Dunellen well enough called him by the nickname given him when Jarrett remarked that Dunellen could find a speck of fly shit in a cave full of guano.

"Hey, you know that, and I know that," Guano said. "Problem is, you executed him before he was tried."

"Shit happens."

Jarrett put his feet on the edge of the motel bed and sat back in his chair, tilting its front legs off the floor. His motel room was in New Providence, where the day rate was within range of mere mortals. Room 19 was exactly 3.6 miles from Meg's house. A copy of Elaine Wilkens's autopsy report was spread out in front of him on the bed. Guano also had a copy.

"Got your fax, for what it's worth," Dunellen said caustically.

Jarrett could see the rotund forensics snoop sitting like a little Buddha in his immaculate stainless steel and porcelain lab, tittering over the discovery of some new piece of toenail or infinitesimal paint chip that could send a murderer away for life. The only thing Guano loved to do more than talk about toenails, guts, and brains was eat a good meal, and he'd done both simultaneously on a number of occasions with Jarrett.

"What do you think of it?" Jarrett asked, referring to the autopsy.

"Not exactly cutting-edge forensics—forgive the pun. Who's this Dr. Mumphrey who performed it?"

"A county medical examiner, local guy," Jarrett answered. "The body was found in a state forest under the jurisdiction of the New Jersey State Police, who called him in. Why?" Jarrett recalled that Guano himself had served a long stint as a medical examiner before switching over to forensics.

"Nothing special, only that, if it's important enough, sometimes they send the body to the state M.E."

"Why would they have to?"

"In the boonies a local M.E. is usually an undertaker with a degree in mortuary science, or some guy who works for a funeral home. Don't get me wrong, there are some good people in the sticks, and computers keep them up to date. But rural areas don't usually have a lot of money for police medical labs. The local M.E.'s don't usually have the equipment to do a thorough exam."

Jarrett had gotten his copy of the five-page report at the State Medical Examiner's Office in Newark for a six-dollar fee. In addition to all the normal categories, the last page detailed the chronology of Wilkens's death, which it listed as occurring at 11:45 A.M., the time at which she was reported missing by the class mother. The M.E. estimated the time of death shortly after that. "I see the cause of death is described as a 'fractured cervical vertebra,'" Jarrett said, skipping to the next-to-last entry.

"Fancy term for a broken neck. This may come as a surprise to someone of your limited mental capacity," Guano said, "but we see that a lot in people who fall off mountains."

"The manner of death is listed as accidental. How did they know she wasn't pushed?"

"How did they know she even died where they found her?" Guano said. "Best they can do is use the local M.E.'s investigation at the crime scene. He'd probably take the victim's body temperature and the air temp, and some vitreous fluid from the eyes and ca ll it a day. This gives him an approximate idea of how long the individual has been dead."

"The average body loses a degree and a half every hour after death, right?"

"I taught you well, grasshopper. Yeah, depending on air temperature, so if he gets to the body right after the accident and the temperature is too low for the circumstances, the person probably died earlier, maybe even some other place. Which isn't indicated here."

"What else would they check for?"

"Signs of rigor mortis. Most people know the physical lock-up happens within two and a half hours or so after death, but not too many know it leaves again after three to four. So your woman shouldn't have been a stiff right away. Same thing with lividity. It takes a while for blood to settle to the lowest part of the body, so she shouldn't have evidenced the reddish discoloring at those places when he got there."

"And according to the autopsy nothing was out of whack in those areas?"

"Not that I can see, no. But let's go through it. Can you hold on a minute?"

Jarrett said he would.

There was some audible rustling at Guano's end. When he finally came back on it sounded as if he was munching on potato chips. "You see the category called 'Marks of Injury'?"

"Yeah. Here on the first page."

"You'd be looking for any external marks on the body which don't seem to fit with the presumed cause of death, which in this case was a triple gainer off a cliff."

"What kind of marks? This section is loaded with them."

"Any improbable wound that wouldn't have been made by objects normally found in the area, say a deep or perfectly round indentation in the head, which could indicate a hammer blow. Rocks aren't as perfectly shaped as machine tools."

"And there's nothing here like that?"

"Nothing I can see that they found. Of course, I don't know what they missed."

"What about clothing?"

"Not too useful unless there's something unusual, like a blouse that was buttoned in a way she wouldn't do it herself. Or if she was wearing stiletto heels on a hiking trip."

"What else comes into play?"

"Enough to fill a Ph.D. treatise." Guano munched another mouthful of chips, swallowed with difficulty, and said, "The brain dissection would show that she could have died of natural causes, say an aneurysm. A crushed larynx might mean she was choked. Everything I see here is covered in a general way, respiratory, cardiovascular, digestive, lymphoreticular, endocrine, urogenital, all that shit. And there's nothing that jumps out. If there was, the death wouldn't have been listed as accidental." After a short wait, Dunellen added, "Only one thing bothers me."

"What's that?"

"There's nothing about what they found in the specimens taken from the lady's body. Blood, liver, stomach contents, like that. There's no toxicology report here, only that they took the samples."

Jarrett hauled his feet off the bed and sat up. "How unusual is that?"

"Not very at the first stage. Like I said before, they probably sent the specimens to a better lab than the one they had locally, and the results came in later. Since they hadn't found anything else suspicious, and with the cause of death looking so obvious, there'd be no sense of urgency to find out about them. By the time the results were ready nobody may have cared to inspect them very closely."

Jarrett had a thought. "If Wilkens were drugged, or poisoned, that's where it would show up?"

"Yeah, anything like that. If you get your hands on the toxicology, I'll take a look at it."

"I have a feeling that's easier said than done, for me at least. What about you calling for me if I can get you a name? Some techie lab guy would probably relate more to a fellow scientist."

"Anyone would relate more to me than you," Guano said. "Okay, I'll help out, but I gotta believe someone would have spotted something like that if they found it."

"Yeah, probably."

"All of which leads me to one question."

Jarrett waited for him to chomp on a few more of whatever he was eating.

"Assuming that all of the police and medical investigators gave the fall a clean bill of health, and since there's nothing suspicious so far in the autopsy report, and no one was around when the old lady tried to fly, except a bunch of eighth graders, why the hell are you still in New Jersey?"

"The question occurred to me."

It was a fair question, at least from Guano's limited point of view. But there was a lot his plump friend didn't know about: the attacks on Meg, the defensive reactions of the school and police to her inquiry, not to mention the butterflies that were fluttering in his chest every time he was with Meg.

"So what are you gonna do now?" Guano pressed.

"Dunno. But I hear it's lovely at the Delaware Water Gap this time of year."

28

Starting as a series of small, snow-fed brooks in Schoharie County, New York, the Delaware River flows southward for 390 miles. The river is an ephemeral mistress, at times shallow and placid, then growing in volume and changing suddenly, as if in a fit of temper, churning, swirling, and spawning whirlpools capable of gouging holes a hundred feet deep in its bed. For much of its length treacherous currents and sharp drop-offs invisible from shore lurk at unexpected points underneath the surface.

As the river gathers momentum, its abundant waters are forced into a narrower channel, increasing velocity and creating a mighty torrent of energy. Suspended within that torrent, millions of particles of abrasive sand make the waters the equivalent of a liquid buzz saw. The moving blade continues downriver, carving deeper into steep-walled valleys revealing their increasing age in a journey back through time at the rate of 3.25 million years per mile of river.

Nearing its southern terminus, the Delaware finally encounters the formidable quarzite ridges of the Kittatinny Mountains. Although the rock is so strong that it is capable of scratching steel, over millions of years the scouring waters have eaten it away to form a river bed three hundred feet wide from shore to shore, fourteen hundred yards across from summit to summit. This is the area that has become known as the Delaware Water Gap. At 1,527 feet, the area's tallest peak is Mount Tammany.

The hour-and-a-half hike to the summit of Mount Tammany was notable for the absence of any sign of civilization along the way. Jarrett's conditioned body responded well to the exercise, but he did not stop to rest, and the light drizzle and slippery rock made the footing painstaking.

By the time Red Dot and Blue-Blazed Trails merged, and the huge knob that formed the actual precipice was visible ahead, Jarrett's heart was pumping as if he'd been chasing a lowlife for blocks.

"Another seventy-five yards or so," Rob Riva, his ranger guide, said, when they reached a clearing in the trees that had precluded their view until then. "We pretty much know the place where she fell."

Park Ranger Riva had scaled the height without breaking a sweat. He was solidly built, tall and with the trim mustache and staunch bearing reminiscent of a Northwest Mountie, sans horse. He'd also been first on the scene at the recovery of Wilkens's body.

Jarrett kicked his boots against a boulder to remove a reddish mixture that was somewhere between mud and clay.

"Lot of schools come here on trips?" Jarrett asked, trying to picture a bunch of eighth graders wending their way up the mountain.

"It's not Mount Rushmore," Riva said. "Only a few groups a season. The trail's not that difficult, but its length keeps a lot of people away."

"Easier on the kids than their teachers," Jarrett said, thinking about Wilkens. "Especially a woman in her late fifties."

"Hell, I've seen seventy-five year-olds make the climb."

The trail ahead was a narrow slash in the wood, rock-strewn and in places a mass of roots. "How close does this get to the edge?" Jarrett asked.

"No one's gonna take a few steps either way and end up in any trouble."

"I haven't seen any hazard markers."

"You won't. There aren't very many anywhere, because of the cost."

A short time later they'd covered the rest of the distance to a clearing in the higher ground and had their best view of the precipice. The top of a rise was thick with evergreens and scrub that grew along the entire ridge like a mop of green hair, then aimed themselves down the center of the forehead to form a widow's peak. Beyond that the slope was nearly vertical and made up of many distinct layers of sediment that no doubt provided a field day for geologists. The mountain's silhouette looked like the furrowed brow of a giant. A man would be about the size of a mole on that forehead.

"The lady didn't make the whole drop," Riva said respectfully, and pointed to the cliff. "She hit the face a few times, then came to rest where the trees start again, about three hundred feet down. If it wasn't for them she would have tumbled the rest of the way. That would have made it harder to find her, but a hell of a lot easier to get to her once we did," he volunteered.

"How'd you hear about her fall?" Jarrett asked.

"A woman in her group looked for her and couldn't find her. She took the kids back down the trail and flagged a ranger at the first rest stop. He radioed headquarters and I was part of the search party that was sent out. I remember how scared the woman who called it in looked," he added solemnly. "The kids, too."

"How long did it take her to find help?"

"The call came in at 11:55 exactly. The woman told the ranger she'd lost sight of the teacher about ten or fifteen minutes before that. Actually, I thought that was a little odd. It must have taken her longer than that to get down the trail to the ranger station. Maybe ten minutes more."

"So you think Wilkens could have fallen earlier?"

Riva nodded thoughtfully. "I would think so, yeah."

A small alarm went off in Jarrett's head. The time mentioned in the autopsy jived roughly with the class mother's
11:45 estimate. If it took her twenty minutes, not ten, to
come down for help she hadn't figured it right, or hadn't
wanted to. But he was probably making too much of an estimate made under extreme conditions. "How sure are you of
the times?" he asked anyway.

"Absolutely. I'd just come on shift, and the call came in
before I had coffee. Eleven fifty-five on the button. Why?
What are you getting at?"

"Just running some numbers," Jarrett said. He made a
mental note to check up on the class mother and refocused
on the trail. "The cliff is what, maybe forty, forty-five yards
from where the trail ends? Hard to tell with all the brush."

"Closer to sixty. But if you keep going you'll find a
smaller path that people made, a little more direct. People
are always finding their own way there, no matter what you
tell em."

Indeed, Jarrett could see a narrower foot trail that led
away from the path in the direction of the cliff. "What was
the visibility like on the day of the accident?"

"Decent. Some pockets of clouds, but mainly dry."

"What about fog?"

Riva tried to stifle a smile. "That's what fog is up this
high, clouds."

"Yeah. I knew that," Jarrett said, clicking a smile on and
off again quickly. "So there wasn't much of a chance a person could have gotten lost because of weather?"

"Zero and none."

Riva stared reverentially at the spectacular scenery. It
was easy to guess why he'd taken the job. "A person in
charge of children would need her own reason to get that
far away from them," he speculated with suspicion.

"Yeah, that's what I figured." *And moving too fast to stop
once she got to the end of the line,* Jarrett thought.

He stepped off the trail into a thicket and pushed his way
through a cluster of low-hanging branches. In a few minutes
he stood only a short distance from the top of the world. He

crept as close to the edge as he could until a wave of vertigo engulfed him. He'd never been fond of heights.

The hand on his elbow belonged to a nervous Riva. "The footing's not very good here. This broken rock can slip out from under you, or the vines can snag your foot." He indicated the spectacular promontory that stuck out, then dropped off and became nothingness. "There's the marker we left." He gestured, and motioned for Jarrett to follow.

When they got to the edge of the flat stone, Jarrett saw a small orange pennant that had been pounded into the ground. "That was a good guess as to where she went over. It was determined from where she landed."

Jarrett looked from the flag along the line Riva pointed out. The flag was in front of the wedge of scrub, the widow's peak, that grew down to the place where the mountain went straight down. Wilkens would have had to fall through the scraggly vegetation before tumbling off.

"Hang on to me," he said to Riva, and held out his hand. "I need a closer look."

Riva braced. "You'll need a rope."

"You got a rope?" Jarrett shot back.

The ranger shook his head.

"That's what I thought. Gimme your hand. I'm not going all the way out, just where the bushes are."

Reluctantly, Riva proffered his arm and Jarrett clutched his wrist. He took a deep breath, crouched, and commanded himself to look at the ground and not think about what lay beyond. A rivulet of sweat ran down his forehead, which was already wet from the climb and drizzle that had become heavier.

Inching his way toward the edge, Jarrett was forced to crawl on his belly for the last few feet. In front of him was the last stand of brush, a mixture of stunted pines and a strain of hearty weed that felt delicate to the touch. As if to make up for its diminished height, it was leafy all the way to the ground. After that, there were a few brilliant canary-yellow wildflowers blooming only inches from oblivion. It was hard to imagine how they took root and lived there, let alone thrived.

Jarrett inspected the fauna for a long time, especially the lowest foliated parts. Something was bothering him, and the longer he studied the area the more intrigued he became. "I don't get it. At some point the lady had to have known she'd gone too far. You'd think that someone about to plunge to her death would have done everything she could to stop herself."

Riva started to get his drift.

Jarrett pointed ahead of him to the drop-off. "At this point she would've been slipping to her death, clawing at any handhold she could find, but there's no sign of anything disturbed here, no torn leaves, no broken-off branches. Even after five or six months, you could still see if the roots were torn up, and these look untouched. With all these places to hold herself back, it looks like she never even tried."

Jarrett locked Riva's wrist in a death grip and hauled himself back to safety, giving Riva time to consider the implications.

"You're thinking suicide? That maybe she jumped?"

"One possibility. I can think of two others. She was dead before she fell off the mountain—"

"—or was carried to the edge and thrown off," Riva finished for him.

Jarrett nodded and tried to trace a line on the ground from where he was to the cliff. According to the autopsy Wilkens weighed something close to a hundred fifty. He wondered what it would take to carry her all that way. And who might have done it.

The class mother still troubled him. If Wilkens was killed earlier than reported, the class mother would have been nearer the scene when Wilkens went over than she reported. It would also have allowed the time necessary for the kids to have been there and back.

Jarrett felt the cold hand of doubt touch his belly.

If the discrepancy had been deliberate, he had his first real indication of a cover-up.

29

Despite what had happened to his desk overnight, William Wesley Gomes had difficulty concentrating on anything but the two men and a woman in the bank president's personal conference room. They were the auditors from Cargill, Lambretta, Ross, who had arrived two days before and would be staying for a week.

Already, something unpleasant was suggested by their pace of work. They'd been in the room continuously, including lunch hours, and were still there when he'd gone home last night.

The oldest auditor was a man in his late forties who worked with a myopic focus. A gaunt and vacant gaze gave him the mien of an undertaker looking for his next cadaver, and he must have had a kidney like a camel's since he never went to the men's room.

The younger one was an intellectual eager beaver who wore paisley suspenders and sipped Snapple peach iced tea all day. A female assistant had also been in and out of the room every few hours. Other than that, no one had gone near the place since the modern-day bounty hunters had begun to devour paper.

There wasn't anything to worry about at this point,

Gomes reassured himself. Paper hunters needed a trail to feed on, and he'd taken pains not to leave one. It wasn't just that his maze was going to be difficult to unravel—there was no maze. His own training at an auditing firm had taught him how to avoid scrutiny. That background was one of the qualifications that had undoubtedly appealed to Keith McVicker, the bank president. It was the same reason that so many big accounting firms hired ex-IRS agents.

Gomes's stomach, however, took no comfort in such assurances. He could feel the heat of the auditors' industry as they fed on numbers like locusts on grain, leaving no stalk unsampled and potential devastation in their wake. At the rate they were moving they'd eat their way to his part of the field much sooner than he'd calculated.

He turned his attention back to his desk and the desecration that had greeted him when he arrived. The cleaning staff had been there overnight and rearranged a number of his things out of their proper places.

For starters, his calendar book was clearly out of alignment with the border of the desk blotter, the two edges far from parallel, as was required. The jar that contained paper clips had been moved a good ways to the right, at least a half inch, so far that it almost touched the Post-it pad.

As always, the disorder made him physically uneasy, and it would prevent him from working until the things were put back where they belonged. A few of the people who worked with him knew of his penchant for order, and he was sure they'd be amused. He knew better. God was in the details, God and Gomes.

With the unused eraser of his number two Eagle pencil, he twisted the bottom of the calendar book to the right until it came into the proper line. He brought the jar back to its correct position, then placed the pencil down on the desk in its orderly sequence among others that were laid out in a line according to length, the printed surface face up, each with a point sharp enough to prick the skin.

The new symmetry pleased him, a place for everything, everything in its place. Disorder was chaos. Chaos could lead to ruin. His use of other people's money was a prime example.

The idea for his unauthorized borrowing was born of necessity. When the money he'd originally expected to fund his new life hadn't arrived, he'd turned to wagering with the intensity of a doctoral student. But after he had mastered his betting system, the immutable laws of chance had betrayed him, and in a short time his debts reached an absurdly high figure. After that, he'd been forced to do businesses with shylocks. When the losing continued, he turned to the only other readily available source of cash: the bank.

The notion of reaching into his customers' accounts arose from an error by one of his loan officers that had shown him the way. The scrupulously honest young woman had accidentally transferred one of her client's funds into the wrong account. With his help, her mistake was redressed before the customer discovered the error, but the seed was planted.

With his debts rising, Gomes spent hours perfecting a fascinating but simple scheme. After the auditors had left the previous time, he set up his own account under a fictitious name and drew funds into it from various customer accounts, replacing each withdrawal by a deposit from the next account and keeping the transaction from appearing on the customer's statement. The bank accommodated his plan by permitting the transfer of funds by telephone with the use of PINs easily accessible to him. The simple authorization of a teller was the only other requisite procedure. To shield his pattern from the tellers themselves, he used them in a random rotation.

The funds from his first transfer came from a merchant, and he covered it two days later with money from a reclusive widow who could be counted on not to inspect her affairs until year's end. From there it was just a matter of moving money around, borrowing and replenishing it, in time to stay a step ahead of discovery. It had been more than two months, and thus far his dealings had not aroused a shred of curiosity.

Naturally, he wasn't foolish enough to think his activities could go on forever. At some point in time, every scheme collapsed of its own weight, as pyramids did. But he'd been certain that the long-awaited mother lode would arrive before that. Then he'd simply even up the accounts, and it would be as if his transactions had never happened.

Unfortunately, the expected funds never materialized. The transfers had gotten larger, and the clock was ticking.

With disgust, Gomes noticed that one end of the scotch tape was protruding beyond the jagged edge of the cutter. It made him unwell to look at it, and he picked up the dispenser angrily. Painstakingly, he pulled off the uneven part so all of the edge was even with the points of the small teeth. He then placed the unit down at a perfect right angle to the Post-it pad.

The tension left his body as soon as things were back in order, but the relief was only momentary and Gomes was again lost in thought. There were better things to worry about than tape and pencils and paper clips. Three things to be exact:

First there was the new middle school teacher, who had continued to stir a pot that could boil over at any time.

There was her crude new friend, that he had seen helping while spying on her, who had put another and potentially more dangerous hand on the spoon.

And, of course, the kids.

At the end of the day, it was the kids who held the key to everything.

Next to the kids, the auditors were a mere annoyance.

30

"I thought we agreed you weren't going to butt into local business," Hudson Perry said with a cold stare from across his desk. "So what the hell were you doing nosing around the Wilkens crime scene?"

Perry's knowledge of his visit to the Delaware Water Gap came as a surprise to Jarrett. Probably it shouldn't have. Knollwood's chief of police had spent decades in New Jersey law enforcement and undoubtedly had friends everywhere in the State Police, possibly even the park rangers' chain of command. One of his friends had found out about his trip there and tipped Perry. Law enforcement was a smaller world than most people realized. Or else Perry had him followed.

"I didn't have any choice," Jarrett said, taking the offensive. "The attacks on Foley have gotten violent."

Perry checked his first reaction and calmed down. "I already told you I was looking into the train incident."

"That's only part of what's going on." For a split second, Jarrett considered telling Perry what he'd found in Timothy Sullivan's locker, but the kid was Perry's grandson, and the way his information had been obtained wasn't going to earn him a citation of merit. "Look, I originally thought Meg Foley was just the victim of a few bad-taste pranks, like you do. But the train was a big escalation. The next time someone could try to kill her, and there isn't any other likely reason for it except her questions about Wilkens."

"We already know what happened to Wilkens," Perry grumbled. "And it's still under investigation, at least techni- cally."

"But it might as well be over, right? Nothing's happened for months. I heard it's dead in the water."

"These things take time, there are a number of jurisdic- tions involved." Perry took a few seconds to make a neat stack of papers on his desk, after which he folded his hands and became a fortress. "So far everyone's conclusion is the same. Wilkens' death was an accident, and that's the way it's going to come out, no matter how long it takes."

Perry's attitude was dispiriting. He could have welcomed or at least tolerated the help of someone trying to make some new headway into the case. He might have had a damn good reason why he didn't want to.

Jarrett knew he was playing a dangerous game. "Just tell me how Wilkens could get sixty yards off the main trail when there was nothing to place her there on her own? And why there wasn't any sign that she tried to stop herself from falling? And what about Volpe's lab accident and the threats to Foley?" He stood and hovered over the big man. "Doesn't all this start to add up to something in your book? Don't you think you should take another look at the individuals who were there when it happened?"

For a moment, Perry kept his eyes on his desk, as if absorbed in thought. Then he slowly looked up at his adver- sary with a stare as cold as ice.

He said it with an amazing degree of control. "If I hear that you even go near any of the children that were on that trip, like you already did my grandson, or their parents, I swear to God I'll lock you up on obstruction so fast your god- damn head will spin. And I'll see that you're prosecuted for criminal harassment after that. Trust me, around here I can make it stick."

A half dozen smart answers flitted through Jarrett's mind. All of them served the interests of justice, none were even worth his breath. His lead suspect was Perry's blood relative and his two best friends. Any further attempt to talk to them would be like talking to Perry directly.

For once, Jarrett kept his mouth shut.

31

Stryker's call came in at 2 A.M. on the button. There was little doubt in Jarrett's mind that his boss had waited until there was no chance that he'd be awake, the latest little skirmish in their personal war. "Who the hell is Hudson Perry and what's he got to do with my life?" Stryker demanded to know.

After the way his meeting had ended with the Knollwood chief, Perry had obviously called Los Angeles and gotten through to the L.A. chief of detectives.

"He's the head cop around here," Jarrett said, stifling a yawn. "He's sitting on a possible crime, and he doesn't want to hear about it from me."

"Not the way he tells it. He says you're impeding the progress of an investigation and causing a public nuisance. Why does something tell me I should believe him and not you?"

"Bad instincts. Listen, Chief, something stinks to high heaven around here, and the police may even be part of it. I don't know that for a fact, but I'm making him nervous by looking around."

"He asked me to call you back to L.A., as a courtesy."

"What'd you tell him?"

"That the last face in the world I wanted to see right about now was yours."

"Really, is that what you said?"

Stryker paused. "No," he said more calmly. "I said that you were on furlough and there was nothing I could do about it."

"Jeez, Elliot. I didn't know you cared."

"Trust me, I don't. Why haven't you called in on the Vasquez fallout?"

"Sorry, I've been busy. So what happened with Vasquez?"

"They're convening a grand jury. No way to stop it. You're gonna have to testify. I was able to buy some time, till things quiet down. A week, maybe more."

"How are things?"

"Thanks to you I'm in the deepest pile of my life. Besides daily demonstrations against police bias, a special commission's been set up to monitor procedure."

"Sorry to hear that."

"So I don't want you within a crotch hair of here until I tell you. I only hope to God the media doesn't find out where you are."

"And what about Hudson Perry?"

"I don't care whose balls you break, so long as they're in New Jersey. I'll tell you when to surface again, and the next life would be too soon for me."

"Roger that, Chief," Jarrett snapped, military style.

"Not that you ever gave a damn what some dumb asshole of a boss ever told you to do," Stryker added sourly.

Jarrett took a few seconds to consider Stryker's remark. "Hey, let's be fair. I never said anything about you being dumb."

32

The Fairmount Halfway House in Hollyhill was a three-story brick mansion dating from the 1890s. In June 1979, it was bought by a benefactor who converted it into a dozen apartments for recovering drug addicts, the first of whom was his son. A few months earlier, the youth overdosed on LSD and thought he recognized a lion at a nearby zoo as a soul mate. The lion, being the more sober of the two, recognized him as dinner and nearly chewed off a drumstick before being beaten back by guards.

Jeremy Lerner strode into the first-floor common room in no particular hurry. He looked to Jarrett the way Paul Haucklin had described him, a pale, gangly kid of eighteen with a lean, studious look. His five-foot-ten frame was crowned by a thick mop of curly brown hair that hadn't been cut since Sergeant Pepper. Floor-length rust corduroys, a frayed woolen sweater, and moccasins completed his ensemble. There was something frail yet menacing about him at the same time, and his dark, tempestuous eyes intensified the mystery.

Jeremy shook Jarrett's hand with the shortest possible contact it took to complete the ritual.

"You want to get out of here?" Jarrett said. "Cup of coffee someplace?"

"I'll make it in my room," Jeremy said. "I don't go out much."

Lerner's quarters were tidy and had a definite cultural ambiance. Classical music posters adorned the walls, including a large photo of a tearful Jascha Heifetz that was visible over Jeremy's bed in the next room. There were books on almost every surface, but only two on a white wicker table in front of a futon in the living room. One was a large-format edition of Mapplethorpe photographs, the other a copy of Thomas Harris's *Silence of the Lambs,* a strange marriage of genres.

"I've seen worse places," Jarrett said after Jeremy poured him a cup of strong coffee. He took his seat on the futon and cautioned himself that this was not a kid to be bullshitted.

"They do a pretty good job here, I guess," Jeremy answered on a more general level than Jarrett had intended.

"What do you do? Is there a schedule or something?"

"All they care about is that you stay clean and hold down a job. After that, you can come and go pretty much as you want."

In Jeremy's case, clean meant sober. Jeremy had developed an alcohol problem in his last two years of high school. It had culminated in a DWI arrest after an accident on graduation night that left his girlfriend seriously injured. Jeremy's choice had been a few months in prison or the Hollyhill facility.

"How's my sister doing?" he asked.

"I think she's feeling better about school. She's got a terrific teacher." Jarrett suddenly thought about Jessie's note. His "feeling better" description was accurate only by degree.

"She really got screwed over by Wilkens," Jeremy said, getting right to the point. "I can't believe everyone just let it happen."

"I'd like to know what went on, from what you heard."

The boy studied him for a moment, then looked away contemptuously. He dug into his shirt pocket and took out a pack of Marlboro's.

Why was it always a pack of Marlboro's with kids?

He lit it, took a drag, and said, "This is the part where you try to find out if I killed the old lady, right?"

"You had a good reason to hate her, plus you had a history with her."

"I never did anything to Wilkens. I'm not into violence."

"It says in your record that you threatened her, in front of witnesses."

"Someone needed to tell her to keep away from my sister. She was torturing Jessie, and no one was stopping her."

Obviously, the months since Wilkens's death hadn't ended Jeremy's rage. Jarrett could only imagine what it had been like at its height. "Your parents were working on it. The school board and principal knew about it and she was being watched."

"Yeah, right, five minutes a day, by a principal whose job depended on keeping the school out of trouble." He took another deep drag on the cigarette and held it in like he was smoking pot. His next words spewed from his mouth on a steady stream of smoke. "It was a lot worse than anyone knew. Jessie told me things she didn't tell anyone else."

"Did Wilkens ever hit her?"

"No, the old bitch was too smart for that. That would leave a mark, and she'd be out on her ass, even with her tenure. It was all mind fucking. She made fun of Jessie, made her look like some kind of freak, until the other kids thought there actually was something wrong with her."

"Jessie told you that? Are you sure she wasn't exaggerating?"

"If Jessie said it, it was true. That's just the way she is. She said Wilkens made her work alone when the other kids had partners. She asked her to do things she couldn't and ridiculed her for failing, stuff like that." He'd begun to raise his voice, but brought himself down again. "Jessie has attention deficit disorder. School is hard enough for her, and Wilkens couldn't deal with it."

"I know, your folks told me."

Jeremy looked unhappy.

"When I'd come home for a weekend, Jessie would cry

her eyes out and ask me how a teacher could be so cruel. She said she couldn't help it if she needed to hear things more than once, and didn't know why Wilkens made fun of her for asking her to repeat something. When that happened, some of the other kids taunted her, and Wilkens let them."

"People who knew Wilkens would have a hard time believing that. She had a great reputation with children."

"I know, that's why she could get away with it." Jeremy stubbed the Marlboro and hunched his shoulders forward. His eyes were dry and radiated intense energy. "I think she went crazy and nobody knew about it. The other kids were probably afraid of her and didn't want to get involved. They just sat there and watched this crazy lady destroy an innocent little girl and felt safe because it wasn't them. I know what it's like in middle school, it's everyone for themselves. No one's got any character yet." He looked at Jarrett without blinking. "Do you know what it must have been like for my sister?"

"I can imagine," Jarrett said softly. He'd thought about it more than once, and had tried not to cultivate an antipathy toward a woman he never knew. In a way, what Jessie went through was also happening to Meg. Meg had also become isolated in a supposedly enlightened community, and was attacked physically and psychologically.

"Assuming it's true about Wilkens, I think most people would understand how a relative of Jessie's might try to stop Wilkens, whatever it took," Jarrett said pointedly. "They could probably see how a person would get so angry that things could get . . . out of hand."

It wasn't the most subtle probe he'd ever tried, but it had worked before. Often the best way to get a suspect to confess was to sympathize with the reasons for his action.

Jeremy leaned back and said it simply. "I wasn't there when she died, and I didn't kill her, if that's what you're trying to make me say. I was working at the hospital, and you can check on it any time you want." His voice was filled with emotion, and when he finished his speech he rose and paced off the anger. "Let me tell you something, and I don't give a damn whether you believe me or not. When I heard Wilkens broke her neck on the mountain I was so happy I had my only drink since I've been here—to celebrate. But I didn't do it. Now why don't you get the hell out of here and leave me alone."

Jarrett picked himself up heavily and stood facing the youth with his hands in his pockets. He'd been listening for something that might show the boy was lying, but so far he hadn't heard it. Jeremy might have been a hell of an actor, and his propensity to explode was a telling trait, but instinct told him the boy was telling the truth.

Jarrett's gaze swept the room one last time. A few dozen CD cases were neatly stacked on the floor next to a player on one wall. A modest-sized TV and old-model Macintosh Powerbook rested on an institutional metal desk near a knee-high refrigerator, like the ones businessmen kept in their offices. The only shelf that didn't hold books had a picture of a pretty but unknown young lady, maybe the girlfriend he'd almost killed in the high school car crash, and two pictures of his sister, one with himself, taken recently. Strangely, there were none of his mother and father.

Over Jeremy's shoulder, in the bedroom, the bed was neatly made and Heifetz was still in a reverie over his music.

Jarrett turned and took a step toward the door when something else in the bedroom caught his eye. The fronts of two heavily soiled running shoes poked out from the neatly made bed. He looked closer and saw that the visible part of the treads was all gummed up with dirt that had dried to a reddish clay color.

He'd seen mud like that before.

At the Delaware Water Gap.

33

The shapely young Starbucks waitress poured a second cup of Java Mocha and wondered why the new customer didn't look up to check her out, the way others his age did.

His weathered good looks stirred her interest, even though he didn't look like he came from the area. He sat alone next to the large front window, staring into his cup and quietly swirling the coffee, yet his quiet intensity permeated the atmosphere. By comparison, the business couple with the briefcases, and the lady jogger in the velour sweatsuit, were merely bits of scenery.

Dan Jarrett raised the huge white mug to his lips and worked on a notion that he'd had even before his visit to the halfway house: what to do with a growing body of purely circumstantial evidence that showed something stunk big time in the Wilkens case.

Jessie's brother had just been the latest in a growing list of people with a possible motive, his motive clear, his indictment caked in mud. Before that, the lack of any physical evidence at the Delaware Water Gap that showed Wilkens had tried to save herself as she fell had spiked his restlessness.

This was the kind of case that always caused him the most trouble, when he felt in his bones that something was wrong, but couldn't prove it. It was when he was prone to allow instinct to rule his actions in haste. He made a silent pledge that this time he'd be a gatekeeper for the house of his own impatience.

A sudden change in the light was accompanied by the crashing sound of something big disintegrating. The power of it sent his head slamming down to the table. Instinctively he covered it with his hands and he was pelted by a thousand splinters of glass. Next to him the giant front window of Starbucks had shattered, leaving one entire side of the shop completely open to the street.

Still holding on to his coffee, Jarrett noticed that his hand was dotted with dozens of pinpoints of blood. As he stared at it, the white mug burst to pieces, and he was left holding only the graceful curved handle.

"Oh shit," he said, suddenly realizing what was happening. He dove from his chair to the floor. "Get down," he shouted, motioning to the other patrons to hit the deck.

The briefcase couple had also been stung by scores of pieces of flying glass and they dove to the floor on their bellies. In a heroic gesture, the man draped his body over his partner's. The jogger screamed hysterically, rolled under a table, and kept on screaming.

Crawling close to the wooden frame at the bottom of the wall, Jarrett angled his body toward the street and reached for his Medusa. He raised an eye over the wood and tried to reconstruct what happened. A second shot had followed the first within a few seconds, but only one. That meant that there might only have been a short time in which to shoot, which suggested that it might have been a drive-by. If it was, the danger had already passed.

Behind him, the piping of the main cappuccino machine suddenly burst open with a *pinging* sound that instantly changed his mind. A loud discharge of escaping steam was followed by a new round of screams from the jogging lady.

"Stay there," he commanded the other customers, then noticed that the waitress who'd served him was standing straight up behind the counter, immobilized by fear, and making herself an easy target.

"Get down, goddamn it," he called again. His order shook her out of her torpor, and she ducked behind the display case that held the pastries.

All the shooting had lasted for less than a minute. There was no way to tell if the shots had come in from high or low because the window was such a large target. There had been no reports from a pistol, so Jarrett guessed the sniper was using either a silencer or high-powered pellet gun.

Lifting his head above the bottom of the wall, he scanned the rooftops of the buildings across the street. When he couldn't see anything moving he dropped his gaze to the vehicles parked directly across the street. There were three from which the shooter could have made the angle to where Jarrett had been seated in the back section. The closest was a large white van with TRU-TEMP AIR CONDITIONING on it, the next a newer model dark Mercedes, the last a Civic wagon five or six years old. All looked empty. All windows were closed.

Jarrett turned and saw the patrons watching him. He had a gun and didn't look like a cop. For all they knew he could be part of the problem. "I'm a police officer," he yelled, stifling the urge to yell, "LAPD."

As his words died out, part of the pastry case splintered into bits, and a piece of plastic flew off the computerized cash register.

"Can you get to a phone?" he shouted to the cowering waitress.

"There's one in back," she answered shakily.

"Call 911. Now."

She followed his instructions and crawled back into the supply room.

Jarrett turned to the street again, his pistol at eye level. He trained his vision on the three cars, watching for a movement or flash of light. The white van was the most likely source, closest to Starbucks. The angle of the sun glinted off the windows facing him.

He checked the Mercedes and Civic again. Something was wrong with the picture this time, but he couldn't put his finger on it. It came to him a moment later, like a lit fuse getting to the powder. The Civic was parked at the same angle as the rest of the vehicles, but there was no reflection in the front window. The window had to be down, and he was certain it was up the last time he looked.

Where were the police?

Swiftly, he brought his other hand to his pistol, steadying it. He stared at the Civic and knew what he had to do. Years before he'd learned the alligator crawl in infantry school at Fort Leonard Wood. It was the best way to move and stay low to the ground. He hoped his muscle memory was still intact.

He pressed himself to the floor and pushed forward, right elbow, left knee. He stopped crawling when he got to the front door and gently nudged it open.

He saw the top of a head drift higher in the driver's seat of the Civic. The tip of a gun was in front of the left ear.

Looking to his right Jarrett checked the car's exhaust pipe and thought he could see it vibrating, a sign that the engine was running. He braced himself, got into a crouch, and flung the front door open all at once.

He left the building in a low sprint, his weapon at his side. A car in the oncoming lane swerved to miss him and continued on with a wide-eyed elderly driver who couldn't believe what he'd just seen in his peaceful hometown.

When he was partway to the Civic, Jarrett saw a hand come up and grasp the top of the steering wheel. The wheel turned in Jarrett's direction and the Civic's front tires moved left.

The sound of the engine being gunned brought him to one knee, and he took the position. He aimed his pistol at the window. "Stop the goddamn car," he shouted at the top of his voice.

The tip of the weapon visible in the Civic turned in his direction and the barrel made the sound of a muffled piston. A puff of smoke shot out of it, dislodging a chunk of asphalt the size of a half dollar next to him.

Jarrett dove to the right as the car careened out of the parking space and came squarely at him. He rolled to avoid it, and scrambled to his feet when it turned away and headed down the block toward an intersection.

What Jarrett saw in the intersection made his blood run cold, a young mother who was halfway across the street pushing a twin stroller. She'd stopped when she heard the car coming and was caught in the middle of the road, frozen like a deer in the headlights.

Jarrett cocked the trigger of his pistol and lowered his sight to the Civic's rear window. His gun hand was absolutely still, but a second later his finger eased off the trigger. The woman was in the line of fire.

The Civic speeded toward the mother, who let out a blood-chilling scream and shoved the twin stroller ahead of her, losing her balance in the effort and falling. The stroller rolled all the way to the curb and stopped with a hard bump, but remained upright.

The woman lay on the asphalt, staring at the car as it approached, unable to move. It was too late to do anything but watch and pray.

The driver sped through the red light. For an excruciatingly long time it appeared as if he intended to run her down deliberately.

At the last moment, he cut the wheel sharply left and made the hairpin turn with his tires burning.

34

"The car belonged to a grandmother from Caldwell who came to town on Wednesdays to have her hair done. The shooter stole it from the salon lot and left it at the train station before her curlers were dry."

Jarrett parked himself on Meg's sofa and sank uncomfortably into the spongy padding. He wasn't much for soft furniture, it made him relax too much. That afternoon Meg had insisted they drive past Starbucks on the way. The shattered window had been boarded up, and the part of the street where the Civic had parked had been roped off with cones and yellow tape that indicated a crime scene.

"Did they go over the car yet?" she asked, coming out of the kitchen holding two Dewars, rocks. The special request from Jarrett was to help usher the morning's scare to the back of his mind instead of where it had stayed all day. The ulcer fairy would have to understand.

"There was one readable set of prints on the steering wheel, probably the grandmother's. The person who stole it must have worn gloves since he knew he was going to leave the car for the police. One of the lab guys came up with a few strands of fiber that didn't match any of the clothing the lady wore that day.

"Does that help?"

"Not unless we catch someone for another reason and can then link him back to the car." Jarrett took a sip of the scotch and felt it burn all the way down. He grimaced and took another swig.

"What are the police doing about someone trying to kill you?"

"They assigned a detective to look into it, that guy named Haucklin who told me he wanted a new investigation into the Wilkens case."

"You trust him more than Perry?"

"I think he's honest, yeah. But I'm not sure what he'd do if his job was at stake." Jarrett stroked his chin thoughtfully and moved his fingers against the grain. He felt the thick, dark bristles of his beard starting to grow back. "One thing that bothers me: He guessed that the weapon was a high-powered pellet gun. He told me they found a gun like that in school recently."

"The middle school?"

"High school." Jarrett reached into his shirt pocket and withdrew a hunk of brass about a half inch long. "After Haucklin left I dug this out from a display case." He held the material out to her, and she could see that it had once been a bullet. The end was blunted and took the shape of five distinctive curls, like a symmetrical metal daisy. "It was a lot longer before it ran into a steel plate in the display case."

"Why didn't you give it to the police?"

"At the time the police consisted of Haucklin. Something told me not to, not yet."

Meg hefted the bullet and felt a grisly fascination with something so small and pretty that was also so lethal.

Jarrett himself was struck by the view of the deadly object enfolded in such a supple hand. He remembered how pliant Meg's skin felt, a strange and random thought at a time like this. "It isn't the kind of ammo you expect to see around here," he said, coming to his senses. "Hollowpoint 357 Magnum, built for expansion and penetration. You see it mostly in places where punks want to out-arm the cops and take them out with a single shot. In this case it was used with silencer, like I thought." He pointed to a smooth section on the casing.

"A silencer because the shooter goes unnoticed and can stay there longer," Meg speculated.

Jarrett nodded and returned the slug to his pocket. "Makes me wonder about Haucklin. His guess couldn't have been further off."

"Remember who you're talking about, a small-town cop who probably never fired his gun on the job."

Jarrett allowed the possibility. "But he implied that it could have been a high school kid. I'm thinking he suspects something he's not telling me."

"You have to remember who he works for, too, and will be after you've gone. Haucklin could be keeping tabs on you." She raised her eyebrows provocatively and reached for her drink.

"The thought had occurred to me." Jarrett watched her move the glass gracefully to her lips. She looked very sleek, almost feline. The soft planes of her face glowed in the muted light and looked as delicate as the petals of a rose. She wasn't wearing lipstick or makeup of any kind, and never had for as long as he'd known her. She had the kind of skin that cosmetic companies could go broke on, and that a man with callused hands felt uncomfortable caressing.

"Did you learn anything new about what happened at the Delaware Water Gap?"

Jarrett's expression turned wary. "I wish I'd spent more time there. There was a lot I probably missed. I tried to contact the class mother who was there. But as soon as I told her who I was, the frost in her voice could have chilled a case of Heineken. I have a feeling the grubby hand of Arno or Melacore touched her, and not lightly."

He caught himself lingering on Meg's face too long again and went for the drink again. He could already feel the calming effects of the scotch. He hadn't noticed when it happened, but at some point Meg had moved closer to him.

Your ex-partner's daughter, for God's sake.

She looked up, frailer than before. "I didn't think anything like this was going to happen. I wouldn't have asked you to come here. I'm scared, Jarrett, for both of us."

His hand moved to her hair with a volition all its own, then he took it away almost as fast. Beth Ellen was with him again. His spontaneous act of near intimacy surprised her as much as it did him.

"I think the shooting says someone sees us both as the enemy now," he said.

Meg let the weight of her head fall against his shoulder. "Maybe we should just let this town keep its dirty little secret and get the hell out."

"That's got to be your decision, I won't help you make it."

She hadn't expected that answer and thought about it. She decided that she was grateful. "I know. I don't want to run again, that's all I do."

"So don't."

She explored his face, which was filled with determination. He was still so confident, even after his close call that morning. In the beginning, a tragedy had brought them together, now they were connected again by a common danger.

"Thanks for being here, Jarrett," she whispered. She arched her head back to look in his eyes, and her mouth came to rest only a few inches from his.

Jarrett felt an electric current pass through his body. He saw the moistness of her lips and heard a voice telling him to run for his life, but his body was beyond intelligent thought. He was drawn to her on many levels. She was like him, a fighter trying to outdistance the past. She was honest and kind and vulnerable. And beautiful.

The narrow window of opportunity to leave came and went. There was the jasmine coming off her hair.

He leaned forward a little, and when she saw it she came the rest of the way. In another moment he did the dumbest thing of his entire life and pressed his mouth to hers.

It was amazing how good dumb could feel.

35

For a while there'd been a chance the lightning storm would skirt the area to the south, but a sudden wind carried the first few drops of rain, and the flashes of light became continuous. Jarrett crept ahead in the darkness toward the Wilkens house with a powerful clap of thunder overhead that added its implicit condemnation of the act he was contemplating.

Meg was probably right, he probably was too cavalier about breaking the law in order to serve it. Already since coming to Knollwood, he'd strong-armed a middle school vice-principal, fingerprinted schoolchildren without their knowledge, and broken into one of their lockers.

His trip into the Wilkens house was going to be the latest violation of the penal code. In the past he'd always sanctioned his illicit actions with some high-minded moral credo, like an eye for an eye. But in the end his reason was much more pragmatic: Good guys need to take liberties to stay even. The matter of his justification, however, was still up for debate.

As Jarrett had learned from the real estate agent, Wilkens's husband had chosen a location among finer homes and she had been unable to keep up with the neighbors. The stone portion of the house had kept its timeless elegance, but the wooden sections that encased it had decayed. Two deteriorating ornate brick chimneys on an aging mansard roof lent the house a brooding aspect.

The grounds were in inverse proportion to most properties. There was a larger sloping front yard and an abbreviated back. The rear of the premises was uncomfortably close to the building next door, separated by a flagstone path and an arching trellis wrapped in wild wisteria. The route to the back door took him under one of the neighbors' bedroom windows, which was partly open, and he was afraid the thunder might rouse its occupants at any time.

As he approached the back door in the rain, Jarrett wondered what his father would think of him now. Thomas Jarrett had been a social services lawyer who saw one truth, the law as written, no exceptions. Using it, he had nailed more than his share of child abusers, blood-sucking slumlords, and tyrannical sweatshop owners. He would not have tolerated for one moment his son's unorthodoxy, no matter what the reason.

Four cement steps led up to the back door, which was locked, but not padlocked like the front. In a routine procedure, the house had been sealed by the county prosecutor's office pending the outcome of the inquiry into Wilkens's death.

The window to the right of the door was the best bet, being severely weathered. Jarrett waited to time his assault with the next round of thunder, and when it came, one forceful blow of his palms lifted the bottom portion off the sill. He slid the window all the way open and hoisted himself into what turned out to be a mud room.

Unoccupied since Wilkens's death, the house gave off the pungent smell of mildew. Using a small flashlight to navigate, Jarrett passed through the mud room, then down a hall into the main living area. He picked his way past a clutter of tables, a sofa, and spiral leg chairs in the living room. On one side, where there was an entrance to the dining area, a large case clock stood in silent tribute to the passing of its owner.

His light played around the room. Judging from the full complement of furniture, no one had shown an interest in her possessions before the court had locked up the place, so there was a chance that some personal articles might still be found.

His search took him quickly to a small carpeted library, wood-paneled from top to bottom. After a swift inspection, the best glimpse into Wilkens's life came from a number of framed pictures in a section of the bookcase. Many of the photos showed Wilkens with groups of students. There were dates on the backs of them. Curiously, or maybe not, given what he'd found out, there were none from recent years.

A large photo showed Wilkens at an official function being handed a plaque by a man who made a ceremonial display of the presentation. Almost all the other mementos in the room derived from her teaching, a few personal notes with warm sentiments, a sports trophy with her name and "Teacher of the Year" inscribed on it, other things from a lifetime of valued service.

There were no family shots. Her students were her family, a sadly ironic fact given the way they'd begun to feel about her near the end.

Jarrett paced quickly into the kitchen, a room older than the rest of the house. The strong odor of soil issued from a linoleum floor that gave under his weight. Yellow metal cabinets that dated back to the fifties were set to one side over a basin sink. When he opened one door, a set of dark blue dishes formed a backdrop for several bottles of various health aids, mostly vitamins.

An outsized plastic pill bottle caught his attention. The prescription on the container was for a drug he didn't recognize, Luvox. Somehow, he had the feeling he was holding an important new piece of the Wilkens puzzle. A call to Dunellen would tell him about the drug. He memorized the name of the prescribing doctor, then put the bottle back in the cabinet and closed the door.

The bedroom was where Wilkens would most likely have kept her personal items. The stairs to the second floor creaked like the door in *Tales from the Crypt*. Another round of thunderclaps overhead chilled the flesh along Jarrett's arms as he used a carved banister to help him up. He noted the curious fact that he was much more at ease bashing thugs than sneaking into a dead lady's boudoir.

The master bath was empty except for the medicine chest. He opened it and focused on the array of pill bottles. As in the kitchen, there was a bottle of Luvox, this one empty. Another behind it had a few pills left and no refills.

Back in the deathly still bedroom, the strong scent of lilac perfume assaulted his senses. Night tables and bureau tops were covered with lace. He expected that at any moment Wilkens's ghost might walk into the room holding a silver tea service.

Jarrett yanked on a drawer at the bottom of an old French armoire. It stuck, but the effort was worth it. One ornately decorated photo album rested inside among embroidered cotton sheets. He lifted it out reverently, feeling lousy about it.

He tucked the flashlight under his arm and opened it. The pictures of the tall and very pretty young woman that greeted him had to be Wilkens as a teenager. She was posed with a woman who must have been her mother and from whom she took her looks.

Two other photos showed her at a Communion and in a rowboat with a broad-chested, mustachioed man rowing her on a lake in the mountains, probably her father. The man had on the kind of white cutaway T-shirt worn by immigrants in those days, and made popular again today by kids and greaseballs.

Thumbing quickly, Jarrett stopped at shots of Wilkens's wedding and saw her then-young husband, a reasonable facsimile of her father, who'd gone on to tend the lawns of her rich neighbors, buy her a house near them, and die soon after paying it off. The scenes of Wilkens with her daughter saddened him as he remembered what Meg had said happened to her.

There were a dozen shots of the child, the last being one at eleven or twelve years of age. Something about her was familiar, but he couldn't put his finger on it. He turned the page, then went back to it quickly with a revelation that lit up his mind like a searchlight.

The doe-eyed child that stared at him from another time bore a remarkable likeness to Meg's student, Jessie Lerner. His mind churned with the astonishing and creepy discovery, something new to factor into the Wilkens/Jessie relationship.

The last section of the album held an eclectic group of photos. A moody shot of her with an unknown man of about forty caught Jarrett's eye. Wilkens was much older here, and the man was stony-faced and athletic. It must have been after her husband had died. The two stood together stoically and in a way that reminded Jarrett of couples in mass Moonie marriages. There was a cabin behind them, possibly a vacation lodge in a wooded area. A lover after her husband passed away?

The album ended shortly after that. Jarrett looked out the window that faced the nearby neighbor and kept his head and flashlight low. A light had gone on in one of the upstairs rooms across from him. If anyone saw his light in the deserted house, a call to the police would quickly follow. He could just imagine trying to explain to Perry what he was doing. To Stryker. Time to stop pressing his luck.

Jarrett's gaze swept the room for the last time and came to rest on a nightstand. It would only take a few seconds, he decided. He might not even need the light now. The lightning was constant again. It sounded like the end of the world outside.

When he opened the shallow wooden drawer he felt as if he'd struck gold. There were two diaries inside. The first opened with the release of a metal catch. He slipped to the floor beside the bed and put the flashlight on it.

How low can you stoop?

In a few minutes, he'd read the entries from a very intelligent and refined woman who had endured more than her share of grief. Her account of her husband's death, and then, only a few years later, of losing her daughter, was heart-shattering. After she was alone, her entries became deeply melancholic, and she discussed the possibility of suicide.

As he read on, Wilkens showed herself to be a star-crossed figure, obsessed with the children in her classes as a last connection to a family, and increasingly bitter about the way they were treating her.

Before he could finish, a blinding blast of light and crash of thunder was followed by an explosion outside, very close by. Jarrett raised his head and saw that the light in the window had gone off. Beyond the neighbor's house the entire area was pitch black. The explosion must have been a transformer that knocked out power to the entire area. All the more reason to leave quickly.

He held the diaries in his hand, tempted to take them, but this wasn't the time to add theft to his list of crimes. He'd find a way to get them legally, when the time came.

Jarrett fought a rising sense of danger and turned the flashlight on the second diary. Some early pages contained reminiscences about departed family members. Later on he found a place that signaled a change in Wilkens's tone.

In this section she'd detailed events in her classroom that had tormented her. Several of the children had been openly challenging her, she said, and were making nasty comments under their breath.

It got worse from there. In a few pages her feelings underwent a dramatic change, from anger and disappointment to something approaching panic. There was a group in her class, she believed, that had been flagrantly insubordinate. On one occasion they'd attacked her verbally as a group. She thought they'd formed a gang and that they hated her and were conspiring to harm her.

The last entry was a mind-numbing disclosure. It contained Wilkens's deepest fear, and was either the raving of a woman gone mad, or the belief of an aging schoolteacher who found herself at the mercy of sinister foes.

The entry read, "I know that no one will believe me, but I'm now certain that the children want to kill me."

The date at the top of the page was October 19.

One week before the fateful class trip.

36

The dread in Meg's voice on the motel room phone was palpable. She implored Jarrett to come over right away, and would only say something had happened that was too sick to talk about over the phone.

Jarrett drove to her house and saw her standing on the deck when he arrived. Her arms were wrapped around herself protectively. Beads of perspiration flecked her forehead. She looked as brittle as he'd ever seen her.

"The door was still locked when I got home," she went off suddenly. "Someone got in and did it . . . in the bedroom."

Jarrett felt her grip tighten when he tried to let go of her hand. "It's okay, I'll take a look."

The scene in the bedroom was chaotic. Meg's clothing was spilled on the floor, as were articles of jewelry and cosmetics.

Her bed had been reserved for a special kind of sickness. The pillow and thin coverlet were still in place but shredded down to the mattress. A face was drawn on the pillow with lipstick, a cluster of smears representing hair like hers.

On top of the desecrated bed selected articles of Meg's underclothing and jewelry had been laid carefully in place, as if she were there wearing them; a pearl choker at her neck, lower down a lace bra, then underwear. The panties were spotted with stains from a substance that had seeped in and left darker circles.

"Was it a kid?" Meg asked disgustedly when he returned to the front room.

"We might be able to find out."

"What kind of person gets kicks out of something like this?"

"I don't know, it was probably done just to frighten you." He shifted his weight. It was a good time to tell her, a potent distraction. "I found out something at Wilkens's place that points to the kids. Wilkens kept a diary. She said she thought some of her students were trying to kill her. It's there in her own writing."

Meg was blank with shock. "How did you get in?" When he returned her question with a sheepish look, she said, "You didn't have a search warrant, did you?"

"When it's time I'll lead the police to it and make them think it was their idea. Remember the newspaper story that said Wilkens had a daughter?"

"The one who died, of a blood disease?"

"I want to show you something," Jarrett said. He reached into his shirt pocket and took out a photo.

She went rigid when he handed it to her. The little girl in the faded picture looked pretty in her period beads, fleecy vest, and bell-bottom jeans. She'd been caught in a happy moment playing with mom and dad—and there was no mistaking who she looked like. "Jessie Lerner?"

"I thought so, too, but I've only seen Jessie once or twice."

"She's not exactly the same, but the resemblance is very strong. Same eyes, same kind of vulnerable look." Meg turned to him. "Jesus, Jarrett, do you think—?"

He was on the same wavelength. "Yeah, if Wilkens really was out of her mind. Maybe she needed to project some sense of injustice on a kid who happened to look like her daughter and was still alive. God knows what she was thinking."

They both went silent.

"What about this one," Jarrett continued, proffering a second snapshot.

Meg stared at it a while, then brought it closer before reacting. "I could be wrong, but I'd swear the man is a young version of Ken Schermer, the head of the Knollwood Soccer Association. I didn't even know they knew each other."

"They did then, and pretty well, it looks like."

"I think he's been married forever, grown kids. How long ago was this taken?"

"Looks like she's around forty, after her husband died."

"Where are they supposed to be?" Meg said, staring at the photo.

"Your guess is as good as mine. Alone, mainly."

"An affair with a married man? Strange that she'd keep his picture after all those years."

Jarrett's expression was sullen. He nodded toward the bedroom. "You have to call the police about this. Sooner rather than later, or else you'll have to explain why it took you so long."

She nodded dejectedly. "I don't think it's a good idea for me to stay here tonight. And I don't want to be alone." Jarrett felt a spark ignite in his loins. "You don't have to be, if you don't want to," he said awkwardly. He watched for further guidance from her reaction, completely uncertain that he wanted to see it.

Her finger was in her hair again, twisting. She gave him a lost look, and he felt his knees buckle. "Is that an offer?" she said as softly as he'd ever heard a woman speak.

"I'll stay here until the police have gone, then . . . we'll go . . . somewhere."

"What if someone sees us," she said, then caught herself and laughed nervously, letting go of her hair and her tension. "Jeez, you'd think I was sixteen and had a curfew." She touched his shoulder and let her long fingers linger. "What I meant to say is thanks, that makes me feel a lot better." She withdrew her hand and looked back over her shoulder into the bedroom. "I don't know how I'm going to be able to go back in there."

"After the police have checked it for evidence, we'll make a huge ball of everything and throw it out."

She smiled with embarrassment. "I wasn't thinking of recycling the clothing."

Once the police were on the way, Jarrett asked, "Did you ever hear of a drug named Luvox?"

"Isn't that something they give to people to calm them down, or for depression? Like Haldol?"

"I found a prescription for it at Wilkens's place. One bottle in the kitchen cabinet, two more in her medicine chest."

"Might not be that big a deal. A lot of people take small amounts of heavy-duty drugs, for lots of reasons."

"I don't think we're talking small amounts here. The first two bottles were empty and the third showed no refills left. The instructions said to take two milligrams a day, but from the date on the last prescription, a few days before she died, it looks like she'd taken a lot more than that."

Meg was perplexed. "What are you thinking?"

"That I'd better find out why she was taking so much, and what an overdose could do to her. I also wonder if there was someone else involved with her medicine."

Meg pondered what he was getting at. "Someone getting her to take more than she knew about?" she finally came up with.

"Yeah, like that. The bar still open in this place?" Jarrett asked out of the blue.

"Only for special customers."

"My turn." He got up. He needed something to clear his head, and the walk to the kitchen was the best he could do at the moment.

He had a brand-new worry now, completely unrelated to the scene in the bedroom, and it shattered his concentration. Given the way things were going, in a short time they were going to end up at his motel room, and he had to figure out what to do once they got there.

There was only one bed in his room, a double.

37

After the police had left, she and Jarrett traveled to the Laurel Motel in separate cars so that Meg could go directly to school in the morning. As Jarrett had feared, the parking lot was full when they arrived, and, as if to underscore his dilemma, the NO VACANCY sign shimmered behind wisps of swirling haze in the humid night air.

Jarrett wondered whether Meg noticed the sign and understood that it signaled that they were on the verge of cataclysmic change. His palms left moisture on the steering wheel when he got out. He hadn't been with a woman for the two years he'd been without Beth Ellen. He hadn't wanted to be, not even once.

He found the opening in the lock to his room on the second fumbling try, and the door glided open. Meg stood behind him holding a small suitcase. There was an uneasy silence between them, but not the kind that created distance. Neither of them had broached the obvious topic. The lighted room revealed the double bed.

Jarrett turned to face Meg without the slightest idea of what to say. Meg smiled and he saw the two women she was at the moment, one world-weary from the traumatic events of the day, the other tense with a guarded and impish anticipation.

The best he could do was, "It's not the Sunset Marquis, but I call it home." He examined the room with her as if for the first time, and noted that the small space produced a further logistical problem. There was no sofa, and aside from a chair in front of a writing table, the bed was the only place to sit. Meg walked over to the bed, plopped her suitcase on it, and turned to look at him expectantly. The ball was in his court.

"I guess we have a slight problem," he said finally.

"I know. I'll bet you anything there's no ice in that thing." She gestured behind him to the key bar built into a cabinet under the TV set. Her smile waned, and she suddenly had an amused, faraway look.

"Something I did?" Jarrett asked.

"I was just remembering a time a boyfriend took me to a place like this. He was so worried about what the manager would say that he wore a tie and borrowed a wedding ring from someone. He was so unbelievably clumsy the manager wouldn't give us a room. Actually, I thought he was adorable."

"How old were you, or is that a bad question?"

"Eighteen. I was a freshman in college. I thought I was in love with him."

"It's a good thing your father didn't know about it," Jarrett said without considering the effect of his reference. He instantly regretted it. He hadn't intended to summon the one presence that would remind them most of why they shouldn't be there.

The mention of Frank had a sedating effect on Meg. She eased herself down on the bed and clicked open her suitcase. Jarrett shed his jacket and holster and felt the same sweep of anxiety he always experienced in the presence of a beautiful woman, his Beauty and the Beast syndrome. It was that way when he'd first met his wife. Then as now, it went deeper than pure physical attraction; a psychic connection of some kind; a sense of destiny, as corny as it sounded.

He stole a glance at Meg from across the room as she took out a few articles of clothing from her suitcase. He recalled the rebellious younger woman he'd first met. She'd tried so hard to appear self-assured, but the soft side showed. The untamed quality had diminished over time, replaced by a sense of purpose. She was a woman in every sense now, intelligent, radiant, and confident in many ways. But in unguarded moments, she still showed the vulnerability that early hardship had brought.

Done with the perfunctory chores of moving in, Meg unclipped a barrette from her copper hair. Under the fabric of her corduroy slacks her limbs looked long and well-formed. Her red and tan plaid shirt was loose around her upper body. As usual, she'd dressed to minimize her figure.

"There's no way in hell we should stay in this room together," Jarrett finally blurted out when the silence had become unbearable. It was a feeble stab at seizing some high-minded moral ground, but the attempt was so transparent he felt foolish.

"You're probably right," she agreed. "I should probably go home."

"That wouldn't be safe. I could get another room, someplace else. Or stay in the car. I've done it a hundred times."

"No, I don't want you to do that."

The exchange was going nowhere.

"Like I said, we've got a problem," he repeated.

She beamed her eyes at him, and there was no mistaking what he saw. "I hear you're good at solving problems," she said, kicking off her shoes.

Later, when they were quiet, he cradled her from behind. Their bodies were slick from spent passion, and he buried his face in her hair. She pushed back against him to make an even tighter seal. Next to her silken body he felt like a barbarian. But at least there'd been no phantoms in bed with them.

"I'm happy about this," Meg said, her face half hidden by the pillow. "I wasn't sure I would be, but I am."

He wished he could say he shared her conviction, but he was awash in conflict. "I never thought about this happening, not in a million years."

"Maybe that's the reason it could. I wonder what *they'd*

think about this," she said with total innocence. "Dad, and Beth Ellen."

The question brought the feeling to the surface again. It had been foolish to think the night would pass without it. Even with Meg so close, part of him felt lost in time and space.

"What was she like, Jarrett?"

For some reason he was able to talk about it. "She lived in another world from the rest of us. Saw a different reality. She believed if she worked hard enough she could make everything add up. I never wanted to be the one to tell her that things were more random than that."

"Was it good between you?"

"In the beginning it was, like we'd found an island just for ourselves. Later on she became disappointed, and I wasn't able to help her. I wasn't there enough when she needed me." *Like when it ended*, he found himself thinking on a bitter note.

"I can't imagine you not being there for someone who loves you," Meg said.

"I couldn't live in two worlds at once. I didn't pick up on it until too late."

"Where are you now on your two worlds?"

It was the million-dollar question, and he didn't have the answer now any more than he ever had. "I know what I lost, and why. Maybe that changes things, I don't know."

Meg ruminated for a while, then said, "Did you ever hear of a singer called Tim Hardin?"

The name rang a distant bell.

"He sang a song called 'Until It's Time for You to Go.' It says that nothing lasts forever, so lovers have to take what they can before it ends. I still think it's the most beautiful and saddest song I ever heard."

Jarrett drew a breath that held the scent of her heated body. Her words touched him, and he tugged on her shoulder until she turned around and they were facing each other.

"Maybe good things don't have to end," she said hopefully, pressing her cheek into his chest. "Not if you're really careful."

She pulled her head back to search his eyes, then seemed to find what she'd been afraid to see, and let her head rest on his chest again. "I think I'm beginning to love you, Jarrett," she said when he couldn't see her face. "It's going to be hard letting you go."

38

Wesley Gomes estimated that the walls were three inches thick and hollow between the studs, with not enough insulation to conform to code. He felt fairly confident about this because, with his ear pressed tightly to the plasterboard, he could hear their moans of pleasure as clearly as if they were in his own room.

The situation was ironic to the point of pain. Only by a caprice of circumstance had Jarrett found himself in the throes of passion instead of on his deathbed.

Jarrett's planned demise had been ordained after Gomes had read the newspaper story about the shooting at Starbucks and observed him further on several occasions. His continuing activities, and his liaison with the young teacher, left no doubt about what he was after. Allowing him time to get closer to the truth was no longer an option.

Not surprisingly, Jarrett was on guard after the recent attempt on his life, looking over his shoulder, checking his truck before getting in, always carrying a weapon under his arm. Thus, following him to his motel had required extreme caution.

Gomes had reserved the room next door to his days earlier, and registered under a false name, paying cash in advance to avoid showing ID. This allowed him to leave whenever he wanted, and without a further transaction.

A quick check of the motel's property revealed that the rooms were all laid out in a straight line. The back walls faced an empty but accessible area of marsh behind the building where there was little chance of being seen at night. Each room had an air conditioning unit that vented warm air from a narrow opening in the wall and took in fresh air from another. The air exchanger operated continuously to provide circulation.

Gomes planned to wait in his room until the cop was asleep, then go to his car, which he had parked in back. He would then attach one end of a rubber hose to his exhaust pipe and place the other snugly into the opening in Jarrett's wall, where the outside air entered. Once he started his car the odorless gas would do its job while Jarrett slept. In a few hours, Gomes would remove the hose and himself and be hard at work at the bank before the body was discovered the next day.

The plan was as foolproof as it was simple—except Jarrett had not come to the motel alone. His arrival with the teacher ruined everything. With two people in the room, there was increased chance that one or both of its occupants would be awake when Gomes started his car, and the sound might make them suspicious. Since he had not thought through the details of a double murder, the added risk was suddenly unacceptable.

Added to this disappointment, the cries of mutual pleasure on the other side of the wall finally became too much to bear. A short time after the couple started to make love, Gomes left his room in a quiet rage and stole to the back of the building for a solemn drive home.

On the way he cursed his luck and the interloper from L.A. who had begun to haunt his thoughts continuously. Jarrett had already narrowed his chances of finding a way out, and it would only get worse with time. He had quickly come to realize that it was Jarrett, and not the teacher, that he had to fear.

Later, as the first rays of dawn lit up the stark walls of his own residence, Gomes thought about the incident at the coffee shop, where someone else had tried and failed to put an end to Jarrett.

Again, he wondered about the hand that had held the gun, and the face behind it. Someone wanted Dan Jarrett dead as much as he did.

He fervently wished he knew who it was, and whether that other person would do his job for him.

If he could wait that long.

39

"What was your boss's reaction to what happened at Foley's place?" Jarrett said to the detective who could pass for his slightly older brother.

"Perry was as pissed as I've ever seen him," Haucklin said. "He's got a thing about sex crimes."

Haucklin still telegraphed his disgust at the perverse act performed in Meg's bedroom. Another officer had responded to the call to her house the night before, and he'd only caught up on the news before Jarrett phoned to meet with him.

There'd been a shift in Haucklin's tone from when he'd greeted Jarrett stiffly in front of fellow officers a few minutes earlier. Now that they were alone in a back room he'd let down his guard and was as friendly as he'd been on the first night they met. Evidently, Haucklin was openly fearful about the consequences of their liaison, a fact that made Jarrett trust him more.

Another lingering concern about him had been resolved. As it turned out, the dispatcher on duty during the Starbucks shooting hadn't broadcast a description of the suspect's car, which explained how the detective could have allowed the shooter to drive by him when he responded to the call. "You must have seen a lot of this kind of thing. You think it was a kid?" Haucklin asked about the scene at Meg's place.

"Your lab guys should be able to tell you that. A sperm count can indicate something about age."

Haucklin sipped coffee from a plastic cup he'd been holding since they'd gotten together at the station house. "I've been trying to figure out who else might have had a motive for killing Wilkens. What about family?"

"The only family anyone's turned up is a nephew who lives in Oakland Park."

"Yeah, I know," Haucklin said, surprised Jarrett had gotten the information. "I heard they weren't too close, but he came to the funeral. He's a banker, and very successful. Don't know what he'd have to gain.'

"I'd sure as hell like to know if he was in Wilkens's will."

"She didn't have a will. I thought you already knew that."

Jarrett registered his surprise. "I assumed it was tied up in probate."

"Uh-uh. She died intestate."

"So anything she left would automatically go to the nephew?" Jarrett asked with obvious intent.

"That's how it works. He was questioned after the accident and got a clean bill of health."

"I should talk to him, too, not that Perry would be crazy about the idea."

"Anything I can do to help?"

A few possibilities came to Jarrett's mind. Naming them was a calculated risk. There was still a chance Haucklin might call Perry and give him up, but proving he'd done something illegal wouldn't be easy. He hadn't been seen and had been careful not to leave any prints. "To start with, you could try to get a court to let you into Wilkens's house. I have a feeling you'll find something that sheds light on what happened to her."

Haucklin's expression turned suspicious.

"Of course, that's just a guess," Jarrett continued with a shrug. "Also, if you happen to be walking by the boys' lockers at the middle school, you might be interested to see what's inside number 316."

Haucklin glared at him. "I presume you're familiar with the section of the penal code that deals with breaking and entering?"

Jarrett feigned hurt at the inference of his wrongdoing. "May I remind you, Detective, that I'm an awwwfficuuur of de lawwwrr," he said in his best imitation of Inspector Clouseau of *Pink Panther* fame.

Haucklin sat back in his chair and made a tent of his fingers. He stared ahead noncommittally for a while, then his scowl deepened and he leaned forward. "And I'm nut a blooond fuuuel," he said, continuing Jarrett's impersonation. His expression turned congenial. "I'll see what I can do."

40

"Elaine Wilkens was suffering from a neurological dysfunction which resulted in clinical depression," Dr. James Rothkopf said emphatically. "It was caused by a chemical imbalance in the brain, for which the recommended treatment is pharmacological."

Rothkopf was the prescribing doctor listed on the pill bottles Jarrett had found at Wilkens's house. A check of the physicians' guide in the phone book showed a James Rothkopf, M.D., P.C., a psychiatrist. His office was at the Murdock Psychiatric Hospital in Lakeland, where he also taught.

From the way he'd come across on the phone, Jarrett had conjured a man in his late forties, frenetic from overwork, with little time for postmortem interviews about former patients. He agreed to a meeting only after Jarrett identified himself as a police officer investigating his ex-patient's death. In person, the doctor turned out to be closer to sixty, stern, but with a youthful face.

"Before her death, a number of people believed Mrs. Wilkens was acting strange at work," Jarrett said. "Some of the parents—"

"I knew about the complaints," the doctor interrupted.

"For a while it was the main topic of our sessions. As you can imagine, the controversy added to her state of depression."

"Did anyone at the school know about her condition?"

"There was no need for that. In my opinion, which I shared with my patient, it would have jeopardized her position and nothing would have been gained. From what I understand she never missed a day, no matter how she felt. I thought she was admirable in that respect."

"Don't you think she owed it to everyone to explain what was going on?"

Rothkopf became annoyed. "If your whole life was police work, and you had a condition that would put you under intense scrutiny, would you want your superiors to know about it?"

Jarrett stifled an impulse to laugh. "Hey, I've been under my boss's scrutiny my whole life. In my case, it's him who's depressed."

Rothkopf didn't allow himself to enjoy the barb. He wasn't going to be Jarrett's buddy anytime soon.

"The accusations about her conduct were very painful to her," he continued. "She was doing a good job not letting her condition affect her teaching, and having her behavior called into question was an unspeakable affront. Teaching was all she cared about. For the most part she spoke of her students with affection."

Except the ones she thought wanted to kill her, Jarrett thought, recalling the chilling entry in her diary. For some reason she hadn't shared that with her doctor.

"She never mentioned any students who were causing her problems?"

"There were a few she thought were a discipline problem," Rothkopf added, after thinking about it some more, "but that's par for the course, I suppose."

"Did she mention any names?"

Rothkopf shook his head. Either he was in too much of a hurry to look in his notes, or he was being faithful to the confidential relationship he had with Wilkens.

"Is there a chance you weren't aware of the way she

really was, in class, I mean? I heard she got very angry, shouted at the kids a lot."

"Doesn't every teacher?"

"Not as abusively as I've heard she did."

"Did any adults see that kind of behavior?"

Jarrett hunched his shoulders. The only adult witness had been Janet Elder, Jessie Lerner's aide. He'd been able to contact her by phone, but, like the class mother on the trip, she hadn't wanted to talk. She verified, though, that Wilkens hadn't inflicted any physical punishment on the students, not that she had seen.

"No, all the reports came from the kids," Jarrett admitted. Slowly but surely he was losing credibility, and he wished he had more concrete evidence. "For the record, I started out feeling the way you do, but I've seen these kids myself. They're still shaken up by whatever happened."

Rothkopf dismissed his hypothesis with a wave of his hand. "Elaine Wilkens wasn't psychotic, and I saw nothing to suggest she was capable of violence, if that's what you're trying to suggest."

The tone of the innocent inquirer suddenly seemed appropriate. "I'm sorry, I don't know much about these things, but could the medicine you prescribed for her have something to do with behavior? Luvox, I think it was?"

His query took Rothkopf off guard. "I don't know how you came by that information, but it was the most effective of the medications we tried up to that point. She was maintaining well with it."

"How many medicines are there for depression?"

"A great many, twenty, thirty. I've never counted."

"How many did she try?"

"Only three, which I considered fortunate. As I said, we stopped when we had some success."

"Isn't Luvox stronger than a lot of other drugs typically given for depression, like Prozac or Zoloft? Is it a new drug?"

Rothkopf checked his watch impatiently. "I really have to bring this to an end. I have a patient waiting."

"Sure, I understand," Jarrett said quickly. "But I have to tell you that a large amount of fluvoxamine—that's the generic name for Luvox, right—?"

Rothkopf nodded.

"—that Wilkens's autopsy showed an usually large amount of it in her bloodstream when she died."

All of a sudden Rothkopf was vastly interested. "How large a dose, exactly?"

Jarrett took out a piece of paper from his pocket and showed it to him. Guano had guaranteed that the plasma level was inordinately high. "And that was approximately twenty hours after death," Jarrett added. He looked up from the paper. "I'm not technical on this, but I found out the half life of fluvoxamine is fifteen hours, so she'd have had to have taken a ton of the medicine that morning to end up with that much in her, a lot more than the average maintenance dose of around one hundred milligrams."

Rothkopf looked like a brick wall had fallen on him. "We started at twenty-five milligrams and titrated it to about seventy-five milligrams. The results of small increases of fluvoxamine can be dramatic, so you don't administer any more than you have to."

"My friend estimated that it would take triple that to produce the reading in the autopsy."

"I don't understand. We watched the dose very carefully. One of the possible side effects was cognitive dulling. Mrs. Wilkens was very concerned about that, especially as a teacher." He regained his irritation and added, "Now I really have to get to my other patient."

Jarrett stood to buy some time. "Are there any other side effects of this Luvox?"

"Yes, as with any of the antidepressants. It depends on the individual patient."

"Like what?"

"The most common are somnolence, dizziness. Some people report nervousness, or even insomnia."

"What about something more serious, say, at higher doses? Could the patient become, say, fearful?"

Rothkopf came around his desk toward the door, forcing Jarrett to back off in that direction. "I believe the contraindications can include a diminution of will. I refer to it as loss of courage." He moved to the door and opened it.

A nervous-looking gentleman in the waiting room looked up expectantly. There was only time for one more question. "What about paranoia?" Jarrett asked, deadly serious.

Rothkopf hesitated, then nodded reluctantly. "It's in the literature, but only in rare cases."

"Thank you, you've been a lot of help."

Jarrett offered him his hand, and the doctor took it. He held on to it when Jarrett tried to leave, then pulled him back into the office and shut the door.

"Just for the record, why are you investigating this now? What are you trying to find out about the accident after all this time?"

Jarrett was struck by the innocence of the question. He'd imagined that someone like Rothkopf would have seen enough in his practice to make the leap all by his lonesome.

"Just why in hell everyone is so willing to believe it *was* an accident," he answered.

41

Jarrett had no great love for the task at hand. He'd wrestled with what to tell the Lerners ever since visiting the Fairmount Halfway House, before realizing he had no choice but to inform them their son might become a suspect in the death of Elaine Wilkens. Jeremy's history of confrontation with Wilkens, his fierce protectiveness of his sister, and the long shot of the red mud he'd seen on the boy's shoes, could easily get fingers pointing at him in any new investigation.

After Jarrett delivered his warning, and as Meg sat in silence, Phillip Lerner looked at his wife in shock and desolation.

"Jeremy has his problems, but he's not a violent person," Carolyn Lerner shouted indignantly. "It's just not in his nature."

"Personally, I'd be willing to bet against it, too," Jarrett replied, "but it's obvious that he's very loyal to his sister. Some people may believe he was angry enough about Wilkens to do something irrational. That's why it's more important than ever for me to talk to Jessie. She may know something that points us in a better direction."

Carolyn still had fire in her eyes. "There's no reason for Jeremy to defend himself. He didn't do anything."

"That's what I'm hoping to find out."

Mrs. Lerner quieted, and this time it was she who went to her daughter, not Phillip as on the first meeting. After what seemed like a very long wait, Jessie returned with her, holding her mother's hand.

"Hi, Jess," Meg said warmly.

"'Lo," she answered, just above a whisper.

"This is Mr. Jarrett," her mother said. "He's a friend of Ms. Foley. He wants your help in finding out something about the class trip." Her statement was cooperative, her tone way at the other end of the spectrum.

Jessie squeezed her mother's hand tightly.

"We told Jessie you wanted to talk to her, but only for a minute or two," Carolyn said. "She says it's okay, if we're with her."

Jarrett leaned forward and lowered his head to the girl's level. She looked as if she were waiting for lightning to strike. At the moment he hated his job. "You can sit down if you want."

Jessie eased onto the sofa and folded her hands obediently. She looked like she had that day at school, Meg thought, when Wilkens's name came up.

"It's all right that you sent me the note," Meg began. "I think it was a very brave thing for you to do, and I'm proud of you."

The little girl's expression didn't change. She was frightened.

"I know you already talked to some people about Mrs. Wilkens," Jarrett went on, "but we weren't there, and we want to make sure we understand."

"She ran away and fell," Jessie blurted out all at once, without being prompted by a specific question. "I didn't see her do it."

"Can you tell me what happened before that? Why she needed to run?"

The question activated Jessie's lower lip, and it quivered as if she were freezing cold. Jessie glanced at her mother, but didn't speak.

"Maybe if you close your eyes and think real hard," Meg suggested.

Jessie shut her eyes on command but still had nothing to say.

"Let me help you a little," Jarrett said with a new idea. "Whenever I say something that's right, you just nod your head. If I make a mistake and say something wrong, shake your head no, okay?"

She nodded and opened her eyes. She liked the idea of not having to say anything more than staying in the dark.

"When the day started you were all on the bus, you and the other kids, and Mrs. Wilkens, and Mrs. Schlag, the class mother."

Jessie nodded, then added, "And the bus driver." It was easier for her to talk when she knew she didn't have to.

"And the bus driver," Jarrett repeated with a smile. "And he took you to the Delaware Water Gap without stopping?"

She nodded.

"Did anything bad happen on the bus, on the way, I mean?"

"Uh-uh."

"All right, so now you're at the Delaware Water Gap. What did you do next?"

"We climbed up the trail."

"I made that trip myself. It's a long walk. Was it hard for you? How were you feeling?"

"My legs were tired," she said, projecting herself back into the scene as he hoped.

"Mine were, too. Help me out a little more. Tell me where you are now."

"At the top of the mountain," she answered quickly. Her eyelids began to flutter.

"Are you all together, the class and your teacher?"

"Yes."

"Where are you exactly? And where is Mrs. Wilkens?"

"She's higher up. I'm at the back of the class."

"How come?"

"'Cause my legs are tired," she repeated impatiently.

"Oh yeah, I forgot. Who's standing in the front of the class?"

"Some of the other kids."

"Can you see who they are?"

"A bunch of them, that's all."

"What's Mrs. Wilkens doing?"

A shadow passed over Jessie's face, and she suddenly had difficulty speaking. "She's yelling at me." She shuddered. A tear instantly formed at the bottom of her closed lid and threatened to leak out.

"What's wrong, Jessie?"

"She's angry because she wanted us all to stay together and I couldn't keep up."

"Was she angry with everyone, or just with you?"

Jessie shook. She was truly back at the Delaware Water Gap and was very afraid. "There were a few others who weren't fast enough, but she yelled at me, like she always did."

A cautionary look from her parents alerted Jarrett to a concern he already had: He was tampering with a very fragile mentality. "I know, honey. I've had that happen to me. Sometimes people get mad at you when it isn't your fault. Sometimes it's because they're unhappy about something else." His offering placated her for the moment. "What happened next?"

"She screamed at me for being so slow. She asked if she had to carry me and told me to come up to her. I was afraid." Jessie's throat closed, cutting off the last few words.

"Why were you afraid?"

"She was screaming so loud. I didn't know what she was going to do," she said mournfully.

Carolyn Lerner turned away so her daughter wouldn't see her own discomfort.

"Did you go to her?"

"I wanted to, but I couldn't move. I was too scared."

Jarrett's pity for her made it hard for him to continue. "We're almost done, Jess. Just tell me what happened after that. What did the others do?"

"They were all looking at me. They were angry, but not at me this time. I wanted to do what Mrs. Wilkens told me . . . but they got . . . ahead of me."

"Who did, Jessie? Who got ahead of you?"

"The three boys."

"What were their names?" Jessie looked at both her parents. As soon as the question was asked the color drained from her face. Her father nodded and she turned back to Jarrett with tears streaming down her face. "Timothy Sullivan and Augie Templeton . . . and Doogie," she sobbed. "They yelled at Mrs. Wilkens, told her to leave me alone."

"And what did she do?"

"That made her more angry. She told them to stop, but they didn't care. They got in front of me."

"Then what?"

"She moved back, but they didn't stop." Jessie's breath came in short bursts. "They ran after her . . . shouting at her. She yelled for them to go away . . . but they didn't. She ran . . . away . . . into the woods."

"How far did she run?"

"I don't know." She was trying hard to go on. "They all kept running, and then I couldn't see where they went."

"Did you hear anything?"

She turned away to look at her mom. "I heard her scream. I stayed there until they all came back, except Mrs. Wilkens."

"The three boys came back?"

She moved her chin up and down. "But not Mrs. Wilkens," she added pointedly. "Then Mrs. Schlag came and made us go back down the trail."

"Thanks, Jess, that helps a lot," Meg interjected to help take some pressure off her. "Just a few more questions and we'll be done."

Jessie didn't look as if she had it in her but agreed. "Did the kids talk about what happened after you left?" Jarrett asked next.

"Everyone was too afraid."

"Did you tell anyone about the boys?" Jarrett said very softly.

"They made me promise not to tell. They said it was all my fault that Mrs. Wilkens died, that it wouldn't have happened . . . if I wasn't always such a problem."

"So you didn't tell anyone? Not even your parents?"

"No," Jessie blurted out. "Not everything."

Carolyn Lerner was in a state of confusion and looked at her daughter with pleading eyes. "I don't understand, honey. You've never been afraid to tell us anything."

Jessie shook her head mournfully. "I made you and Dad so unhappy already. I didn't want to make it worse."

A small sound caught in Mrs. Lerner's throat. She and her husband exchanged woeful glances.

"Then why did you write the note?" Jarrett asked, just above a whisper.

Jessie's eyes welled up. "The bad feeling wouldn't go away." She tried to go on, then had trouble speaking.

"Sometimes its easier to tell someone else, isn't it, Jessie?" Meg offered. "Even though you know how much your parents love you."

Jessie nodded limply. Her mother leaned forward and stroked her arm.

"Thank you for trusting me so much," Meg said.

"You were afraid of what the others might do, but deep down you knew it wasn't because of you," Jarrett added.

Jessie made a choking sound and buried her face in her mom's lap.

Jarrett gazed at Jessie with tenderness. He'd seen that look before, but in women who were afraid, some of violent men, sometimes wives who lived in fear of husbands who'd battered them and might again. He'd never seen it in a twelve-year-old girl before.

He let out a deep breath and relaxed his body. The ordeal was finally ending. "Before I tell you how brave and smart I think you are, would you do me one last favor?"

Through tears, she shrugged.

"Would you mind very much giving me a hug? I really need a hug." He held out both hands to her. Jessie stifled a last sob and looked up at him from her mother's lap. When he slipped off his chair and came to her on one knee she let herself come off the chair and be drawn to him. Her body shook several times, as if ridding itself of the burden of guilt she had carried for so long.

Jarrett held her and rocked her back and forth. Her parents held back a flood of emotion, as did Meg.

"It wasn't your fault, Jessie," Jarrett whispered in her ear. "None of it, Jessie. It wasn't your fault."

42

"A man like him is capable of anything," Meg said, with a disdainful look at the girls' soccer coach, Ken Schermer. She remembered the photograph of Schermer and Wilkens that Jarrett had showed her. It had been taken long ago when he was married and had kids in the school system. He still had the same manic look in his eyes.

She shot a woeful glance at Jessie Lerner, who was hunched over on the bench with her hands folded. It hadn't been enough for the child to endure a siege of terror in the classroom, Meg thought. Jessie had the further misfortune to have a coach who, even at the middle school level, was legendary for his need to win, at any cost to his players.

"He's known for sitting out lesser players all the time. He thinks that children would rather be benched on a winning team than play a lot on a team that loses. He couldn't be more full of crap," Meg said with annoyance.

Schermer's concept flew in the face of current research on kids' self-image and sports. He had the two most odious characteristics a tyrant can have, she thought, strong and wrong.

Jarrett studied Schermer from a different perspective. He'd come to the match to observe him up close because, in his experience, men revealed themselves under the pressure of competitive sports in a way they never did off the field of battle. "At least he knows the game," he said when the first half ended.

"That's all he knows," Meg said angrily. Jessie hadn't played at all, even though the score was lopsided in her team's favor. "The kids don't call him 'Iceman' for nothing."

When the game was over they watched Jessie get off the bench to slap the hands of the returning heroes in a victory to which she had lent only a precious few seconds of playing time and her voice. She was being a good sport.

Jarrett caught up to Schermer as he was lugging a heavy net full of soccer balls back to his car. The back of his T-shirt read, "Soccer Isn't Life, It's Better."

When Schermer had loaded the balls in his trunk, Jarrett introduced himself as a private investigator, which was true, and said he was following up on the Wilkens accident, which was a triumph of understatement.

The muscles in Schermer's cheek pulsed as he clenched his jaw. "What's there to investigate?" He stood next to the car ramrod straight, reminding Jarrett of a marine D.I.

"How she died, for one thing."

"You don't think it was an accident." Schermer trained his cobalt eyes on him, his mind working.

"I didn't say that."

"Yes, you did, by saying you were investigating it."

"Let's just say there are some loose ends."

"Who are you working for?"

Jarrett had expected the question. He was prepared to claim it was a relative who didn't wish to be identified.

Before he could lie, Schermer cut him off. "Why are you asking me about it?"

Jarrett reached into his pocket and took out the photograph of him and Wilkens. Schermer studied it for a moment without expression, but he snuck a peek around him to see if anyone else was in the vicinity.

Jarrett knew he'd touched a nerve. "I take it you knew her socially at one time."

"We were friends, but that was a long time ago, not that it's any of your business. We met through," he hesitated, searching for the right words, "a social club. We had similar interests."

"And how long were you both *club members?*"

"We attended meetings for about a year," he said more sharply. "Then the group broke up and we lost touch." He gave the picture back resentfully. "I don't know how that could be part of whatever you're investigating." He opened the door of his car.

Jarrett took a step closer. "I'm not interested in prying into your past. I'm only trying to find out anything I can about Wilkens."

Schermer got into his car, but the window was open.

"I can't figure out why she had a picture of you in her diary after all this time," Jarrett said, leaning next to him. "I'm also curious about the candles."

Schermer started the engine. "I'll make you a deal," he snapped back, as he put the gearshift into drive. He held on to an icy control worthy of a Mafia don in a Senate hearing. "You don't worry about that, I won't worry about how the hell you got the picture in the first place."

When Jarrett didn't have a fast answer, Schermer gunned the gas, and the car shot forward so quickly Jarrett had to jump out of the way.

43

In his three-year stint on the force, Paul Haucklin had never seen Chief Perry show so much emotion, not when he was named "Citizen of the Year" by the Knollwood Chamber of Commerce, not even when he won a trip for two to Hawaii in Summit Suburu's "Hit the Road Jackpot Sweepstakes." The only time anyone could recall him raising his voice was when he passed three kidney stones at St. Luke's Hospital one Christmas Eve. Even on the rare occasions when he fired an officer, Perry, like the businessman in Bob Dylan's song, had learned to smile while he killed—until now.

"I knew the son of a bitch was gonna be trouble," Perry snarled, "just like I knew about the schoolteacher. They're the type that are pissed off at authority of any kind, and they both have wise mouths. Two of a kind."

Haucklin made a snap decision to keep his own mouth shut. For some reason Perry had chosen to confide in him and not others on his staff that he'd known much longer. For that Haucklin at least owed Perry his objectivity.

But he also owed Jarrett. He'd reached out to him, not the other way around, on a matter of conscience. "Somebody *did* try to push Foley in front of a train," he finally volunteered. "And somebody took shots at Jarrett. I think that might give them the right to be pissed." Defending Jarrett was a dangerous game, but it was the honorable thing to do.

Perry clamped beefy hands to his broad belly, a way some fat men had of checking their girth every now and then. He drilled his young detective with a calculated glance. "The fact remains that none of this would have happened if they'd kept their noses out of our affairs. You agree with that, don't you?"

Haucklin's halfhearted nod didn't quell Perry's concern, but it was deferential enough. Haucklin suddenly wondered if his boss had found out about his tête-à-têtes with Jarrett, and if this impromptu get-together was a loyalty test.

He tried to remember if anyone was around the night he first spoke to Jarrett in the parking lot and came up with two names: Peter Kirn, a friend who felt the way he did about the Wilkens incident, and Manny Lasario, who'd also been working the late shift and was a kiss-up of the first order.

"I did some checking on Jarrett," Perry went on. "He's been a screw-up for most of his career. Word is he's been censured more times than anyone on the force. They finally exiled him into something called the Threat Management Unit, which is a fancy name for an antistalking force that protects movie stars. A week ago, in the middle of a stakeout, he beat the crap out of a suspect on live TV. The guy died and Jarrett is in it up to his neck. That's probably the reason he left town and came here."

"The guy he killed was supposed to have murdered his partner in cold blood," Haucklin interceded in Jarrett's defense. "My brother lives in L.A., and he told me about it. Most of the force thought he was a hero. And Jarrett was also the one who captured that serial killer called 'Starman' last year, when no one else could."

Perry shot an evil glance at him. "You seem to know a lot about him."

"I'm trying to figure out who we're dealing with, just like you."

"Okay, so maybe if I was fighting World War III in L.A. I'd

want someone like him on my side," Perry allowed, "but Jarrett's a misfit here, like a barracuda in a lake full of sunnies. And he's tied into the Foley women. For all we know he's poking her and running her errands in return, one of which happens to be an unusual interest in Wilkens."

When Haucklin didn't answer, Perry opened a drawer and lifted out an El Producto. It was bigger around in the middle than at either end, like him. He put it under his nose to smell the tobacco.

"I found out that he went to the Delaware Water Gap claiming he was an investigator and asked a lot of questions about the accident. When I talked to him in person he said he thought Wilkens's death could be tied to the attacks on Foley." He engulfed the cigar in flame from a large wooden match and seemed calmer once he got a hit of nicotine. "I want you to watch Jarrett, try to become asshole buddies with him. Keep me posted on what he's doing on Wilkens, and keep it between us," he added with a sly wink.

Haucklin felt the burden of his divided loyalties. Normally the confidential assignment would have been a major vote of confidence for an officer who served at Perry's pleasure. But Elaine Wilkens, and Jarrett's investigation of her, wasn't going to go away. Sooner or later Jarrett would get to the truth, whatever it was, whoever it touched—including maybe Perry, it had crossed his mind.

An earlier worry returned. The chief was a lot cagier than people gave him credit for. If he'd gotten wind of his and Jarrett's liaison, he might have dreamed up an ingenious way to kill it off by forcing him to rat him out.

"He's not stupid," Haucklin said. "What if he's on to something, and it sticks?"

Perry took a deep drag of the stogie. Not all of the smoke made it out of his mouth and he hacked for a good five seconds before clearing his throat and recovering his ability to speak. "We already know what happened to Wilkens. Don't forget, my grandson was an eyewitness. Timothy may not be a choirboy, but he's honest with me." He stubbed the cigar, thereby squandering the fifty or sixty cents it probably cost. He looked up and said, "You with me on this?"

Haucklin knew there was only one answer to that question. He gave it, without delay and with conviction.

"Absolutely. Timothy's a great kid."

44

Wesley Gomes left his desk and paced nervously toward the teller cages. He had the distinct impression that he was being watched. He did an abrupt about-face and shot a glance at the customer waiting area. One of the heads that had been looking in his direction swiftly turned away, at least he thought it did. He wondered what his blood pressure read at the moment. He could actually feel his blood.

The youngest of the four female tellers smiled officiously at him when he approached. "I'd appreciate it if you'd take care of this right away, Sara," he said in a voice that carried equal amounts of nonchalance and authority.

"Not a problem," Sara said cheerily, her crinkly smile set firmly and permanently in place for the day.

From his desk Gomes had observed the perpetually pleasant young African-American woman in the robotic performance of her duties, taking paper, stamping paper, giving paper. He'd chosen Sara Geiger this time because he'd had to escalate his borrowing and needed to continue his rotation of tellers. Also, she was new, and her inexperience made it unlikely that she'd spot anything amiss, or report it if she did.

Beyond the safety issue, he'd actually begun to fantasize making love to Sara. He'd never had a black woman, and this one was particularly pretty. He thought about copulating with her in the safe deposit box room, or on the bank president's sofa. He conjured it continuously while talking to her, as his eyes caressed her body.

Today she looked younger than when he'd first interviewed her, making him wonder if she'd lied about her age to get the job. She'd come to the bank from a vocational school in Newark and was nervous to the point of pain. Actually, she was one of the more intelligent rookies. More importantly, as far as his current need was concerned, she was indebted to him.

Gomes realized that his hand was trembling slightly as he held the transfer slip with an ample five-digit total at the bottom, a figure much larger than the disastrous bet at the blackjack table. He pushed the paper through the slot in the sturdy Zone Defense bandit barrier and watched the woman's eyes for signs of suspicion.

Instead, in a show of procedure for his benefit, Geiger checked the document for the proper authorization, put a perfunctory dot by his signature to show that she'd looked for it—*good girl, Sara*—then put in under the machine that stamped the time and date. She handed the receipt copy back to him, showing all her nicely shaped teeth.

"It's a business doing pleasure with you," Gomes joked when he had the requisite authorization for the transfer in his hand. For a moment Sara seemed confused, then her smile broadened and she blushed at his suggestive play on words.

Gomes winked at her—*big plans for you, girl*—and pivoted on his heels. He'd taken only a few steps away when Sara's honeyed voice wafted over him.

"Uh, Mr. Gomes!" she exclaimed. She was embarrassed, but in a pleased way. "Don't you think you'd better look this over again?"

Something about the way she was looking at him when he turned gave him pause. "Why, what's the matter?"

"I don't think this is going to go through," she continued, waving the original copy of the deposit slip.

A cold hand clutched at his heart. She looked at her copy of the transaction and then back at him, her open smile augmented by a brimming sense of discovery.

"Joseph Vacarro, the furniture store man?" she continued, waving the paper. "That's the account you're transferring the money from?"

Gomes nodded. His knees had started to tremble. "What about it?"

"Just that Mr. Vacarro was just in here at lunchtime, when you were out. I remembered the name 'cause I have a cousin named Vicars, and it made me think about how I haven't seen her since her wedding to this fella from Seton Hall." She noted Gomes's impatience and got to the point. "Anyway, Mr. Vacarro made a large withdrawal from his account and I was thinking, how could someone just about clean out his account and then call up and make such a large transfer of funds?"

Gomes's mind worked quickly. Out of nowhere he was suddenly close to the abyss. He spoke slowly, with control. "Are you sure it was Mr. Vacarro?"

"Absolutely. He came to my station. I could find the receipt if you want—"

"No, that won't be necessary," he said, starting to panic. The last thing he needed was for someone to call Vacarro and alert him to the scam. The idea of getting caught by a rookie teller filled him with a sense of irony.

"Do you think Mr. Vacarro is trying to pull something funny?" Sara asked in a whisper.

A hazy notion floated around in Gomes's mind and finally took shape. He needed time to think through the details, but there wasn't any time.

He molded his tense expression into something more social and leaned closer to her. "Nice going, Sara," he announced ceremoniously. "You passed with flying colors."

His change of tone caught her off guard, and her face screwed into a question mark. Just as quickly, her smile came back. "You were testing me? You did this on purpose?"

"It's one of the things we do around here," Gomes said, without missing a beat, "to keep tabs on our most promising people."

Sara's complexion was infused with shades of lavender that indicated pride.

Gomes came close to the barrier and beckoned her with a finger. "I'll see that this goes into your record when it's time for your review. Now, you can give me back your *test paper*, eh?" He motioned to the deposit slip.

Sara looked at him, unsure. A quick series of images passed through his mind: him being escorted out of the bank in handcuffs, his fiancee Christine crying and throwing her ring at him, her father, a brutish man when he needed to be, shaking his fist contemptuously in the background.

He focused on Sara's long and delicate fingers clutching the receipt. He'd imagined those fingers encircling his lower parts, now they'd were nearly around his neck.

Gomes reached for the paper, but Sara didn't move her hand forward to give it to him. A bead of sweat zigzagged down the hollow of his back.

"If you'll just give it to me now, I'll tear it up," he repeated more sternly.

Sara continued to stare at him, until her lips curled cutely again. She shook her head in a mocking, scolding way. "Still testing? Mr. Gomes, I know the procedure. "'Once the document is stamped, the transaction is completed and cannot otherwise be annulled,'" she repeated by rote. "I'm supposed to keep it in the drawer and let my supervisor do that," she announced triumphantly.

Gomes's stomach clenched. His gambit had backfired. Sara was playing his game, too well.

"So Mrs. Shapiro must be in on this, too."

"Yes." He recovered quickly. "I'm going to tell her how well you did, but it's better for now if she doesn't know I told you."

Sara thought about it. She shrugged cutely and handed the original back to him.

Gomes struggled not to show his relief. He felt a heavy

weight lift from his chest. "I'm very proud of you, Sara," he said coolly, "very proud indeed. Keep up the good work."

Sara beamed. Her teeth formed the center of a perfect smile. "It's been a business doing pleasure with you, too, Mr. Gomes."

45

"You got a piece of this place or something?" Jarrett asked from his side of the booth in the back of Tramps Lounge in Kendall.

"I like the atmosphere," Detective Paul Haucklin said.

"Yeah, right."

Haucklin had insisted they meet well off-campus, and the earthy bar and grill twenty miles from Knollwood qualified. The lengths he'd gone to for privacy spoke to his fear of being seen with Jarrett.

"Some stuff has come up I can't handle by myself," Jarrett said. "Wilkens isn't just a private little war anymore."

"You didn't help yourself any by going to the Delaware Water Gap. Perry's still got a bug up because of that. He knows who you talked to and the questions you asked. You gotta remember how long his arms reach."

Jarrett remembered Taffy Eldridge's quote from Mrs. Cuesta, *monos con navajas.*

"He says he's gonna take you down if you try to bring up any more crap about Wilkens, and he wants me to be the angel of death."

"Funny, I can't picture you with wings."

"I wouldn't take it too lightly."

187

"Are you still interested in what happened to Wilkens?" Jarrett asked directly. "If not, all you have to do is walk away, no discussion."

Haucklin's answer was immediate. "I'm still with you. I don't know why, but I am."

"I know why."

Haucklin furrowed his brow. "Eagle Scout as a kid. I guess I never got over it."

"Not that I don't appreciate the support, but you don't really have a choice. What you know will probably put you in a bad place later on, when the truth comes out."

"Were you going use that on me if I decided not to hang in?"

"Yeah, if I had to. Did your guys learn anything about the break-in at Foley's?"

"No, at least not for sure." He adjusted himself in his seat and his eyes darted left of Jarrett to the door, then jagged back. "There were some prints that didn't match Foley's, but they could belong to anyone, housekeeper, previous tenant, or a recent guest," he added, narrowing his thick brows salaciously.

"I've been working with her there. What of it?"

Haucklin put up his hands between them. "Hey, you don't have to convince me."

"Any prints that might have belonged to a kid?"

"Could be."

"What about the sperm count?"

"In the normal-to-high range for an adult, but the guess is, it's a kid who already went through puberty. Too bad we don't keep reference files on sperm like we do with prints. If we ever get a suspect, we could use it to prove he was there, if we could get him to whack off."

Haucklin was more complex than Jarrett had realized. A strong code of ethics mixed in with a healthy dose of cynicism. His kind of guy. "If I had some ham, I could have some ham and eggs, if I had some eggs," Jarrett joked.

"It's a shame we can't legally fingerprint kids, without good cause. Somebody spewing his jism on somebody else's underwear isn't the basis to check every schoolboy."

"What if I could get you some prints, from a few selected kids?"

"Oh, shit," Haucklin shot back. He was right with him and not liking it.

"Hey, all's fair, and all that bullcrap."

"And, of course, you'd need someone to help you compare them to the ones you *might* be able to get."

"Something like that."

Haucklin looked at the door again. Two people had come in after them, no one else in the place had left. He was getting more nervous by the second.

"I have something that might make you feel better," Jarrett said. "Wilkens was taking some potent medicine for depression, stuff called Luvox. Her autopsy report showed a bunch of it left in her body, a lot more than the dose her doctor prescribed."

"What's your point?"

"Two points. One, how did she ingest so much in the first place, as in, did she do it on purpose or did someone slip it to her? And two, could it have caused some fairly flaky behavior? According to her doctor, it might have brought on paranoia."

The bulb in Haucklin's brain burned brighter. "You think her students were telling the truth then, that she was off her rocker?"

"Could be."

"Who could have given it to her?"

"Dunno, maybe things got so bad with her that she kept increasing the dose herself, but her doctor doesn't think so. If it was someone else, he or she would have to be thinking long-term. And it would require being with her a lot."

"A close friend?"

"Didn't have any. A schoolteacher named Volpe comes closest."

"A relative?" Haucklin guessed.

"Yeah, like the nephew, at the bank. Wesley Gomes."

A pleased look spread over Haucklin's face. "I can help you out there. I went to take a look at him after the last time we spoke. He's not just a VP at his bank, he's a first vice-president, whatever that means."

"About another fifty grand, probably. What does he look like?"

"Late thirties, blond hair, little round wire-rimmed glasses. Squirrely, or maybe intense is a better word. I watched him awhile and he was totally anal, you know, everything in its place, to an obsessive degree. I'll bet he writes down when to take a leak."

"What did he stand to gain from Wilkens's death?"

"That's the interesting part. Since Wilkens died without a will, we know he could put an airtight claim on her house, which is worth maybe half a mil."

"I was told it was closer to seven hundred thousand, but it would take a bundle more to fix it up."

Haucklin eyeballed him suspiciously, then went on. "Anyway, he was checked out after the accident, and naturally the house came up. He said he'd been told it would be his after all the red tape was cleared away, but he blew everyone off when he said he didn't want to sell the place and take the money. According to the transcript, he said he was thinking of renting it to a poor family he heard about who needed a place to live. He even named the family. We checked it out and he'd already told them. It was all true. But nothing's happened with the house yet 'cause its disposition is tied to the investigation, which is still officially ongoing."

"Hell of a guy."

"He can afford to be, he makes over a hundred and sixty at the bank. Oh, yeah, another thing—Wilkens had a safe deposit box, and Gomes's name was the only one on the list of people who had access to it besides her. We didn't get to the box till four days after she died, and it was still full of cash and jewelry. He could have taken it."

"How much was in it?"

"In cash, about ten grand. Jewelry, maybe another ten or fifteen."

"Nothing compared to the house," Jarrett said. "Ever hear of a guy named Ken Schermer?"

Haucklin cocked his head. "He with the town rec department or something?"

"He's a marketing consultant who coaches part-time for the Knollwood Soccer Association. He likes to win, and usually does. Turns out he had a relationship with Wilkens a long time ago, when he was married. Don't know how heavy it got, but I suspect they were doing the deed. It was ancient history, but maybe the medicine did something to her brain that brought back the good old days. Maybe she threatened to bring a skeleton out of the closet and he freaked."

"You talked to him?"

"Yeah, he's a slippery S.O.B. Word is, he wants to chuck his consultancy and open a soccer school full-time for kids."

"Enough to kill someone who threatened his moral standing in the community?"

"Maybe, if the timing didn't conflict with one of his games."

Haucklin pondered the idea, then said, "If it's not him, that leaves us with her students again. They might have been able to get to her medicine if she took it during the day and they knew where it was."

"Yeah, but why mess her up more, when she was already busting their chops?"

"Maybe to send her over the edge—bad choice of words—in a way that everyone else could finally see." Haucklin shook his head. "I still can't believe we're talking about thirteen-year-olds."

"Did you check out that locker I told you about?"

The detective's expression tightened and he was suddenly pissed. "I was going to—until I found out whose goddamned locker it was."

"I wanted you to see it for yourself."

"Perry's grandson, for Christ's sake. Why didn't you just tell me to go fuck myself and save me the trouble?"

"The kid had articles of clothing from Wilkens, and possibly Foley: a handkerchief and a pair of pantyhose."

"Little asswipe pervert."

"I'd settle for that." Jarrett placed his hands on the table.

"Listen, I need your help. And I need it right away. It's getting pretty thick and I'm more sure than ever somebody took out Wilkens. I need you to go back to the Gap and look around, now, before Perry can get any more of his friends on the warpath."

Haucklin's head literally snapped back.

"I want you to go to where she fell and take your time looking around for anything I might have missed, any evidence a kid could have left near the cliff on a route I didn't take. Maybe something you find will match up to a few of the boys I'm thinking about. Fibers of clothing stuck on the bushes, a candy bar wrapper. Even a joint. Kids are always losing things," he tacked on sarcastically, "and it's pretty dense up there. Maybe there's still something left after the winter."

"This may come as a surprise, but I'd hate to be seen there myself."

"You got friends there, too?"

"No, but who knows?"

"Just don't talk to anybody, and don't go as a cop. Be a hiker or camper or something."

"I can't use my car," Haucklin said.

"I'll loan you mine for a few hours. We'll meet someplace out of town and make the switch."

"What if somebody recognizes your car?"

"Yeah, right, with a thousand green Explorers around here. And no one will be looking for you in mine, especially if I rent another one just like it." When Haucklin remained silent, Jarrett said, "Hey, listen, I'm not all that thrilled getting you involved in this, but there isn't any other choice. This thing can escalate at any time."

Haucklin nodded limply.

"Why is it that the more I scratch the ground, the more people turn up with a possible reason kill a poor old lady schoolteacher? I thought this was supposed to be a nice, friendly place."

"It is," Haucklin returned with a grim look. "So long as nobody scratches too deep."

46

"Nice to see you, too," Jarrett said, when Meg literally pulled him into the living room without a more intimate greeting.

The last time he visited with Meg was right after her house had been invaded, and she was like a little girl who'd been to the Haunted Castle before she was old enough. This time she was bristling with positive energy.

When she turned to face him she stopped twirling her hair. "Sorry, hello." She bent forward to kiss him hard on the lips, then launched into it. "You're not going to believe this. Remember the drug you said they found in Wilkens's body? Luvox? I just found out that someone used to pick it up for her at the drugstore. A man."

"What's his name?"

"I wish I knew. A kid who works there has a bit of a crush on me, I think, or a big mouth, I'm not sure which. I worked the conversation around to Wilkens and asked if she'd been a customer. He told me she bought her medicine there and had given her permission for a man to pick it up for her. But he couldn't remember who. It was an informal arrangement. They didn't keep a record or her request."

"Any description?"

"About thirty-five or so, blond hair, the boy said, with

small round glasses. The kid said he was overly neat. He saw him tidying up one of the cosmetics shelves while he was waiting for the prescription."

Jarrett's head moved up and down vigorously. "Wesley Gomes, Wilkens's nephew."

"You think he could have been overdosing his aunt, tampering with her medicine? Could an overdose kill her?" Meg said in a hushed voice.

"I guess it's possible, only I can't figure a motive. He was one of the first people questioned in the investigation. The only thing Wilkens had of value was her house, and he planned to rent it to a destitute family for a token amount. I don't think you kill someone just to become a landlord."

"How do you know he wasn't lying? That he wasn't really going to turn around and sell the place?"

"It checked out. The family he named was contacted, and they said he'd agreed to let them live there at low rent. Gomes even signed a paper to that effect, a kind of preliminary lease, pending getting the place. They were very grateful to him."

"That's totally bizarre."

"Maybe he did it to impress his fiancee, whose father, by the way, is loaded. A smart investment in long-term goodwill. Between his job and his father-in-law-to-be, I don't think Gomes is too worried about his financial future. Or maybe he's just a hell of a nice guy."

"I wish someone would give me a house to live in cheap." She looked up at Jarrett provocatively.

"*Mi casa es su casa*," he responded, "if I had a *casa*." He stepped to the living room window and looked out. There was nothing to see but trees, nothing to hear but crickets. "I was told this morning that some extra security is coming along with me on the class outing," Meg said when he returned, "to keep tabs on me, no doubt."

Jarrett was just as incredulous as he had been the first time he'd heard about the trip.

"I think you're out of your mind to be going. Where's it to?"

"About as safe a place as there is, the Essex County Courthouse. It's a twenty-minute trip, a little way into Newark."

"It doesn't matter how close it is, it's who you're taking with you, or who's there when you arrive. We've threatened a lot of people in a short time."

"It could have been worse. It was supposed to be the Statue of Liberty, but nobody was comfortable with anyplace that high up, for obvious reasons." She attempted a smile, but it was overshadowed by nervousness.

Jarrett could see the tension under the surface. Her good intentions had put her in jeopardy again. He also knew there was nothing he could say that would change her mind about going.

Their expanding world of uncertainty held them in silence until Meg said, "Maybe this is a lost cause and we should let it go. Maybe I should just get the hell out of this town and start over somewhere else. Again," she said, exasperated. She calmed, then touched his cheek. "What have I gotten us into?"

Jarrett felt a warm current caress the small of his back. "A jewelry store, for one thing," he said. He reached into his jacket pocket and brought out a small white box that he hadn't had time to wrap. Her mouth opened in delight.

"Don't worry, it's not a ring."

Under the white cotton padding there was a simple necklace made of a strand of beaded gold link chain and an oval gold pendant. There was a heart etched on the pendant, and inside an inscription that read *D.J. likes M.F.*

She looked up at him with eyes as moist as her lips.

"M.F. likes D.J., too."

47

Paul Haucklin kept a tight grip on the steering wheel. His palms were slick with perspiration, and his body battered from fifteen minutes' worth of potholes in the eroded roadway. Aside from the concern that he was on Perry's payroll and Jarrett's mission, there was no other particular reason for the intense unease that he began to feel right after he left the Interstate.

At a fork in the narrow road he finally saw a sign for Mount Tammany, but the marker itself presented a further problem. It looked as if it had been hit by a vehicle and was bent sideways, making the choice of which way to go unclear.

Haucklin muttered a curse under his breath and went deeper into the forest to the right. The new road was even narrower than the one he'd been on, and he was certain he'd made the wrong call. There were no more signs, except for one that indicated a campground, which was deserted when he passed it.

Also, he hadn't begun to climb yet. It was just after four with a somber afternoon sky that threatened rain. The thickness of the vegetation encroaching on the road cut down on what little light there was overhead and required him to flip on his headlights for visibility.

A vehicle that appeared a short time later in his rearview mirror reassured him that at least he was not alone. The gray 4Runner crept up behind him and stayed a respectful distance away. It felt good to have some company in a place that time had forgotten.

The road itself was a single lane that appeared to have been hacked by hand into the bottom of the mountain. Its narrowness required a driver to pull off to one side if two cars approached each other, but so far there hadn't been any oncoming traffic. Haucklin pondered how long it would take him to walk out to civilization if his engine quit on him. He wondered if the place was patrolled by park rangers, and then remembered that, given the reason for his visit, and Perry's long arms, a ranger was the last person he wanted to run into.

Involved in that last thought, he was startled when his rear wheels slipped on some loose stones, and he skidded a few feet sideways before the tires gripped the surface again. He slowed down and looked at his gas tank. It read three-quarters full, enough to get where he was going and back, if he was on the right road.

His departure had been held up by an unscheduled briefing by Perry on another matter, and now, given the lateness of the hour, there was already some doubt that he'd be able to do what Jarrett asked. Even if he found the path up the mountain, climbing might take longer than he figured, especially if the trails were marked as poorly as the roads. Once at the top he had to search an area several acres across not knowing what he was looking for. It would be a race against darkness.

He knew exactly why he'd agreed to the trip in the first place: Things had been going too well. He, his wife, and their two daughters were doing just fine before Jarrett came along. He was making his sixty-eight a year and would continue to, with modest raises, into the foreseeable future. Managing his affairs prudently, the state college for his kids was within reach, and, unless he screwed up, his career was safe in an insecure world. A sizable pension at the end would be an agreeable reward, and after that he could hire himself out as a private investigator. Making obscene amounts of money, as many Knollwood residents did, had never been a priority. All things considered, he'd be comfortable.

Except he'd never been the type to get comfortable when an issue of conscience was concerned. Sometimes it was more of a curse than anything. A hardworking carpenter father and a social services mother had instilled their values too well, and the Wilkens case was made to order for someone with a low threshold of ethical discomfort. For better or worse, he was stuck with who he was and what he needed to do, and he knew Jarrett had spotted his Achilles heel a mile away.

The unlikely specter of a traffic light ahead in the gloom ended his introspection. The signal flashed a red warning, and he slowed to a stop. A single bulb, for which electricity had somehow been miraculously provided, illuminated a sign that warned him to be alert for oncoming traffic and to wait for the green. In this desolate place, the notion of oncoming traffic seemed as ludicrous as a traffic light itself.

A few seconds later the driver of the 4Runner pulled up behind him, and the two of them sat there waiting. Their proximity gave Haucklin a chance to try to verify that he was headed in the right direction. The idea of making a human contact was also appealing.

He got out and started for the 4Runner, recalling a famous bumper sticker, "Real Men Don't Ask Directions." When the Toyota's front window went down, the face that stared out examined him with diligence. The young driver was unkempt, with a dusky complexion. His body gave off the scent of perspiration mixed with a sweet cologne, and his expression held a brooding quality, probably from the same impatience Haucklin himself felt waiting for a light to change in the middle of nowhere.

"Am I going the right way for Mount Tammany?"

The driver didn't answer, but only stared back at Haucklin. It was possible he didn't understand English.

Coplike, out of the corner of his eye, Haucklin inspected the front and back seats of the truck, but they were empty.

"Is Mount Tammany this way?" he repeated more distinctly, with a pause between words for clarity.

The gloomy face relaxed in sudden comprehension. "Ah, Mount Tammany," the man said with an easy nod.

With an indication that the two of them did indeed inhabit the same universe, Haucklin placed an elbow on the 4Runner's window ledge. "How far is it from here?"

"You missed the turn," the driver said, with a slight inflection that Haucklin took to be South American, Mexican maybe.

The driver opened his window all the way and leaned out, looking behind him at the road. He took a hand off the wheel and pointed. "There was a sign. Don't know how you could have missed it."

Haucklin turned to look where he indicated. "I wasn't sure which way it was pointing." He was still searching the distance behind them when the driver's hand shot to his skull. "What the hell—" Haucklin started to say, but with a lightning-fast move the driver grabbed a handful of his hair and yanked his head toward him, smashing it against the side of the truck. Haucklin cried out in pain and tried to twist his head away, but the stranger's hand held firm. Dazed, Haucklin reached up to the man's wrist and tried to wrench it loose.

The driver's other hand instantly went toward Haucklin's throat, holding a pristine five-inch hunting knife with a serrated edge. Unable to move, Haucklin felt the instrument cut deep into his flesh. The blade severed one of his two carotid arteries and he was awash in his own blood. From someplace he heard a cry that reminded him of a sheep bleating loudly as it was being slaughtered, then realized that it was he making the sound.

The last thing he heard came from a more distant place, and it made no sense, no sense, no sense at all.

"Go to hell, Jarrett," the faraway voice said.

48

Jarrett closed the door to his motel and walked cautiously to the second green Explorer he'd rented since coming East. He bent down and peered at the undercarriage of the vehicle, then cautiously lifted the hood and looked inside. Ever since Starbucks, he'd developed the habit of checking the truck for any little present his would-be assassin might have left.

Satisfied that the vehicle hadn't been tampered with, he started out for the United Bancorp building in Oakland Park, and returned to the catalog of issues that were bothering him. Highest on the list were all the contradictions about Gomes.

For one thing, the relationship between Gomes and Wilkens was difficult to figure. At best, Gomes had been a shadowy figure in her life until recent times. Volpe, the person closest to Elaine Wilkens, said she'd mentioned him only once or twice in the past, but in a way that indicated to him that they weren't very close. Ken Schermer, the soccer coach, had made it into Wilkens's picture album, but not Gomes.

On the other hand, Gomes was her only living blood relative, and over the years Wilkens had distanced herself from her deceased husband's family. Obviously, from what Meg had learned at the drugstore, he was someone she trusted. But then, too, she hadn't drawn up a will to leave him anything. Why?

Gomes's essential giveaway of Wilkens's house, at least for the time being, was an even greater paradox. If Gomes was really that altruistic, could he also be capable of murder? And if he didn't want the money a quick sale could bring, what possible reason did he have for killing Wilkens? Had she injured him in some way in the past? Or his mother, Wilkens's sister, who'd died many years earlier? Did she know something about him that could compromise his career or future marriage in some way?

Jarrett's concern over Meg's upcoming class trip had also become a consuming distraction, and that was tied to Meg herself. In a short time Meg had begun to fill the place left empty since Beth Ellen, and it was getting harder and harder to be away from her. At some point he knew that their relationship would require a resolution, and the thought of going either forward or backward with her scared him equally.

The task of trying to protect someone he cared for this much was just another negative thrown in for good measure. It was the worst possible circumstance in which to make objective decisions.

The bank was already active at 9:40 A.M., when Jarrett pulled into a spot that afforded a partial view inside. Five minutes later he still hadn't gotten out of his truck, debating how far to go with Gomes, how much of his hand to tip.

The short burst of a police siren abruptly tore him from his decision. A radio car that had pulled up behind him had "Knollwood P.D." emblazoned on its side.

The name tag on the young officer who arrived purposefully at his window read "S. Clarke." He had his hand on his hip near his pistol, a subtle act of intimidation Jarrett was familiar with. "Please step out of your car," Clarke ordered.

"What's going on?" Jarrett said through the open window.

"I said get out. Chief Perry wants to see you," he boomed,

with no attempt to conceal his disdain. Perry's antipathy, or something else, had seriously infected him.

The slight readjustment of the officer's hand closer to his pistol quickly raised the stakes. Whatever he wanted, it was important enough for the Knollwood P.D. to take action out of its jurisdiction.

The standoff was interrupted by a screech of tires. A second and third radio car came into view and raced up behind the Knollwood cruiser. The new cars belonged to the Oakland Park P.D., but neither of the officers got out. Their presence was enough.

"Whatever," Jarrett offered with a shrug.

He left the Explorer, and Clarke stood menacingly close while he got into the cage in the back of his car. As Clarke walked around to the front, Jarrett stole a look into the bank. A cluster of people were at the front window. The bank personnel staring out at him were probably wondering what kind of criminal it took police from two towns to arrest.

With a quick scan of the faces, Jarrett thought he recognized one that could have been Wesley Gomes, but Clarke threw an arm over the backrest and put the cruiser into reverse before he could be sure.

"Whatever happened to *semper fidelis* and all that stuff?" Jarrett said sarcastically.

Clarke locked his foot on the brake and the car jerked to a stop. "Listen, you son of a bitch. They just found Paul Haucklin's body in the Worthington State Forest, what was left of him," he shouted with bristling rage. "And he was driving your truck. If I were you, I'd keep my mouth shut before someone shuts it for you."

49

Hudson Perry looked like a man who'd lost a close family member and gone on a three-day binge. Jarrett felt even worse. A burden of responsibility pressed down on him with the weight of Paul Haucklin's coffin.

The air in the office was thick, this time not with the odor of cheap cigars, but with grief. The immediate explosion that Jarrett expected didn't happen when Clarke shoved him into the room, then closed the door and remained outside.

"Do you know how they found him?" Perry asked incredulously. "What someone did to him?"

Jarrett struggled to keep his equilibrium. He'd thought that nothing Perry could say could make him feel more miserable than he already did, until his lead-in.

"Some goddamn bastard cut off Paul's head, and left it on the roof of his car, like it was a flasher," Perry said mournfully. "I saw him. It's the worst thing I've ever seen." He choked on his words and swiveled around in his chair until he was in profile. His head drooped at an unnatural angle over his paunch. "How in God's name do I tell his family?"

Jarrett wanted to say something. He'd only been with Paul Haucklin a few times, but he respected his honesty and had decided that he could trust him. He remembered their conversation at the out-of-town bar where he'd badgered Haucklin to go to the Delaware Water Gap in his place. He'd played on Haucklin's conscience, and now Paul was dead. Neither he nor Perry knew who killed him, but both of them probably knew who'd put him in a position to be killed.

"What in Christ's name was he doing there?" Perry groaned.

"He went to look for evidence that could show Wilkens was murdered. I asked him to help."

Perry turned to face him, full of fury. "*You* asked him? What in hell gave you the right to ask him? I warned you to stay out of it."

Jarrett averted his glance.

"Why didn't you go yourself if you had to? And why did he go in your car?"

"We figured it would be more discreet if Paul went, and he didn't want to be recognized." Jarrett wanted to add what Haucklin told him about Perry's friends in Sussex County, but didn't.

"How could he do a thing like that without telling me?"

"He was bothered by the way the investigation of Wilkens's death came out and wanted to help. He came to me on his own, that's just the way he was. He was an honest man."

For the moment, the appraisal tempered Perry's anger, but he was still perilously close to the breaking point.

"For what it's worth, he was very conflicted about going behind your back," Jarrett added.

"The killer mistook him for you. That's what it was," Perry shouted.

Jarrett nodded sorrowfully. "The person who shot at me must have followed me to Starbucks, so he probably knew what I was driving, checked the plate. I should have thought of that. Haucklin and I look enough alike for the killer to have made the mistake."

"How the hell could you have put him at risk with some-one like that after you?"

The accusation hit home on two levels at the same time. Haucklin wasn't the only good man Jarrett had put at risk who had ended up dead. He'd done it seven years before, with his partner.

Jarrett turned away and rubbed the side of his face, forcefully enough to take off skin. "I didn't think there was a chance in hell of this happening. I can't tell you how lousy I feel."

"I don't care how you feel." Perry slammed his fist down on his desk so hard it should have cracked in two. "Why put his head on the roof of the car? What in God's name would make someone do that?"

Jarrett understood the extent of Perry's bewilderment. In the end he was only a small-town cop who hadn't seen the mayhem Jarrett had, more times than he wanted to remember.

"Who do you think was involved in Wilkens's death?" Perry said in a sudden change of tone. "Elaine was my friend for thirty years. She was my teacher when I was a kid, for Christ's sake."

Jarrett was taken aback. Perry's question indicated a radical shift in his thinking. It had taken Haucklin's murder, but for the first time Perry was allowing the possibility that he'd been wrong about Wilkens. His tone also showed his tacit agreement to become the student.

In the next few minutes Jarrett detailed his suspicions about Wesley Gomes, Ken Schermer, and Jeremy Lerner. Judiciously, he left out the name of the kids most likely to have helped Wilkens over the edge, if it was the kids, since Jessie Lerner's account was all he had to go on. It was obvious that they were part of the equation.

All of the new names surprised Perry. "Why Gomes? We investigated him, and he had nothing to gain. The worst thing he ever did was sixty in a forty-five zone."

"Where was he at the time of the accident?"

"As I recall, he was out of town on business. Someone checked it out."

"There was something strange about his and Wilkens's

relationship. I have a feeling about it. It's possible he was fooling around with the medicine she took."

Perry took notice and said he'd look into Gomes again. He didn't mention anything about the other two. He ended up staring out the window. Outside, the wind pressed against the upper branches of a towering tree. They were bent back in submission, like the chief himself.

"Tell me what in God's name I can say to Ellen and the kids about Paul," he said after a long silence.

Jarrett shook his head but didn't respond. Over the years he'd witnessed just about every kind of inhumanity one human being could inflict on another, and in the end all he could do was try to show those touched by a loss that he'd evened the score a little. But in all that time, he'd never found an answer to the question Perry asked.

50

"What's going on out there?" Gomes said to Sara Geiger, who was craning for a view into the parking lot. He'd been working off a case of nerves caused by pieces of crumpled paper the maintenance staff had left on his desk blotter. It had triggered a bout of nausea, until he swept the filth back into the trash and washed his hands.

Geiger stood at the back of the cluster of bank personnel who'd been freed from their routines to watch a scene that could have been from *NYPD Blue*. There was representation in the group from all departments, with the exception of the auditors, who stayed at their posts to ferret out the condemned.

"They must want that man real bad," said Sara, clicking her tongue. "Two more police cars just showed up. They have him surrounded."

Sara gave way to Gomes, who peered outside. "Any idea what he did?"

"Uh-uh, but he looks like a shady type, that's for sure. Maybe he came to rob the bank." She was very excited about the concept and put a hand over her mouth.

Two people in front of Gomes moved out of the way, and he had his first view of the suspect. When he recognized him, his blood ran cold and he felt panic spread through his body. There was no doubt in his mind that Jarrett had been on his way to see him. If he'd gotten through, it could have been disastrous. The L.A. cop was a crude and driven individual, from what he'd been able to observe. He reminded Gomes of a jackal who, once having gotten the scent, would pursue his prey to the death simply because his nature required it. Jarrett was a formidable enemy.

Gomes returned to his desk before the drama in the parking lot was played out. He wiped perspiration from his brow, then folded his handkerchief into a perfect square and returned it deftly to his suit jacket pocket, making sure none of the hanky protruded over the top.

He tried to enter some notations on the margins of a loan status report, but his hand was shaking so much he had to put the pen down.

Only circumstance had saved him from an encounter with the one person he feared more than the auditors. He surmised that denying him an interview would have looked too suspicious, and the cop was much more practiced in that art than he. Even with the proper responses, some unplanned gesture would have put the lie to his answers. He was thankful that fortune, which had cursed him at the gaming tables, was with him this morning. He vowed not to allow Jarrett a second such opportunity.

Shaken, Gomes made his way to the rest room to put cold water on his face. The room was empty and reeked of chlorine. He stood in front of the sink, studying himself in the mirror. Puffiness around the tops of his eyes showed the strain of events and lack of sleep. His mouth was slack. His fiancee, Christine, had already noticed the changes and asked him about it. He'd told her it was because of late work, and it was—but not the bank's. She had admired his drive and gave him the best sex of their relationship.

The water from the faucet helped him calm himself. In a few moments he allowed that his concern about the auditors might have been premature. As far as he knew they were still not delving into his area, and he wasn't sure they would at all on this visit.

On the other hand, if they did get the scent and started asking questions, he now had to worry about the Geiger woman. That was a problem that could be solved, but not at the bank.

The cop was the most serious danger by far. Sooner or later the jackal would reappear. He would not tire until he found what he was looking for.

The one saving grace was that there was still time to get the needed money, the mother lode, and buy into a brand-new set of options. He could replace what he owed the bank, or not, and live the good life someplace far away, with or without Christine. Even the bookies would never be able to find him.

To get to that point, however, there was only one course of action possible. It was a distasteful act, and one that he wouldn't have chosen to perform, but it had now become a matter of survival.

Gomes shook cold water from his hands and dried his face with a stiff paper towel. He vowed to stop thinking about the auditors and loan sharks and a filthy jail cell that he could not possibly endure.

The time to act in his own defense, more decisively than at the motel, was at hand.

He had things to do, places to go.

People to kill.

Again.

51

"So whaddaya think? Our old pal Augie gonna rat us out?" Timothy Sullivan said to his new best friend, Doogie McMillan. He was facing Doogie holding a basketball to his chest, and said it as though Augie Templeton wasn't even standing with them at five o'clock on a Tuesday afternoon on the middle school basketball court. Doogie didn't say anything and didn't look at Augie.

Without warning, Sullivan threw the ball hard at Augie. The ball slammed into his belly, and he doubled over, the wind knocked out of him.

"Oops," Sullivan said. "Gotta work on my passing."

"I just wanted to talk about it," Augie said, catching up with his breathing. "It's getting too weird."

"You're getting weird. Talk to who?"

"To each other, that's all."

"Is that what your shrink is telling you to do?" Doogie offered, choosing the safer side as usual. Sullivan's pleased grin reinforced his decision.

"We thought it had gone away, but it hasn't," Augie answered. "I'm sick of feeling crappy about it all the time."

"That's a good one," Doogie clucked, recognizing some kind of play on words. "Getting sick of feeling crappy." He looked at Sullivan, who wasn't laughing, and reined in his gaiety.

"Nothing's changed, except you," Sullivan shot back.

He stared down the smaller boy, waiting for him to avert his eyes as he usually did when they had a confrontation. This time Augie stared back without blinking.

There was definitely a new component in his attitude, Sullivan recognized. As much of a wimp as he was about Wilkens, he'd found the courage to take a stand now—even though he knew he could get the piss beat out of him for it.

"What's bothering you?" Sullivan finally said, in a more conciliatory manner.

"That policeman Ms. Foley knows talked to Jessie Lerner. My mom told me. He's talking to everybody. He's gonna find out about us."

The revelation shocked Doogie. "What's the big deal about that? Jessie didn't see anything."

"She saw us chase her."

"So what? We were just trying to keep her away from Wilkens."

Augie seemed stymied by the boy's illogic. He picked up the basketball.

"Yeah," Sullivan echoed. "What if she did tell him? So what?"

"Nothin's gonna happen, like before," Doogie shouted, mainly to reassure himself.

"I know he's gonna find out about it," Augie decreed. As if to confirm the opinion, he launched the ball at the basket from where he was standing at the edge of the key, and it was nothing but net. The perfect shot spooked Doogie.

Sullivan snagged the ball on the bounce and held on to it. "Bullshit. My grandfather will stop him if he has to."

Sullivan hadn't wanted to use this information. He was told never to say anything about how his grandfather, the police chief, felt about things. But it sort of slipped out. That *poor impulse control* again.

The disclosure temporarily shut Augie down. There was always an unspoken assumption about help from above, but this was the first time it had been said out loud. "Is that true?"

"Swear to God and hope you die. My grandfather hates his guts. I heard him say he'd be gone in a few days, and without him around Foley ain't gonna do squat."

Doogie was very pleased at the continuing revelations about the police chief.

"Which leaves only one problem," Sullivan added with a sinister edge. He and Doogie set their eyes on Augie simultaneously.

"Don't worry about me," Augie responded, but not with conviction.

Doogie failed to make the distinction. He came forward with a "cool," his hands in the air. He got fives from both of them, then plucked the ball from Sullivan's hands and started dribbling. He planted himself for the jumper, and the ball arched gracefully, but it was off the mark and ricocheted to the left off the rim. It kept going off the court and found its way to the parking lot, coming to rest at the gate.

"Get it," Sullivan commanded Augie.

Augie stood perfectly still. He knew the request was a test. Sullivan wanted an act of submission.

"C'mon Augie," Doogie urged. "Get it."

Augie was deeply conflicted. The plain fact was, the three of them were in this thing together, and they needed to be able to depend on one another. But there was no doubt now that Sullivan saw him as the enemy. He'd been taking more and more crap from Sullivan, and there was only one way he knew of to stop a bully. Still, he couldn't risk a fight with him.

Augie turned away and walked toward the ball in the parking lot. He stopped for a moment and looked down at it, then glanced back over his shoulder. The two of them were waiting expectantly. "Go to hell," he muttered, just loud enough to be heard. He stepped over the ball and kept going to the street.

When he was out of view, Sullivan shook his head at Doogie. "You wait here," he said, and took off after him.

Alone, Doogie was shaken by a look on his friend's face that he'd never seen before. Timothy's skin had gone bright red, and his eyes were so narrow Doogie wondered how he could see. His hands were two tight bloodless fists. He looked scary, really scary.

Doogie waited for what he considered a long enough time for one or both of them to return. When they didn't, he gave up and headed for his own house with a bad feeling.

PART THREE

52

"Paul Haucklin's been killed," Jarrett said with a vacant look. He stepped past Meg into the living room and slumped onto the sofa.

She pushed the door shut feeling lightheaded, then fearful.

Jarrett pressed his hands to his face and spoke through them. "He wouldn't have been there if it wasn't for me. It's my fault."

"What are you talking about? What did it have do with you?"

"I convinced him to go to the Delaware Water Gap and look around. I couldn't go myself because Perry alerted the rangers to me. Haucklin took my truck and somebody murdered him thinking it was me." He glanced up at her, bereft. "I don't want to tell you how."

She moved next to him on the sofa, but he was in his own separate world.

"He must have been defenseless against the animal that did it. What the hell was I thinking?"

Meg didn't know how to respond. She'd never seen him like that, except one other time. She forced the painful thought out of her mind. "Can I get you something? A drink?"

"Had a few, didn't help."

They sat quietly for a while before he raised his head and sat back. "Someone out there is scared enough to kill a cop."

"Has to be the one who killed Wilkens."

"Or someone who knows who did and is trying to protect him. Or them. But this time it couldn't have been a kid. Haucklin was butchered."

A look of alarm hardened Meg's face. "It could have been you," she said. "This is the second time. Sooner or later—"

"I have to figure out how to keep you out of the way," he interrupted. "You can't go on the trip tomorrow."

Meg realized that he'd quickly turned the topic from his safety to hers and was touched. "We've been through his before. I have to go."

"Haucklin's murder changes that."

"Are you saying someone might try to kill me?"

"I don't know how much of a threat you are to whoever did this, or how desperate he is."

"Well, that's just great. If you wanted to scare the hell of me, you just did."

"Good. You're too damn stubborn as it is."

Meg drew away from him, in a state of confusion. "I'll be on a bus with two or three adults, and then in a courthouse. No one in his right mind is going to take a chance with all those police and judges around. And hundreds of people."

"We're not talking about someone in their right mind. For all we know he might think he's better off in a crowd."

"Which means I'm not safe anywhere anymore, right?"

"Yeah, that's where I come out."

"So what do I do, lock myself up in jail?"

"No, you do the smart things, that's all. The trip isn't one of them. I never liked the idea, and a lot less now."

"You know I have to go." She folded her arms defiantly, but she was scared. He could see that easily.

"Goddamn it, Meg." He grabbed the sides of her arms, but she was rigid.

"Then I'm coming along, to make sure you're all right."

His suggestion took her by surprise. "What are you going

to do, sit with me on the bus and hold my hand?"

"I'll follow the bus and stay in the background at the courthouse. You won't see me, but I'll be there."

Meg considered the idea again, trying to be objective. In truth, she was frightened; she had to be after what had happened to Haucklin. She'd been too hasty in rejecting Jarrett's protection. "Okay . . . fine. So long as you don't make it too obvious," she finally conceded. She leaned closer to him, wanting to be held.

Jarrett had other things on his mind. "Perry will be watching your house from now on. There'll be enough police presence for anyone after you to have second thoughts."

"Why don't you stay?"

"I'm not sure I can even be with myself tonight. I gotta work some things out."

About Haucklin, she understood. She got up with him when he went to the door and pressed herself into his shoulder when he opened his arms.

The ringing of the phone made her jump. It ended the much-needed intimacy. "See you tomorrow," she said with a pleasant but artificial lilt.

"No you won't, but I'll be there."

The woman on the other end of the phone got right to the point. Barbara Templeton, Augie's mother, was very frightened.

"Augie didn't come home from school today, and I'm calling on the chance you might have overheard him say where he was going."

Her question was laced with equal parts of control and desperation. Asked so late in the evening it was all the more foreboding.

"No, I'm sorry, I don't remember anything."

"Did he act unusual in any way? I'm calling all his teachers."

"I really wish I could help you. Augie did look a little tired, now that I think about it, but nothing else besides that."

The sigh in the receiver was mournful. "He's never done

this before. He always calls to let me know. He knows how worried I get." After a short hesitation she added, "We've been looking for him for hours. I'm afraid something's happened to him."

Meg's heart went out to her, but she couldn't let herself believe that Augie was in danger. It would be too much to deal with, especially after Paul Haucklin.

The idea that the two events might be connected gave her a sudden fright, and she made up her mind to call Jarrett as soon as she hung up.

She searched for a way to help Barbara Templeton and came up with only one not-so-brilliant idea. "I'm sure you thought of this already, but have you asked Timothy Sullivan?"

53

The bedroom was frigid from air conditioning turned on full blast all night. In the shower, the steaming water was nurturing, and it took a great effort to turn it back to cold to rouse himself. Even though one of Perry's men was supposed to watch her house, after getting a call from Meg about the Templeton kid, Jarrett had gone back to cruise Meg's neighborhood until well into the morning, just to make sure.

When he got back to his motel room he was past the point of no return. His mind raced and fitful sleep came sometime after five. The alarm woke him at seven, but the blinking display showed there'd been an interruption in the current, and his watch read a few minutes after eight. He wondered why Meg hadn't called again about Augie Templeton, and took it to be a good sign. A rushed shower won out over breakfast.

He'd been over the route the school bus was going to take to the Essex County Courthouse in Newark many times. The bus was scheduled to leave at 8:30 and arrive at the courthouse around nine. Once in the building he would blend into the crowd without taking his eyes off Meg, or anyone who came near her. He checked his Medusa for the third time.

An insistent pounding at the door startled him. By the time he slipped on his jeans, the unknown visitor thumped the hollow door as if he were using a battering ram. Jarrett reached for his piece and removed it from the holster. He tucked it into his jeans behind his back and didn't bother putting on his shirt.

Knollwood patrolmen Ed Catallo and Pierce Roland stood there like two storm troopers. At least six-four, Catallo was easily the biggest member of the force, good-looking in a John Wayne way and a study in composure. His partner was a buzz-cut head shorter, stocky and mean-looking. He looked like the missing link. Perry had sent the shock troops. One of them smelled of Old Spice.

"Let me guess, I'm under arrest again," Jarrett said sarcastically.

"Get dressed," Catallo answered, deadpan. He wasn't looking for a fight, just obedience.

Jarrett asked what it was about with the feeling he didn't want to know.

"Get goddamn dressed," the ape cop shot back.

Catallo took a step into the room and looked around, staying cool. Jarrett kept his eyes on Roland's hands. At the moment his thumbs were hitched safely into his belt.

"None of this would have happened if it wasn't for you," Roland raged. "First you get Paul killed and now this. What kind of cop are you?"

"What happened?" Jarrett repeated.

"A boy named Augie Templeton killed himself sometime last night," Catallo announced stoically.

Jarrett literally rocked back on his heels. He'd taken punches to the jaw that hurt a lot less.

"His body was found in a place near his house," Catallo continued, "by his father. There was a suicide note."

"The note said he did it because of you," Roland spit out. "Some fuckin' cop."

"Perry wants you to see where he was found," Catallo said. "Let's go."

The news about Templeton was so sickening Jarrett's

whole body hurt. But the idea that somehow he might have had a part in the poor boy's death left him more stunned.

The idea didn't play. The only times he'd seen Augie Templeton were in Meg's class or at the schoolyard from a distance. He never knew the child had even been aware of him.

With a start, he tried to imagine the impact the news was going to have on Meg and her class. A second death for her and the kids to deal with, this one so much more personal. She couldn't have known about it yet or she would have called.

"There was a class trip scheduled for today, Templeton's class. Do you know if they canceled it?"

"I heard someone say they were letting the bus go, to give them time to set up something for when they get back," Catallo said. "This all just happened."

Another thought burst into Jarrett's brain like exploding shrapnel. He was going to miss the trip. That would leave Meg uncovered.

It came back to him, what Roland said about the suicide note, about Templeton naming him as the reason. Someone was trying to set him up, it had to be that. "I swear I have no idea what this is about. I never even met the boy."

Neither of them reacted until Roland moved by him and went to the only closet in the room. Jarrett followed his short journey, and saw him take a shirt off a hanger, turn, and throw it at him. He caught it with one hand and noticed Roland staring at his back in alarm.

"Put your hands in the air. I'm gonna take your weapon," he barked.

Roland was holding a .38 police special and pointing the barrel at Jarrett's throat.

He looked as if he'd have no problem using it.

54

Meg could feel twenty-four sets of eyes on the back of her head, one set in particular. She looked over her shoulder at the students from her seat behind the driver and immediately saw Timothy Sullivan staring at her. His haughty expression contrasted with the somber faces that surrounded him and gave her a case of the willies. She faced front again and vowed not to let him get to her.

Jessie Lerner wasn't with them on the trip. Her mother had called the attendance office to inform them without offering any reason, and no one pressed her for one. Meg was starting to question the idea of the class trip herself. Given everything, it probably should have waited another month or two. She'd acted impulsively in going along with the idea, especially in Jessie's case.

The day got off to an ominous start with a deeply disturbing piece of news. Word filtered down that Augie Templeton hadn't come home the previous night, and no one knew where he was. At first, the other students were abuzz with the information, but their initial excitement ebbed quickly, and they'd settled into a cheerless mood. Their memory of what had happened the last time they set out together had to be preying on their minds. The silence lent an eerie ambiance to what should have been an exuberant ride.

Before they left, Meg was disheartened to see Lester Arno climb the steps to the bus after everyone else was seated. He took his place across the aisle from her without so much as a nod. Arno's authoritarian presence spoke to the uneasiness of the parents as well as the administration's concern for safety. She was sure there was major concern about her, too.

Arno tapped his foot nervously as Meg tried not to think about Timothy Sullivan's beady little eyes, though she could still feel them.

Jarrett was the one comforting thought she could muster. At that moment, he would be somewhere behind the bus, following from a distance that wouldn't attract any attention. When the bus reached its destination, he would park in a different part of the lot and follow her wherever she went with the students.

Nothing would escape Jarrett's scrutiny. If the unlikely happened, and the person who killed Paul Haucklin tried something, there was a good chance that Jarrett would catch him. It was a remote but titillating possibility that could put a sudden end to all the horror. She wished she'd taken a seat at the back where she'd be able to sneak a reassuring glimpse of Jarrett out the window.

She took a deep breath and tried to relax. She prayed that Augie Templeton would turn up, that he'd only run away from home. She hoped that, despite the way the day had started, despite Sullivan's eyes and Arno's tapping foot, the trip to the courthouse would turn out to be exactly what the doctor ordered. Uneventful.

55

Like Elaine Wilkens's house, the vacant old estate where they'd found Templeton's body sat at the edge of the more prosperous section of Knollwood. There was a post-and-beam barn behind the main residence, and it was from there that Augie's body had been removed. He'd been found hanging from the barn's rafters, less than a block from his own house.

Patrolman Pierce Roland opened the back door of the squad car, and Jarrett got out. The three men hadn't exchanged a word during the sixteen-minute trip from the motel.

Half the Knollwood police department swarmed over the barn and seemed to turn as one when they saw Jarrett arrive. Jarrett made his way through the gauntlet and went into the rough building.

The place was big enough to accommodate a small airplane and smelled of old oil stains on the broken cement slab floor and rotting wood above. Perry waited with two civilians who were no doubt forensics officers. If possible, he looked worse than he had in his office when he and Jarrett met about Haucklin.

Part of Jarrett was relieved to see that the boy's body

was not in evidence. The detective in him wished it were.

"His father found him here this morning hanging by his neck," Perry said accusingly. He looked up at beams once used to support a platform below the roof of the barn. His jaw was rigid, his teeth clenched.

At the place Perry indicated, one end of a long electrical extension cord was strung around a rafter close to one side of the barn. The dangling piece was fashioned into a noose, open wide enough to have permitted the boy's head to get through it when they took him down. "Where's his father now?" Jarrett asked dryly.

"With his wife at the hospital. She collapsed after seeing her son."

Jarrett studied the beams and how they were connected. Access to the one the boy used to hang himself wasn't obvious, no ladder or other contrived structure that he'd stood on to get height. A voice told him that something was majorly wrong. "How did he get up there by himself?"

"Over here. He could have used the studs." Perry pointed to the wall behind them where a series of crisscross two-by-fours went all the way up to the roof. At some point they'd been added to reinforce the sagging side.

The beam itself was one of six that ran from the front to back walls. Templeton had chosen the closest one, which he could have reached once he'd climbed up the studs.

"The noose was probably already around his neck," Perry surmised.

"Who let him in here in the first place?"

"No one. The lady who owns the place is in a sanatorium. The local kids use it now and then as a clubhouse. There's no lock, and it wouldn't matter if there was."

Jarrett braced himself and said, "Your officer told me there was a suicide note that mentioned my name. I have a hard time believing that."

Perry's anger surfaced with sudden fury. He took a step toward Jarrett, and his breath swept his forehead. "It was in his shirt pocket when we found him. He confessed to killing Wilkens and said you were after him." Without warning he shoved Jarrett's shoulders hard enough to push him off balance. His hands were quick for someone his size.

"If he believed that, it's only because someone made him believe it," Jarrett countered, finding his balance again. "Where's the note, and how do you know he even wrote it?"

"His mother identified the handwriting."

"Let me see it."

"I read it, that's all you gotta know. Nobody touches it until it's examined for prints."

"I swear I never talked to him, or anybody else about him. I give you my word on that. I don't know how he got the idea I was after him."

"You think the kids killed Wilkens, everybody knows that."

Jarrett couldn't deny it. Templeton was one of the kids who'd charged Wilkens at the top of the mountain, according to Jessie Lerner. "I was never convinced of that. I don't think it happened that way now."

Perry was still tormented by the thought. He had reason to be. "My grandson was there. He said they didn't touch her. I know he told me the truth."

"Maybe the confession is a fake, like the part about my causing him to do it."

Perry didn't have an answer, any more than Jarrett did.

"You've got to talk to the other kids."

"I already did, the first time."

"Talk to them again. They might tell you a different story . . . after this."

The suggestion ignited Perry. "Why, so somebody else can get scared enough to kill himself?"

Jarrett's mind raced. "Did you stop to think that this isn't what it looks like, that maybe the suicide was staged? That someone forced Templeton to write the note?"

If Perry had he didn't show it.

"What's the M.E. saying about cause of death? Is there a chance the boy didn't die from hanging? Did he examine the body for signs of a struggle?"

Jarrett could see he had pushed a button. Perry was

bothered. Jarrett looked up at the noose, which had caught a gust of wind that came in from the open doors and swung back and forth eerily.

"There were abrasions on both wrists," Perry admitted finally. "There's no way of knowing how they got there."

"He could have been caught and suffocated." Jarrett said in a flash. "Someone could have picked him up after he was unconscious—or dead—and carried him up to the beam."

Perry shook his head. "That's a long shot," he said, though he considered his next thought carefully. He appeared to be trying to keep an open mind. "There is something, but it's not evidence. Before she collapsed, Mrs. Templeton claimed she didn't believe her son was capable of killing himself, especially not this way."

"Why not?"

"Augie had asthma as a child, and never got over the fear of not being able to breathe. He was still so phobic about it that he carried an inhaler with him, even though he grew out of the condition."

"So the last thing he'd want to do was suffocate himself," Jarrett concluded. "How long before an autopsy can be done?"

"Two, three days." Perry shook his head, and his anger returned in full force. "No matter what, one of my officers and this boy are dead, and until I can find out who did it, I'm holding you responsible."

Jarrett had more counterarguments than he needed, but he was caught in an impossible position. Denials wouldn't do any good. The only thing that could help was evidence, and the way things were going there was a good chance he wouldn't be free long enough for it to surface.

"I'd like you to get the hell out of town, but you're going to be needed for the inquest."

"There's a killer out there who doesn't give a damn who he murders to shut people up, and he won't go away, even if I do."

Through a wall of distrust, his words resonated.

"Let me help you find him before anything else happens," Jarrett pressed. "Maybe I made things worse, but maybe they would have happened anyway. All I know is, I owe Haucklin and Augie Templeton my best try at finding out who killed them. Both of us owe them that." He waited for a response, unsure if his offer meant anything or just sounded self-serving.

Before Perry could answer, Jarrett thought of a more convincing argument. "This could have been someone else, in place of Augie Templeton," he said. "You know that. And it may not be the end of it. For God's sake, let me help."

The thinly veiled reference to his grandson caught Perry off guard. He considered it seriously. "If anything else happens because of you, I swear—"

Jarrett didn't wait to hear any more. He checked his watch and saw how late it was. He was a half hour from the Essex County Courthouse, not counting the time it would take to get a ride back to his truck. He made a mental note to ask that Meg be kept under twenty-four-hour surveillance when she returned from the trip. Perry would have to agree to that now.

"I'll do everything I can," Jarrett said. "I give you my word."

"Just get the bastard who's doing this," Perry said forcefully. "I don't care how."

56

By the time Jarrett arrived at the courthouse, he was almost two hours late and felt as if he'd drunk twenty cups of coffee. The morning had turned warm, so at first glance nothing seemed unusual about a large cluster of children standing on the courthouse lawn—until he saw Lester Arno at the building's entrance conferring with three uniformed guards. Arno was waving his arms around and looked stressed out.

Jogging the distance to the kids, Jarrett could make out two women and a man standing next to each other watching over the children. There was no sign of Meg. By the time he got to the vice-principal his pulse was on rapid fire.

Arno turned and actually looked interested, if not pleased, to see him. Inside the building, another officer was leading a spirited exchange with two subordinates. Judging from their uniforms, they were part of the local security force.

"We don't know what happened to her," Arno said awkwardly, assuming Jarrett already knew what was going on. "We were told about Augie Templeton and were getting ready to go back to school. Everyone was on the bus before we realized she hadn't come back."

A numbing dread took hold of Jarrett. "Meg's missing?"

Arno was brought up short by the question. He looked at Jarrett oddly, then realized that Jarrett had no way of knowing.

"How long?"

"Half an hour. When she didn't come out of the building we went to look for her. The security guards—"

Jarrett didn't allow him time to finish. He bolted to the entrance of the courthouse in a full sprint.

"—are still searching," Arno continued in a monotone, to no one.

57

After a frenzied drive to Oakland Park from the Newark courthouse, Jarrett's second attempt in two days to enter the United Bancorp building succeeded.

Even though many of the bank's employees had witnessed his arrest the day before, none of them seemed to recognize him as a free man.

By the time he entered the building, he was despondent over Meg's chances, and desperate to talk to Wesley Gomes.

After being directed to Gomes's office, one of several lined up next to one another on the fringe of the main lobby, Jarrett spotted two men and a woman inside it shuffling papers. Neither of the men looked remotely like Gomes. A quick survey of the rest of the premises showed no sign of him. Jarrett stuck his head in and asked the men if they knew where Wesley Gomes was. His question was met with cold hard stares, and finally a shaking of heads.

A corridor to the right of the teller cages led to the only formal offices that were visible. A secretary clocked him hurrying by, looked at him suspiciously for a second, then went back to the crossword game on her computer.

Personal assistant Ann Browning stiffened when Jarrett came up to her post and put his hands on her desk confrontationally. A sign on the closed door behind her read SCOTT MCVICKER, PRESIDENT. Jarrett requested to see him immediately, and Browning went into her schedule book with a frosted pink manicured fingernail, looking for a nonexistent appointment. Jarrett lost patience and bolted past her. He got into McVicker's office just after the buzz of her intercom.

McVicker was startled at the intrusion, but calmed after a fast apology and a look at Jarrett's badge. He waved his secretary back to her desk and instructed her to leave the door open. Ann looked at Jarrett as if he had a contagious disease, spun on her heels, and left frost where she'd stood.

The bank president was a tall, handsome man of about fifty-five with an easygoing but confident bearing. He led them to chairs around a small conference table. "I'm very sorry to hear that," he said after Jarrett had filled him in on Meg, "but what does this have to do with the bank?"

"Meg Foley and I were involved in a investigation of a teacher's death in Knollwood a few months back. Elaine Wilkens."

McVicker nudged his memory. "The one who had an accident on a class trip?"

"Yeah, only it's looking less and less like an accident. I think the person who was responsible for Wilkens's death abducted Foley this morning."

"I still don't know why you're here."

"Wilkens had a relative who works here. His name is Wesley Gomes."

McVicker sat up straight in his chair and stared at him. His expression was hard to fathom.

"I came here to question him, but he's not around. I was hoping you'd know where he is."

This time McVicker's countenance turned gloomy. "We don't know why Wesley didn't come to work today. We've been trying to contact him, and haven't had any luck."

"He may have had something to do with the kidnapping. I need to find him."

McVicker remained silent for a short period. He was a

deeply troubled man. "You mind if I smoke?" he said after a while.

"It's your office."

The bank president found a pack of Lucky Strikes in his suit jacket pocket. He took a cigarette out, then changed his mind and put it back in. "First ones I've bought in twenty-five years," he said, embarrassed. He paced to the door and closed it, then said abruptly, "I need to talk to Gomes myself. Something has come up, but I'm not at liberty to discuss it now."

"I take it it's something you didn't expect," Jarrett probed, with several possibilities suggesting themselves.

"I'm trying not to go off half cocked. Gomes has been with us for six years. He was made a vice-president faster than anyone else ever has. There were plans to let him run a branch."

Jarrett noticed the use of the past tense. "I saw some people in his office going through his papers. I'm probably out of my element here, but a vice-president doesn't show up for work, you can't get in touch with him, and all of a sudden he's off the fast track? Sounds pretty serious."

McVicker's expression showed he was not a man who should play poker. He was uncomfortable in his own body. "Really, I can't discuss it. Maybe in a few days."

"I haven't got a few days. Can you at least tell me who the people in his office are? Are they bank officers?"

McVicker shook his head. "I'm sorry. I'm wish I could help you, but I have to end this."

"You said you haven't been able to locate him. Where have you checked?"

"His home, and his fiancee's home. No one's seen him, but it's only been a few hours. That's all I know."

The next thing out of McVicker's mouth was going to be goodbye.

"Look," Jarrett tried quickly, "I know you're not running a grocery store here, and what your responsibility is. But I didn't tell you everything. Besides the kidnapping, a police detective and a young boy were murdered. I don't know whether it involves Gomes or not, but something you tell me might help."

McVicker listened intently, but was deeply conflicted.

"I give you my word nothing goes any further than us," Jarrett added.

McVicker turned his back to Jarrett and faced his desk with his arms folded. He didn't move for an endlessly long time. Eventually Jarrett noticed that he was staring at a picture of his family, all five of them, including a son only a few years older than Augie Templeton was.

"How old was the boy who was killed?" McVicker asked.

"Thirteen. Who are the people in Gomes's office?" he repeated.

McVicker sighed deeply. "We were here well into the night going over the records and came in early this morning to check again. The implications of what we found were serious. We were going to talk to Wesley as soon as he came in." He faced Jarrett with a defeated look. "There are irregularities in his accounts. Evidently they go back quite some time and involve a large amount of money."

Jarrett nodded respectfully, aware of the trust that was being placed in him.

"The people in his office are outside auditors. I was about to meet with them when you came in, to go over the records." He shook his head in disbelief. "I'll have my assistant give you Wesley's address, but I'm relying on you to keep your word about confidentiality."

"You don't have to worry about that."

The two men stared at each other. McVicker went into his pocket for a second time, and this time he lit up his Lucky Strike.

"If you find him, I'd appreciate your letting me know where," he said, taking a deep drag. "I'd really appreciate it."

58

He knows. The bastard knows.

From behind the drapes at a front window, Wesley Gomes anxiously watched the interloper as he sneaked up the incline toward his residence. He'd been just about to leave his condo when he saw the green Explorer pass by and stop a short distance down the block. He had to admit that, for once, he'd been incredibly lucky.

Gomes never left his home anymore without a peek outside. There were too many unhappy loan sharks who'd lost patience with his payback schedules. Physical threats had been made, so far none of them kept. If possible, he was even less anxious to see this new visitor.

When Jarrett's searching eyes confirmed the number over the condo's front door and he looked at the windows, Gomes guided the curtain slowly back into place. He had answers prepared for the loan sharks' emissaries, plus a little cash stashed for just such an emergency. But now he had a new decision to make that he hadn't had time to calculate. He felt as if he were spinning out of control, like a metal ball on a roulette wheel, not knowing which slot he would land in.

Think it through.

He peered outside again as Jarrett came closer. There was still time to deal with the situation. The woman was tucked away upstairs in the little room he'd prepared for her. She was tied and gagged securely, not likely to alert Jarrett unless he came too close and she make a noise. He could deal with that by being with her, just in case. He wondered why he'd taken the chance and let her live at all.

Gomes made his first decision. He climbed the stairs that led to the second floor, crouched, and waited on the landing.

A moment later a loud thump on the front door made him jump. The jackal's formal announcement of his presence was confusing. Jarrett would not likely have a warrant. Wesley Gomes had not been accused of any of his crimes. If and when a warrant was issued, Jarrett was not the one who would serve it. He was only a private citizen here with no authority. More likely, he had come on his own, to try for a voluntary talk. If that were the case, he might just leave when no one answered.

When the knocking stopped, Gomes saw the locked doorknob turn, counterclockwise a half turn, then a full turn the other way. Gomes sat absolutely stationary, a cold pool of panic forming in his belly. Suddenly he was consumed by a sense that it was all beginning to unravel. Total loss of control, the ultimate weakness.

Orderly mind. Concentrate. Outthink him.

Gomes thought about the back door from the kitchen that led down to the garage and considered escape. But the garage had an electric door, and raising it was a slow process. Even if he sped away before Jarrett got there, the cop would give chase. It was a bad bet, like others he had lost lately. But the kitchen was a good idea for another reason.

When Jarrett's shadow left the glass panel on one side of the front door, Gomes slipped down the stairs and darted to the kitchen. He opened a drawer where he kept the knives and dug until he found the largest one. He was about to leave, then faced the center island with a better thought. The meat cleaver hung in an open cubby under the marble countertop. He put the knife down and grabbed the cleaver's handle.

By the time he was back at the stairs an explosion shook the front door, accompanied by the sound of wood splintering. Gomes launched himself up the stairs, two at a time, and reached the landing as the next blast came. By the sound of it, the door would not hold much longer.

In full flight, he hurried along the upstairs hallway until it went right and ended at a sunken bedroom. Before the bedroom, on the left, there was a small chamber built for storage. The panel door used a magnetic lock and was built seamlessly into the wall. Without any knob, and in the muted interior light, the existence of the secret room was almost impossible to detect.

Gomes pressed on the panel, and it clicked open toward him.

The woman was there where he had left her, curled on her side, the gag still in place. Her eyes were narrow with the sudden light, but when she saw the cleaver they widened and she let out a whimper and pushed herself farther back into the confining space.

Gomes crept in on his hands and knees until his head was next to hers. "Not one sound," he whispered. "Do you understand?"

She stopped moving.

Two carry bags were on the back of the door. Gomes reached behind them and found the hook that held them, then used it to pull the door shut, making a perfect seal. He turned back to the woman and felt for her thigh in the dark. He pushed on it, compressing her body and making more room for himself.

He could feel the heat coming off the teacher. He could smell her fear. Fear had its own scent, like electric wiring carrying too much current. When the woman was as compact as he could make her, he drew a calm breath of stale air and waited.

The third shock to the door resulted in the sound of metal clanging on the ground, a piece of the lock mechanism. Faint footsteps followed, and the atrium closet door opened and closed softly. Jarrett was inside, searching. He had no reason to suspect the owner was at home, unless he saw the car in the garage. Until then, this was Gomes's advantage. And the woman. And the cleaver.

For practice, Gomes hefted his weapon and slashed at the air. The instrument felt as if it weighed thirty pounds, although it couldn't have been more than six or seven. It made up for a lot, but was no match for a pistol. He'd have to be careful, choose the right moment.

His fingers played along the same edge he used to sever the bones of chickens, of large ribs of beef. He kept it razor sharp, sharp enough now to cut human bones when the time came.

In the stillness of the room, Gomes pondered what he had to do once he had dealt with the intruder. The idea of removing the man's bloody body, and cleaning up the mess, revolted him. He'd kill Jarrett, then the woman, and leave them both in the room until he could figure something out.

If he could kill him. If he got the chance. If he could do it.

Gomes stared at the glowing hands of his watch until a few minutes had passed. The sound of his breathing filled the small space and commingled with the woman's. He debated hitting her with the flat end of the cleaver, one sharp, powerful blow, to assure her silence, but Jarrett was already nearby, and she might make a noise before she went unconscious.

"Not a sound," he repeated, putting his hand on her breast. She shivered but didn't move. He could feel her heart beating. He was certain she wouldn't betray him.

Two more minutes went by without further sounds from below. Perhaps Jarrett had regained his reason and become afraid that someone saw him breaking in. Caution might have convinced him to leave.

The sudden creaking of floorboards dispelled that naive notion. Jarrett was clearly beyond making intelligent choices, a creature driven by primitive instinct, as he had surmised.

The new sound came from the top landing. Gomes hadn't heard him come up the stairs, but now he was in the hall only a short distance away.

More footfalls, a blunted click of a leather heel on wood where the runner ended.

Coming closer.

Gomes's mouth was dry. He had a scratchy feeling in his throat that threatened a fatal cough, but he managed to stifle it. His forehead and underarms were awash in perspiration. He found Foley's face and pressed his hand over her mouth. Her skin, like his hands, was moist. He wondered if he could hold on to the bludgeon when it was time to use it.

A footstep sounded directly in front of him, but only one. Another board groaned with the weight of a man pressing on it. The cop was there, on the other side of the thin door, not moving anymore. For some reason he hadn't stepped down to the bedroom.

Gomes held his breath. His body vibrated. At any moment Jarrett might spot the panel. Maybe he was looking at it now. Gomes thought he could hear him breathing.

Suddenly, take him by surprise.

He would wait until Jarrett went down into the bedroom, Gomes decided quickly. He would throw open the door and be on him before he could react, delivering a devastating blow to his head, or his back, a larger target. Once Jarrett went down he would strike again. It would take only a few seconds.

Gomes took his hand off the woman to reach for the hook on the back of the door. He increased the pressure almost enough to open it, and pressed the cleaver to his chest. Outside, a heel squeaked as it rotated on the floor, then a single footstep went farther away, back from where it came.

Not going into the bedroom.

Another heel sound, weaker, on the stairs. The pressure of Gomes's finger slackened on the hook. Another board on the bottom landing, then silence.

Gomes's breathing became more even. He felt a strong

urge to urinate. Still, he held himself absolutely motionless. It was going to be all right, he thought. He had controlled the situation and saved himself the risk of attacking a dangerous enemy.

He waited ten more minutes, just in case it was a trick.

When sufficient time had passed he opened the door only enough to admit a sliver of light. He listened again.

There were no more sounds.

He knew he had won.

59

"Any chance she could have taken off on her own, that something set her off?" Perry asked without conviction when Jarrett got an urgent call to meet with him early in the afternoon.

"There's no way she'd have left the kids unless she was forced to," Jarrett laced into him.

"What about her car?"

"Still in the school parking lot." Jarrett was at the end of his patience with Perry, who was in a state of denial. "I found this in a stairwell at the courthouse when I was looking for her." Jarrett held up the pendant he'd given to Meg after their first and last intimate night together.

Perry squinted at the inscription but had a hard time without his reading glasses, until Jarrett drew it back. "It was a gift. She must have left it for me to find."

"You think that's where she was abducted?"

"It's the easiest way to leave the building without being seen. They use the stairs to move prisoners in and out for safety, or when they don't want to deal with media. They go to the ground floor."

"Where were the other adults?"

"Outside. None of them saw anything. Security questioned everyone who was in the area and drew a blank."

Perry pulled at his chin nervously.

Something else besides Meg was troubling him, Jarrett suspected. "I can't tell you why, but Wesley Gomes has gone to the top of my list. Did you follow up on him?"

Perry nodded prophetically. "After I put his name out he turned up in the ledgers of a bookie who was raided in Newark. Gomes owed the guy over twenty grand. I was about to tell you."

Jarrett remembered what McVicker told him at the bank. The debt might explain a lot of things.

"After I found out, I had some people put the arm on a few other operations we know about. One of them had Gomes as a client, too, until he was cut off at five figures. The guy must be in pretty deep if he's been dealing with these types."

"Anything else?"

"He's engaged to a rich lady in Essex Fells, big money, expensive tastes. Maybe he was trying to keep her in style, and it cost more than he made, even as a banker."

"What about Ken Schermer?"

Perry grimaced and he waved him off this time. "Hell, he's clean, as far as we know. If he had an affair with Wilkens that's probably the worst thing he ever did. Look, I know the man. If I make waves it'll ruin him. I can't do that based on what might have happened twenty years ago."

"You're goddamn right you can," Jarrett shot back. "Or do you want to find out that Meg Foley may have died because you care more about protecting an adulterer?"

Perry didn't answer.

"Well, do it discreetly," Jarrett conceded. "Talk to him privately, verify where he was when Templeton was killed, and where he was this morning."

Perry agreed with a weak grunt.

"Jeremy Lerner was working at a hospital at the time Wilkens was killed," Perry continued. "I spoke to the supervisor of the ward he was assigned to."

"He could have left after he checked in."

"Uh-uh. He signed out for lunch at noon, and Wilkens

died before that. There was no way he could have entered his name before or after the fact because the attendance book is supervised."

"Okay, good," Jarrett said, relieved and not surprised. "That gets us back to the students. What about Templeton's confession? I hate to say it, but he wasn't alone there."

Perry pressed on the desk and pushed his chair back for more room. "Timothy is my grandson," he said sorrowfully. It was the only answer he had to offer.

"I'm sorry, but he was one of boys who chased Wilkens before she died, according to another student who witnessed it."

"I can't believe Timothy had anything to do with it."

"I don't know that he did, but maybe he knows something about who did. That's why I have to talk to him."

Perry looked bleak. At the moment he was a grandfather, not a cop. He took in a vast amount of air and let it out, making a rumbling sound in his chest. "I know the boy better than anyone. In some ways I'm closer to him than his parents. He looks up to me. I know he's not the easiest kid in the world, but there's no way he could do anything like this."

Jarrett had heard that speech a thousand times. Perry was like every relative who was ever told that a younger member of their family did something terrible. "We're talking about two murders, now," Jarrett was forced to say, "not counting Haucklin's."

With Timothy's name still hanging in the air, his implication was clear about a connection to Templeton.

"I got a call from the medical examiner," Perry said. "The autopsy isn't complete, but blood evidence indicates that Augie Templeton was dead for six or seven hours before he was found. That puts the actual time of death somewhere between ten and eleven the previous night."

"What was the cause of death?"

"Suffocation, but not from the wire. It looks like someone choked him and carried him to the barn to make it look like he hung himself—like you guessed."

"And forced him to write the suicide note," Jarrett said, shaking his head sadly.

"There's something else," Perry began again. "Timothy has a friend named Doogie McMillan. My daughter and his mother talk, and she told her that Doogie had been acting strange, even before Templeton. He was crying at night and complaining of chest pains. They took him to a doctor, but they're all at a loss to explain it. But I can't imagine he was involved in anything. He's a scrawny kid and not too gutsy. A follower."

"How did he react to Templeton's death?"

Perry settled deeper into his chair and his face turned gaunt. "His mother said her son had a panic attack. She was nearly hysterical herself from worry. Doogie told her that he and Augie Templeton"—Perry stopped short, hardly able to get the words out—"and my grandson chased Wilkens and she fell over the edge of the cliff. He was afraid of what would happen to him if he told."

Jarrett took the news with deep concern. He'd heard the story from Jessie, but had never been able to believe it was that simple. If it was, his theory about Gomes had just gone out the window. "What are you going to do?"

"There hasn't been time to do anything. I found all of this out just before you got here." Perry stared at Jarrett, unable to conceal his anguish. He was looking for help.

"We have to talk to Timothy," Jarrett said with deference. "He might know something. Maybe it can lead us to Meg Foley."

Perry looked at him blankly. His eyes were vague and wandering. "Yeah, I know," he said with effort. "But I think maybe he should see a lawyer first."

60

That night, Timothy Sullivan sat at the far end of a sofa in the family's comfortable TV room. He looked shrunken and fearful, not the brash bully Jarrett had met only a few days before. His eyes were bloodshot, and he had a large pillow pressed to his lap. For all his size and swagger he was still a little boy.

Perry had met with his daughter and son-in-law and talked to Timothy alone before allowing Jarrett to come to the house. They were all aware that, with Doogie McMillan's confession, Timothy was now a suspect in Wilkens's death, if not Augie's.

The other possibility was more frightening. If someone else was responsible for the murders—like Wesley Gomes—Timothy could be next. Convinced of their son's innocence, and fearful for his life, the Sullivans knew it was time to cooperate, not be protective. They waived the right to a lawyer in the interest of expediency.

"I know you want us find out what happened to Augie," Jarrett said to the boy. "We need your help to do that."

Timothy looked at his mother with pleading eyes. Anne Sullivan made a move to comfort him, but Perry waved her off. "Tell Mr. Jarrett everything you told me, the same way," he instructed him.

"I didn't do anything to anybody," Timothy blurted out before Jarrett had a chance to speak.

"I believe you," Jarrett said, giving him the benefit of a big doubt for the time being. "What about Ms. Foley? Did you see anything at the courthouse?"

Timothy bit into his lower lip. "I wanted to look at what was going on in one of the courtrooms. I got in, but a guard kicked me out. I went back to the bus after that."

"Did you see Ms. Foley on the way?"

"Yeah, but she didn't see me. I didn't want to get into trouble 'cause I didn't stay with the group."

"Did you notice anyone around her, someone talking to her maybe?"

"We went over it," Perry volunteered. "He thinks he remembers someone."

Timothy sat easier on the sofa. The exercise had begun to divert him from his anxiousness. "There was a man, maybe, I don't know. Ms. Foley was looking into one of the rooms, and there was someone across the hall from her. I think he was looking at her. There were a lot of people in the way."

Jarrett felt a surge of adrenaline. "Anything you can remember about the man? Did you ever see him before?"

"Uh-uh. I think he was skinny, about as tall as my dad, I think. I'm not sure."

"What color was his hair?"

"Brown or blond. He was going bald."

Light hair, balding, Haucklin had said.

"Anything about his face that was unusual?"

Timothy shook his head. "I was just trying to get past there."

"Then what made you notice him?"

"I had to get close to him to get by without Ms. Foley seeing me. He was leaning against the wall cleaning his glasses with a tissue, cleaning them a lot. When I went by him I bumped his knee and he dropped them, but it wasn't my fault."

"What were his glasses like?"

"Round, I guess, like circles."

"Wire or the thicker kind?"

"I can't remember."

"Anything else?"

"Yeah, he was very neat-looking."

"In what way?"

"I mean, he was dressed nice. It was real hot, but he still had his suit buttoned."

Obsessively neat, Haucklin had said.

"Where you saw him—was there an exit nearby?"

Timothy searched his memory. "Yeah, I think so, down the hall a little. I thought about using it to get to the bus."

"Why didn't you?"

"It said it was for emergencies. Had one of those handles that sets off an alarm."

Jarrett's heart raced. He clearly remembered the door that led to the stairwell and that the alarm hadn't been working. Near the bottom of the stairs he'd found Meg's pendant. He was suddenly manic about finding Wesley Gomes.

"The last thing I need to talk about is Mrs. Wilkens."

Timothy's calm vanished in an instant. He glanced woefully at his mother.

"Just like you told me," Perry admonished.

"Doogie McMillan is saying that you and he and Augie were responsible for Mrs. Wilkens's accident," Jarrett said, choosing his words carefully. "I know you guys may have frightened her at the mountain, but I have a hard time believing what Doogie said is true. Want to tell me your side of it?"

James Sullivan made a move to protest.

Perry saw him and said sharply, "I trust my grandson." His words had the force of blunt object, and James sat down. Perry checked his daughter for her concurrence and got it.

Timothy's eyes were wet and getting wetter. He dabbed the corner of one with the cuff of a sweatshirt. The water was quickly replaced. "We were angry at her. We thought she was going to do something bad."

"To you?"

"No, to Jessie Lerner. Mrs. Wilkens hated her."

"What did you think she was going to do?"

"She was always doing something. She was mental about Jessie."

"What about this time?"

"She asked Jessie to come next to her. Jessie said no, and then Mrs. Wilkens screamed at her, and then at all of us. We didn't care so much, but Jessie started crying."

The Sullivans locked eyes in a pained glance. Perry was as relieved now as when he'd heard it in private from his grandson earlier.

"What did you think was going to happen to Jessie?"

"Dunno, maybe get hit."

"Did she ever hit Jessie before?"

"No, she only yelled and tried to make her look stupid in front of everybody. She made fun of her for not understanding things in the lessons."

"How many times?"

"A lot."

"Did Jessie do anything to make her angry on the trip?"

Timothy thought about it, real hard. "She was slow, that's all."

"Slow because of her learning disability?"

"Uh-uh, slow getting up the trail. That's what made Wilkens yell at her, because she didn't walk fast enough."

"What did you do after she called for Jessie to join her?"

Timothy swallowed a gulp of air. He spoke only after his grandfather's nod. "We were mad. Something was wrong with Mrs. Wilkens. A few of us . . . we decided we wouldn't let her punish Jessie anymore."

"Who? Which few of you?"

"Me and Doogie. And Augie."

"How could you do anything? She was the teacher."

"There were three of us. We told her to leave Jessie alone."

"What did she do then?"

"She thought we'd back down, like always, but this time

we didn't. I didn't mean to but—" He stopped himself, very anxious. "I cursed her off. It just came out. I don't know if she heard me. Then the others started yelling, too, all of them. That made her stop screaming."

"It sounds like everyone was scared. And that's why you chased her."

Timothy set his mouth in a flat line. "I didn't say that."

"Doogie did, and Jessie Lerner."

"Did you or didn't you?" his father ordered, the first time he'd spoken. "Tell the truth, son."

Timothy made a wounded sound. He struggled for air, but finally was able to speak. "We didn't mean to, but she wouldn't leave us alone. She started to run and we did, too. I don't know why," he said, sobbing. "Nobody thought about it."

"How far did you run after her?"

"Just a while. We stopped but she kept going."

"What happened then?"

"We heard her scream. We were scared of what we'd done so we went back." His lips trembled, as if he were freezing cold. A tremor racked his young body, then another.

"Then what happened?"

He turned to his grandfather. "The scream sounded like it was going away. We knew she fell . . . over the edge. We thought we made her fall off the mountain." The boy gagged on his words and buried his head in his hands, sobbing uncontrollably. "We thought we killed her."

Jarrett sat back with a sigh and allowed Timothy the space he needed to collect himself. No one in the room moved, except to lower their heads. In time the boy's crying subsided.

"You didn't actually see her fall, did you, Timmy?" Jarrett said just above a whisper.

"No," Timothy murmured.

"You didn't push her, did you Tim? You never even touched her, just like you told your grandfather."

Timothy moved his head from side to side and made a feeble sound.

After the boy's cathartic exercise, the Sullivans stared at

Jarrett anxiously. Jarrett recalled the area before the cliff and the foliage on the way that showed no sign of a group having trampled it. Timothy's story had matched Jessie Lerner's, enough to convince any jury, and him, but it didn't explain why Wilkens hadn't tried to save herself. And suicides don't usually scream.

He thought about Timothy's description of the man near Meg at the courthouse. Suddenly he had better things to do than third-degree the wretched little boy who sat before him. "Look at me, Timothy. Listen to me."

Reluctantly, the boy raised his head.

"I believe you," Jarrett said. "I don't think anyone's going to bother you about this anymore."

With his final pronouncement there was a palpable change in the room. In a moment, Timothy managed to stop sobbing, and his mother held him. Perry looked as if he were recovering from heart surgery. In a way he was.

A short time later, Timothy wiped the last of the moisture from his cheek with a palm and looked up at his interrogator. "Talk to Doogie," he said falteringly. "Please. He must be really scared."

61

The recurrent dream wasn't a nightmare, only a replay of an old reality.

He was racing down the street in heavy traffic, urging more speed from the Land Cruiser than it could possibly produce; heartbroken, repentant, nearly blind from crying, all the way down Santa Monica Boulevard to L.A. General and his dying wife.

At her room they were still wiring her to more machines and monitors than he'd ever seen in one place. He wasn't allowed in for a long time.

When he was finally at her side she was at rest, her head bound by an absurd amount of bandage. He held her limp hand and spoke her name over and over, manipulating her fingers one at a time, as if that simple act could regenerate life.

He held on to her for the five more hours it took for her to lose the struggle. In the end, she never knew how brokenhearted he was, how contemptible he felt, how much he wanted her forgiveness. How much he loved her.

The dream haunted him as he pulled up to Gomes's residence again the next morning. He was trying to save the life of another woman he'd begun to care for deeply. Like Beth Ellen, Meg had trusted him and he'd let her down.

The door to the generously sized condo stood open behind a uniform Jarrett recognized as Roland, the plug ugly officer who'd rousted him at the motel. Roland stepped aside contemptuously, but only enough to let him pass.

In the foyer, a framed photo of Gomes sat on a table beneath a large bronzed mirror. The shot was taken at a low angle, which made Gomes look taller and more imposing than he'd been described. His arms were folded in a pretentious show of bearing, and a smug smile played across his lips. He looked every bit the part of the successful young banker, a man on his way up.

Two detectives were at work, one dusting for prints in the living room, another with a handheld vacuum sucking up potential evidence. At the moment Jarrett missed his self-indulgent forensics friend, Guano, and wondered if he himself had left any evidence of his illegal visit. He'd worn gloves to search, but fibers from his clothing and scuff marks from his shoes left him vulnerable to a trace, just as they would for any intruder.

He caught sight of Hudson Perry at the top of the staircase. Perry noticed him and beckoned, "I think you'll be interested in this."

Jarrett climbed the stairs and was led down the hallway toward the master bedroom. Perry stopped at an opening in the wall that Jarrett had missed in his hurry to inspect the premises. Jarrett ducked down and peered into the narrow space.

"We found it by accident," Perry said. "One of the men knocked into the wall and it sounded hollow. Someone must have been on the floor." He pointed at floorboards at the back near the wall. "There were human hairs stuck in a few of the joints."

"What color?" Jarrett asked quickly, his heart thumping.

"Reddish brown."

Jarrett's heart sank.

"Gomes's hair is light, and the strands were too long to be his."

"Any prints?"

"Two sets in here, same two plus a different set downstairs."

Jarrett's face was a portrait of pain. The thought that Meg had been there while he stood unaware on the other side of the door was tormenting. He drew a mental picture of Meg huddled as Gomes's prisoner. She would have been gagged or beaten, maybe drugged to prevent her from making any noise—or something unthinkably worse. There were no signs of a struggle, no scuffed pieces of wood, at least. He said a silent prayer that she'd been alive then, and still was. "You could get a sample of Meg's hair at her apartment and compare it."

"Yeah, I know," Perry said, aware of Jarrett's switch to the woman's first name.

Perry was doing his job, Jarrett thought, even though he'd been the walking wounded ever since they found Haucklin and Templeton. Nothing like this had ever happened to him.

"I don't get it," he said. "It looks like Gomes is in this up to his neck, but why? What in hell is in it for him?"

Jarrett shook his head. If he'd been able to come up with something himself, maybe the whole thing would have ended before Meg's life was in the balance.

Fifteen minutes later the tour of the condo ended in the garage and Gomes's black BMW. The detectives had been over it earlier and were unimpressed with their findings. Their discussion was cut short by an imperious interruption by Roland. "Call for you on the radio, Hudson. I told them to put it though to the house." He didn't look at Jarrett.

"Who the hell is it?"

"Not a clue. They said it was important."

Perry turned to Jarrett. "What are your plans?"

Jarrett looked as if he were trying to stand against a strong headwind. "I don't know, do some checking around on my own, then go back to the motel and try to think of something. If there's a way for Meg to get in touch with me, that's where she'd try. Gomes, too, I guess."

Perry gave him a respectful nod.

"Can you get a remote trace on my line there? I don't want any uniforms around if Gomes is watching."

"It'll take a few hours."

"You'll check the places Gomes might have gone for a car?"

Perry's withering look told Jarrett he wasn't that stupid.

"I'd also like to know what the lab says about the hair."

Perry agreed, then left to get to the phone in the living room. Jarrett saw him ask a detective if it was all right to touch the receiver, then he picked it up.

Roland was back at his post at the front door, and he stepped into the entrance to block Jarrett when he approached. He gestured to a damaged part of the door sash and tapped it with a fat knuckle. "Looks like someone was in a hurry to get in here before we did."

Jarrett aimed a bored glance at the spot. "My, will you just look at that."

Some of the blood drained from Roland's face. A shout from the next room broke the icy tension between them.

"Jesus," Perry said loudly, still holding the phone. "Are you sure?" He swung his weight around and glared at Jarrett from halfway across the room. "It's a friend of mine from the county prosecutor's office," he announced. "I think we just found out what's in it for Gomes."

62

"Bobby Benjamin is as good as they get, which is why I asked him to put a trace on Gomes. Once his antennae go up they stay up," Perry said when they were outside the condo, out of earshot from Roland.

Jarrett telegraphed his impatience.

"Benjamin was in the area when his assistant Brenda got a call from a claims investigator from Pennsylvania who said his company was being pressured to pay an old claim that's been held up by red tape. He said he's been called by the claimant off and on for months."

Jarrett came alive.

"It gets better. His assistant tells Benjamin she's also been getting calls from a New Jersey lawyer about the same case, and the guy's being a real pain in the ass. The lawyer says he's working for the claimant and wants the county prosecutor's office to press for a faster resolution. By then Benjamin has his ears on."

"Let me guess," Jarrett said, suddenly angry at himself. "The insurance investigator is calling about a claim on Elaine Wilkens. The lawyer's client is Wesley Gomes. Jesus!" he shouted, punching one hand with the other.

"The claim is on Wilkens, all right, but this lawyer doesn't have any clients. There's not even any lawyer listed in New Jersey with the name the guy gave. Benjamin figures it was Gomes himself calling, from wherever he is."

Jarrett felt heat course through his body, ahead of another wave of self-reproach. "How much is the policy for?"

"Two million."

"How the hell could he have taken it out without Wilkens's knowing?"

"By forging her signature. It wouldn't be the first time, especially with an insurance company that does most of their business by mail, like this one does."

"What about a medical exam? Wouldn't Wilkens have needed one? At her age?"

"Not every company requires one, especially for limited-term policies, which this one was. They just won't cover pre-existing conditions, and they jack up the premiums sky high to cover themselves."

"But they'd need to investigate the death themselves before paying out that much cash."

"They did. According to Benjamin, they sent a letter to the prosecutor's office asking if the beneficiary was charged with a crime, which is routine. Since at that time no one had even heard of Wesley Gomes, the letter was sent back giving him a clean bill of health. And by the way," Perry went on, "we're not talking about Prudential here. This is a small company in another state. And they already had a police investigation being conducted for them for free—ours—so they sat back and waited."

"Sooner or later Gomes had to know his name would come up."

"Which it did, but not because of the policy. We talked to him later after finding out he was a relative from one of Wilkens's teacher friends in the school."

"What about Gomes's alibi, the business trip?"

Perry let out a deep, sheepish sigh. "I went back into the original interview with him. He was out of town on business when Wilkens was killed, like I thought, and we confirmed he was at the meeting. But now I'm wondering, if he drove early and got to the summit of the mountain ahead of time, he might have been able to kill Wilkens and still make the appointment in South Jersey. It would have been tight."

"Jesus Christ, didn't you think to check it out any further?"

Perry shook his head dejectedly. "At the time, it was enough that we confirmed he made the meeting. Like I said, everything about the guy looked clean."

Jarrett couldn't hide his disdain for the sloppy police work, even if it was a small town force. He thought for a moment, and the last piece fit in place easily. "And that's why, just in case there was trouble he couldn't plan on, Gomes was willing to rent out Wilkens's house cheap, and not cash in on it, just to throw off anyone checking on him at a later date. It didn't matter, because he had a bigger payoff down the line that no one would think to look for by then, especially since the cause of death seemed so obvious. This bastard life had all the bases covered."

"Yeah," Perry allowed. "He came close to getting away with it."

Jarrett looked up to the facade of Gomes's condo and remembered the smug expression in his photo. There was no doubt now that Gomes had killed Wilkens, and probably Templeton and Haucklin. When the insurance money on Wilkens was held up because of an investigation that wouldn't officially end, he killed the boy and used his forced confession to her murder to throw suspicion off himself and bring the case to a conclusion.

The sudden returning image of what Gomes had done to Haucklin made Jarrett sick with new fear about Meg.

Perry was rattled too, for his own reasons. "I guess I was pretty slow about all of this."

Jarrett shook his head absently. He was thinking again about the secret room he'd missed when he crashed into Gomes's place. He could have rescued Meg and not risked losing her.

"Welcome to the club," he said bitterly.

63

Wesley Gomes heard the noise his pretty schoolteacher made against the lid of the trunk. The intensity and duration of her struggle surprised him. The woman was trying to break open the lock with her feet, a gesture of futility. He would have thought by now that she was used to being a bird in a gilded cage.

When he came to the intersection of Oak Knoll and Pingry, Gomes's watch read six minutes after midnight. It felt as if he'd been driving for days. He was pleased with his decision to rent the Oldsmobile Cutlass. The nondescript gray car bought him anonymity.

He was also satisfied with his choice for their final destination. With so many locations susceptible to police surveillance, a middle school in the early morning hours, her school, was certain to be their own private world. He had a key, of course, compliments of his new friend in the trunk.

Having to cart Meg Foley around all day had posed a few interesting logistical problems. Still bound, she had to be attended to like a helpless child, fed and exercised and allowed to eliminate before she made a mess. For a while he'd considered doing away with her. There were any number of places nearby where her corpse wouldn't be found

until after he was long gone. He had decided on strangula-
tion because it was clean. Also, there would be no stains
that, in the unlikely event he was apprehended, would be
traceable on his clothing or under his nails.

In the end, the decision to keep her alive came back to
Dan Jarrett. Everything came back to Jarrett. The cop's visit
to the house made it clear that he was on to him and that it
was no longer safe to remain there. Jarrett and those he
enlisted to help would be stepping up their search for his
precious girlfriend, and her kidnapper, in a big way. It was
only a matter of time until someone ferreted out his connection to the insurance policy, and that would be the end of any
hope for the money. With great reluctance, he had finally had
to give up all thought of cashing in on Wilkens's policy.

Fortunately, he'd found himself a new insurance policy.
Using the schoolteacher to bargain with wasn't as clean a
proposition as his departed old aunt had been, but he was
certain he could pull it off.

The new scheme was ironic. In the end, the unlikely person who was going to bring him the money was the cretin
cop himself. Separate from that, because Jarrett could be
counted on to follow him even after the final transaction, it
was necessary that Jarrett not survive it.

Beyond the practical considerations, Gomes had to
admit that Jarrett had become somewhat of an obsession.
He abhorred his brawling street mentality. He had actually
begun to look forward to demonstrating that, in the more
highly evolved of the species, superiority resided in the
mind, not the large muscles.

For a while, as with the teacher, the only question had
been how the denouement would happen. It could not rest
on a final test of physical strength. Jarrett had to be trapped
in a position in which he'd have to make himself a willing
victim, a blood sacrifice, so to speak. So the decision to keep
the teacher alive was a result of the most obvious of reasons:
Live bait catches more fish.

The day's only scare came when he left her at the cheap
motel he'd found near the airport for the overnight stay and

drove to the bank before it opened. He had hoped for one final transaction to tide him over, but had spotted the auditors' cars in the special spots reserved for them, and well ahead of their normal time. A bright red flag.

His one and only drive-by in the Oldsmobile gave him enough of a view through the front windows to make out a group of people inside his office. Two were sitting, the third was McVicker, standing. Gomes left the area as soon as he saw them.

The thumping from the truck brought Gomes back to the task at hand. The digital clock on the dash read 12:16 A.M. After a number of passes there was still no sign of life in or around the school. Gomes veered off the street and pulled to the front of the staff parking area with his headlights off.

He stayed in his car, studying the building. There were no lights on in the rooms that faced the street, only a faint glow from interior hallways. No sound issued from the building or the adjacent yard. No insomniac was walking his dog.

The only noise came from the back of his Oldsmobile where his pet still thrashed about now and then. It was time to let her out, he decided a short time later.

Time for teacher to go to school.

64

The time he spent locked up in his motel room since he returned in the evening was as hard as any he'd ever spent. He watched it get dark, and checked in with Perry and McVicker every hour. McVicker still hadn't been able to get a lead on Gomes either, and from what the books now showed conclusively, he had good reason to locate him.

By nine o'clock, at least, the tracing apparatus was in place, confirmed by a test with a technician on the other end of the line. At ten, the food he'd had delivered remained uneaten.

Jarrett became stuck on the thought that Gomes had brutally murdered his victims without any regard to their age or sex, which added to the probability that he'd have no compunction about killing Meg. Gomes also knew that he himself was on to him, and close enough to have raided his home. This made it more likely for Gomes not to put up with the added risk of a companion.

So much time doing nothing made Jarrett languish physically. His body demanded rest but his restive mind countenanced no possibility of sleep. Every instinct compelled him to get out to the street, to create something out of nothing. He had confidence that Perry was doing the legwork he had

asked about before he left him: questioning Gomes's neighbors and acquaintances, trying to luck out about where he
was staying and what he was driving. Perry could use his
contacts all over the state to help.

It was also a safe assumption that people on McVicker's
side of the equation were hard at work trying to trace the
steps of an embezzler. At some point, if not already, the FBI
would be called in on behalf of the federally chartered bank,
not to mention the kidnapping, which now appeared to be a
certainty.

Compared to this dual effort, Jarrett could bring little
more to the party than he already had. In reality, his best
chance of helping, as anguishing it was, was to stay put.

The sudden jarring ring of the telephone just after
eleven was like being touched by a live wire. Jarrett spun to
face it, then held himself in check. The police and Bell
Atlantic technicians needed as much time as possible to
activate the trace, and the longer he waited the better.

He stood in place terrified that the caller would give up.
He broke for the receiver at the fourth ring, his heart racing.

"You wanted to know what the lab had to say about the
hair," Hudson Perry said in a monotone from the other end.

Jarrett's head pounded in disappointment. "Yeah, what
is it?" he said limply.

"The closet hair matched what we got from Foley's
shower. There's no doubt that it was her in Gomes's place."

It was an assumption Jarrett had already made. "Any
idea how long they'd been there?"

There were two reasons for wanting to know: to figure
how much lead time Gomes had on them, and to find out for
certain whether Gomes had been at the house when he was
there, so he could torture himself some more.

"Within the last twelve hours. There were pieces of tissue
from the roots still moist, and the amount of evaporation
indicated that's how long they'd been separated from the
scalp."

"Anything on what kind of car he's driving?"

"Uh-uh. Looks like he didn't rent anything local. If he

used a phony ID we won't find out until the car is reported missing, and that could take days. I've got three men looking into places he might have stayed, and they all have copies of Gomes's picture, but God knows how much of a search radius we need. He could be anywhere. He had enough time."

"Did he have another residence? A cabin in the woods, or a friend with one?"

"No other home. We're trying to find out the rest."

"What about his fiancee?"

"That was tough. The feds were already there about the missing bank money. I wish you'd told me," he added sourly.

"I gave my word."

"Anything from your end?" Perry said, as if he already knew the answer.

"Nothing. I'm going out of my mind just waiting around."

"I wish I could think of something."

"Yeah, right. Stay in touch."

Jarrett let the receiver dangle from his hand after Perry hung up. He stared vaguely at the wall before he focused again and put it down. He was drained of energy. There was no way he was going to be able to sleep, even though he'd gotten only a few hours the night before.

He sat back on the bed and hoisted his feet up, then made the mistake of closing his eyes. Every time he did he saw Meg's eyes searching his with the same question. *How could you let this happen?*

The phone shattered the silence again—probably Perry with something he'd forgotten. Just in case it wasn't, he waited the four rings.

"Are you listening closely, Mr. Jarrett?" the clear and confident voice said.

Jarrett sat up so fast that a stab of pain laced his back. "Who the hell is this?" he fired back. The skin on the nape of his neck was tingling.

"Just shut up and listen. I have her, you want her. I propose a trade."

The caller's absolute calm was unnerving. Jarrett churned

for a point of attack, but held himself in check. He was dealing with a dangerous mentality, too dangerous to threaten.

"I can't do anything until I know who you are, and what you've got."

"Don't insult me with your stupid little game. You know who we're talking about. I was at the house when you broke in."

The reply was convincing. No one else could have known about his visit to Gomes's place except Gomes. He hesitated before answering. He guessed it had been about fifteen seconds.

"And don't worry about keeping me on the line. This is a cellular call. It can't be traced." Jarrett's fear spiked. What Gomes said was true. There was no way to trace a call from a mobile phone as there was from a land line. Cellular signals were bounced off a satellite down to towers that served a broad area. The technology required to trace satellite signals to a specific point was still years off. The killer had thought it out.

"What do you want, *Gomes?*"

"What everyone wants, of course. Money, freedom. And, oh yes," Gomes said, as if a casual afterthought. "I'd also like to enjoy your teacher friend again, if you give me the time."

Jarrett cursed into the receiver before he could stop himself. The room was going dark, like something in his brain had burst.

But Gomes sounded too placid. No one could be that calm in this situation unless he was crazy, close to the edge.

"What kind of trade are you looking for?" Jarrett said, remembering the opening gambit.

"Your teacher for a million untraceable dollars. You get one hour to bring it to the middle school. If you show up with anyone I kill her. You'll be watched." Gomes waited a few seconds, then repeated, "I said untraceable dollars. Believe me, I know the difference."

The figure was insane. It might as well have been a billion, Jarrett thought. "It's the middle of the night, for Christ's sake. You must be crazy asking for that kind of money."

"That's why it isn't more. I wanted to make it easy."

"You're out of your mind."

"Generous is the word I would have used. It's a bargain, considering what you've already cost me."

A reference to the two million in insurance money, Jarrett understood. Gomes wasn't even trying to hide it. He must have had plans to go someplace where he'd never be found.

"Even if I trusted a kid killer, where the hell am I supposed to get the money?"

"I'm sure you'll think of something. Fifty-eight minutes before Foley dies."

The threat forced him to actually consider Gomes's demand. A ludicrous picture flashed into his mind. A middle-of-the-night visit to McVicker, pleading with him for a mil in unmarked bills. Jarrett repressed a lightning-hot rage.

Depersonalize. Get something.

"How do I know she's alive?" he said, the word coming hard.

"You're so predictable."

An unintelligible murmuring followed, Gomes with his hand over the mouthpiece.

A moment later, Meg was on the receiver. "Jarrett?"

"Are you all right?"

She didn't answer, then said, "I'm here at least. He hasn't—"

"It's going to be okay, I'll work it out," Jarrett said before she could finish. "I'm coming to get you."

"He killed Augie Templeton," she cried suddenly. "And Wilkens. He was waiting at the top of the mountain, and followed her when she ran. He threw her off." Her words were cut off by a loud sharp slap.

Jarrett fought for control when Gomes came back on the line. "How do I know you won't kill us both, even if I get the money?"

"Killing cops gets some people very angry. Extradition and all that. A head start will do just fine."

"I don't believe you."

"That's the best part, it doesn't matter what you believe."

Footsteps outside the motel door twisted Jarrett around. He saw the light change under the door and drew his Medusa.

Gomes's voice came through the receiver again. "Hurry, Jarrett. Your friend is looking very lovely at the moment."

A click ended the connection.

Jarrett gripped the phone as tightly as if it were Gomes's neck, then put it down. He slipped to the door and placed his hand on the knob, and jerked it open.

A tall, gaunt man was caught standing there, his gaze riveted to the barrel pointing at his right eye. "Take it easy, mister," he said with a quivering mouth. He couldn't stop looking at the pistol.

Jarrett recognized him as the night manager and lowered the muzzle. "What the hell do you want?" He grasped the man's shoulder to hold him in place and stuck his head outside, looking right and left. No one else was around.

"A man paid me to give this to you. I don't want any trouble," the manager stammered. He held a box that could have contained shoes and was tied with a ribbon.

Jarrett took his hand off him, and he backed away a few steps. The box weighed almost nothing, too light for an explosive device. He holstered his gun and said, "Take off."

The manager managed an obedient salute and scampered away.

Jarrett stepped back into the room from the doorway where he was backlighted and undid the bow cautiously. The container was a plain cardboard box with no markings on it. He slipped off the lid. There was a small note card on top of tissue paper inside, the kind that comes with flowers. The note read, "*Tempus fugit.*"

Under the tissue paper the shoebox was filled to overflowing with human hair, long copper brown clumps.

He could smell the jasmine.

65

"We spoke yesterday at the bank, about Wesley Gomes," Jarrett stated, as contritely as possible.

"Couldn't it wait?" Scott McVicker said in a sleep-thickened voice.

"Someone's life is at stake. You're the only one who can help."

A long pause, then, "Go on."

"Gomes is holding the kidnapped teacher for ransom. He killed Elaine Wilkens and the young boy in Knollwood. And probably a police officer. I know where he is and what he wants."

"My God." There was a long gap, then McVicker said, "You really think Gomes will kill her? I can't believe—"

"He has nothing to lose."

"Where is he?"

"I can't tell you. Or the police. His threats were very clear on that."

"What does he want, money?"

There was no way to cushion the blow. Either he would or he wouldn't. "A million in untraceable bills. He says he knows which ones they are. I have less than an hour to put it together, no time to go through red tape. He's counting on that."

McVicker made a distressed sound, but didn't give an automatic *no.*

"It's presumptuous to think I can solve your problem. Maybe if I talked to him—"

"Not an option."

"You understand it's not my money. It belongs to depositors, other institutions. I don't have the legal authority."

"I know. It's a hard call."

A period of silence was followed by "It's a lot to ask. I'd need time."

"I wish I could give it to you. The deadline is an hour, and I've just spent a few more minutes of it."

"Jesus."

Disastrous repercussions had to be looming in McVicker's mind if he lost the million dollars. "You'll get the money back. I don't plan on using it, but I have to show up with it."

"Can you guarantee that?"

Jarrett was tempted to lie. "No, I can't."

"Too bad. I was hoping you'd say you could. That way it would have made it easy for me not to trust you." He let out a heavy breath. "What do you want me to do?"

"Meet me at the bank as soon as you can. I'll need the bills and something to carry them in."

"I'll try. I don't know if this can happen, but I'll try. At the very least I'll need to document this with your superior in L.A., otherwise I can't help you. And that's an absolute, too."

"You mind if I ask what for?"

"For one thing, to make sure you exist. I'm not giving a million dollars to someone who doesn't check out."

"Good point," Jarrett allowed. He could imagine Stryker's reaction to the bank president's message, but had no choice. "No problem. I'll give him a call and your phone number," he said, casting his eyes heavenward.

"No, tell me his name. I'll get in touch with him."

McVicker didn't get to be a bank president by accident. Jarrett gave him Stryker's name and his private phone number. McVicker also insisted on the number of the LAPD headquarters.

"He won't know enough to go along with this, but at least you'll get a witness out of it," Jarrett added.

"Better than nothing. It won't get me off the hook if I have to tell our shareholders I gave a million dollars of bank money to a murderer, but it's better than nothing." The sound of a match igniting and McVicker sucking in smoke said he was getting hooked again. "Damn it, I can't believe I'm agreeing to this. I've only known you for ten minutes."

"If you need another rationale, there's a good chance you'll get Gomes out of the deal."

"If you check out, I'll see you at the bank in a half hour," he said wearily.

"Could you make it twenty-five minutes?"

"As soon as I can, goddamn it!"

Jarrett put down the phone gingerly and uttered a silent prayer of thanksgiving.

66

The early-hour meeting with the bank president went one up on Fellini for surrealism.

Arriving with his personal set of barrel keys, and the disarming code for the alarm system, McVicker led Jarrett into the dim building. The man who accompanied them was an austere silver-haired vice-president who'd worn a tie and a ghostly pallor for the occasion. He carried a simple tan gym bag and made Jarrett sign a legal form before admitting him to the vault. A few minutes later he counted and handed over a million dollars in cash, including every small bill he had on hand.

McVicker had contacted Stryker at home after verifying that he was a chief of detectives at headquarters. After a lengthy dose of bombast about Jarrett, Stryker informed McVicker that if anything went wrong with his favorite detective's plan he was on his own—as if he even had to say it.

Pacified by proof of Jarrett's legitimacy, McVicker agreed to go ahead. His need to find Gomes and justice, plus his basic human decency, reminded Jarrett of Haucklin, God rest his soul.

When he was alone in his Explorer with McVicker's

money, Jarrett stepped on the gas and drove through the deserted streets of Knollwood, past houses spotlighted to show their stately lines and the bounty of their landscaped acres. A cluster of bushes that fronted one home was draped with silver foil balloons, the remnants of a recent birthday party. It was nice to know that joy and gaiety were still being celebrated somewhere.

Eventually, an opening in the trees showed the large brick middle school building. A lone car was parked in front of the main entrance, the only one in the area. If it was Gomes's car, the audacity of parking in plain view was the hallmark of a killer who knew he held all the cards.

Pulling up alongside it, Jarrett killed his engine and reached for the gym bag. He opened the door and stepped out, tracing the planes of the building with his eyes.

A combination image from the past and present played in his mind. Frank and Meg, father and daughter.

Don't let me lose them both.

67

Gomes stood behind her holding a silver aluminum case in one hand, the rope that he'd removed from her legs in the other. The case had been in the trunk all afternoon with her. For a long time she had thought it contained a bomb.

When her slow pace displeased him, Gomes grasped the back of her neck and shoved her shoulders ahead too fast for her legs to catch up to. Meg catapulted toward the floor and, with her wrists tied, was forced to break the fall with her elbows. She hit the cement and it felt as if she'd fractured them. She writhed in pain, but didn't give the killer the satisfaction of calling out.

"I'm only letting you walk out of the goodness of my heart," Gomes stormed. "Make it easy or you'll lose the privilege—and I'll put the gag back on." He gathered her loose shirt in his fist and hoisted her off the ground.

As soon as she stood she pivoted toward him and spit in his face. Gomes lashed out with a medium punch that caught the back of her skull and knocked her sideways. "Last warning." He raised his foot to her spine and used it to shove her forward harshly again. Only the wall kept her from a second headlong plunge.

On the way to Melacore's office Gomes shut off each of

the lights in the hallway as they passed by them. When they got to the principal's door he found it locked.

He rapped on the beaded glass that formed the top portion of the door, judging its thickness, after which he took a measured step back and sent his foot crashing into the lock. The metal held, but the glass exploded into the room. He reached inside, turned the latch, and the door swung open.

With the help of a final push, Meg stumbled into the first of the two rooms. The office was the school's nerve center, with computers and copiers, a fax, and desks for administrative assistants. The back wall contained a large bulletin board, next to it various switches for temperature control, fire and theft alarm systems, passing chimes.

Gomes guided her to the door of the principal's private office, which connected to the front room, and this knob turned with a soft click. Inside, Meg was directed to sit in Melacore's oversized desk chair, and Gomes used the rope he'd removed from her ankles to retie them.

"They know about you," she said, desperately searching for a way to reason with a murderer. "You could still get away."

He ignored her and put his silver case on the desk in front of her. He opened three locks. If it was a bomb, she guessed that he was about to arm it.

"They know you killed Mrs. Wilkens," she tried again. She thought of Augie Templeton but was afraid to say his name out loud and remind Gomes of his hideous crime against a child. It would only make it easier for him to murder her.

Gomes stopped working with the case to look at her with smug contempt. "My dear old aunt was off her rocker. It was a mercy killing."

"She was your family. How could you do it?"

He leaned close to her ear and whispered, "With a little push at just the right time." He smiled insanely, but he wasn't insane. "After the medicine didn't do the job," he added for effect.

He returned to the case and removed an object that

looked like a giant staple gun. If it was a weapon it was the strangest one Meg had seen, the size of the controllers kids used to operate TV video games, only much deadlier-looking.

"Air taser," Gomes announced proudly, holding it up for her inspection. "Amazing what you can get surfing the Net."

With a shudder, she got the general idea. She'd seen a demonstration of a stun gun on a news program and had been repelled by it. Electricity was her pet fear. Firing electrically charged darts into a human body seemed like an electrocution, and Gomes's taser looked like a super-charged model.

Opening a chamber in the taser's body, Gomes plucked out two triangular pieces of metal connected to black wires, then wedged out a cartridge labeled "Compressed Air."

"Fifty thousand volts does interesting things to a person's central nervous system." He glared at her maniacally. "Ever watch a wasp try to control its limbs after it's been sprayed with insecticide?"

It was obvious that he was visualizing Jarrett.

"This is crazy. Why do you have to torture him?"

Gomes's clear blue eyes spun in their sockets. "Because I want him to watch what I do to you, and not be able to move," he said matter-of-factly.

68

Three stories of darkened windows overhead, and good odds that one of them had a set of eyes behind it, watching him and his bag full of money.

The backs of Jarrett's hands bristled like they did when someone pointed a gun at him. If a bullet didn't find him there in the parking lot, it could easily be waiting once he poked his head inside. His best chance was to get out of the streetlights and remain a moving target for as long as he could. Other than that he was royally fucked.

Dashing forward he shot a glance to the roof. It was mansard style, too steep to walk on, with a low brick parapet that formed its perimeter. On another occasion he'd seen a narrow fire escape that led up to a second-floor library window behind the building, but the window had bars. He didn't have time to explore alternative ways in. His deadline was down to a few minutes away.

At the main entrance the heavy front door was unlocked and showed no sign that it had been forced. Using the suitcase, he pushed the door back and stepped into the hall, his senses alert to any sudden movement. The foyer was lit by a single fluorescent bulb that flickered slightly. There was no sign of Gomes and no niches in the walls he could see in which he might be hiding.

He felt the reassuring bulge of the Medusa, which was stuffed into his belt behind his back as it had been at the motel. There was a bullet in the chamber and the safety was off. It wasn't the most brilliant ploy, but if he got the chance he might have an instant to reach for it and catch Gomes off guard.

Jarrett thought about other times he'd entered a deserted building not knowing who or what was waiting. As nerve-racking as it always was, he usually had a partner for insurance. Now he was alone, and, in every move he made, Meg's safety had to come ahead of his own, the worst-case liability.

Darting ahead, he found that the first part of the hall ended in a T, forcing a choice. Entering the open section was the moment of greatest risk because a shot could come from either side. He had no idea which way to go, or why he wasn't being told.

Pressing himself against the corner he mentally flipped a coin and turned left, then crept ahead again. The wall opposite him contained a built-in glass case with drawings from art class and a bulb that buzzed continuously. One student had used columns to show perspective, another did a Cubist portrait good enough to hang in a museum. Not an ordinary school, not like the ones in South Central.

The corridor was a brooding tunnel that could easily hide a shooter. Jarrett debated calling out to him, but decided not to. It would only tell Gomes where he was, and there was still a minuscule chance that he'd gotten into the building without being seen. All he could do was keep walking, like entering a cave wired for explosives, and waiting to catch a trip wire.

He'd traveled another dozen yards when a loud crackle sent him to the floor with his hands over his head. The sharp noise came again, but this time it was like static from a public address system. Jarrett stood up and pressed his back against the wall.

A short time later a male voice boomed from an unseen speaker. *"Welcome to first period. We've been waiting for you."* The voice reverberated with a Satanic echo.

We meant Meg and him, Jarrett assumed. His hand found the pistol grip behind his belt, and he stood tight against the wall. The corridor was silent, but a hum from the speaker showed that the PA system was still on. The microphone had to be in the administrative office, a longer way in the opposite direction. If that was true, Gomes couldn't see him. He must have guessed where he was at the moment.

Jarrett looked over his shoulder in the other direction. The path was dark at the far end, at least a hundred feet away. It was a similar distance after that to the office, Jarrett estimated. It was possible Gomes had turned off the overheads and was waiting for his target to arrive.

"I hope you brought what I ordered, Officer Jarrett."

"Keep talking, lowlife," Jarrett muttered under his breath. Gomes was playing it to the hilt, ridiculing him, maybe to impress his prisoner. It had obviously become personal to him, something besides the money.

Jarrett spun around and started for the probable source of the voice. Being cautious, it would still take him a while to get to Melacore's office.

A bigger problem was that he had no clue what to do once he arrived.

69

With the help of a small flashlight placed on Melacore's desk, Gomes removed a roll of silver tape from the case, tore off a piece, and pressed it over Meg's lips, making a tight seal. When he turned his attention back to the taser, she tried to move her legs. By alternating the pressure on the opposing heels and toes of her feet, she was able to buy an inch of separation between ankles, but the next fraction of an inch took all her strength. She could work on loosening it some more if she was given the time. The cost would be a few more sections of skin rubbed raw, an insignificant price to pay.

Meg prayed that Jarrett had disobeyed Gomes's instructions and brought help. She fantasized that at any moment a legion of police would burst through the windows that Gomes had closed off with blinds. In reality, she knew Jarrett would never risk it.

Gomes held the assembled taser with an air of nervous anticipation, then bent down to place the empty box out of sight under the desk. Meg quickly twisted her ankles around each other to pretend to tighten the rope that no longer performed its full function.

He rose without lingering under the desk, his eyes intent

on the hall. In a moment he maneuvered the visitor's chair behind hers and sat down with her between him and the door, effectively turning her into a shield.

It was impossible for Meg to think of a way that Gomes would not succeed. First he'd torture Jarrett, then kill him. Her turn would come soon after that. All she had to work with was her chair and a small space between her ankles.

The muffled clicks of leather on the cement hallway floor chilled her to the bone. Jarrett had gotten there faster than she'd guessed he would. Frantic, she studied the desk. It was sturdy, with a metal crossbar that served as a structural support.

The spark of an idea flickered to life. Slowly, she slouched down in the chair, as if fearful of the approaching confrontation. Gomes took note of her feeble attempt to get out of the way with a condescending glance, then turned his attention back to his weapon. In another minute she had coiled her knees as much as she could against the brace.

The footsteps sounded as if they were only ten or fifteen yards away in the hall. At any moment Jarrett would be at the door to the first office. Gomes started to hum softly. He was supremely confident, and had reason to be.

When she guessed that Jarrett was almost there, Meg pulled one ankle against the other and felt the rope slacken. Then she straightened her legs all at once. Her heels shot forward into the metal, and the counter force moved her chair backward so quickly that it took Gomes by surprise. The hard back of the chair crashed into both his knees. He lit up with a loud groan.

Gomes needed both hands to push her chair away, and dropped the taser, which spilled harmlessly to the floor. Meg pushed the rope the rest of the way off one ankle and stood before he did. She started for the door and screamed a warning to Jarrett through the tape, but it was muffled pitifully.

Sparing a valuable second, Meg looked back and saw Gomes with the taser in his hand. He was loping after her. She bolted into the front office, hoping that Jarrett would charge in with his own gun.

In her rush, her thigh caught the corner of a computer table with force and she stumbled. When she regained her balance she was staring at the complex of switches on the back wall, and remembered that one of them was a fire alarm.

Changing direction, she raced to the metal lid that covered the switch. Even though her hands were tied, she was able to flip the metal cover open with her fingers.

Gomes's arm was suddenly around her neck, powerfully prying her away. Without hesitating, Meg shot her hands forward and slammed the switch with the heel of one palm.

For a heart-stopping moment the two of them froze and stared at the switch, waiting for the siren.

Nothing happened.

Gomes released her neck and shoved her head to the right, in front of another box on the wall. "Wrong one," he said triumphantly. He pressed the taser to her neck.

Meg closed her eyes and gagged, bracing for what she knew was the end of her life. She closed her eyes. Before the taser discharged, she imagined another presence in the room behind Gomes. Inexplicably, Gomes pushed her away from him with tremendous force and her head hit the wall. She slumped to the floor, fighting darkness.

After what seemed like an endless time, she lifted her head, but had trouble clearing her vision. She didn't know if she was hallucinating or had suffered a concussion. Gomes's face was contorted and there was a hand clasped over his mouth, the thumb stabbing into his eye. Another hand held his wrist and was forcing the taser upward. Gomes thrashed wildly, but couldn't wrestle himself free. His strength was no match for Jarrett's.

The pressure on Gomes's wrist increased, and the taser moved steadily higher. With unrelenting effort, the hand that enclosed Gomes's wrist rotated it a half turn and forced the front of the weapon to his temple. A finger moved from his face to cover Gomes's on the trigger.

The explosion came with a flash of pure blue light. Two small silver-tipped darts burst from the taser and imbedded themselves deeply into Gomes's skull. One entered at the hairline, another found a place near the center of his ear.

Gomes's eyes and mouth popped open simultaneously, but his scream was obliterated by the buzz of fifty thousand volts coursing through his brain and nervous system. Once open, his eyes never closed. His body jerked in a spasm of terrible pain, and he collapsed as if he were only a pile of clothing.

Meg's eyes followed the stricken body to the floor, feeling revulsion and gratitude. It took another second before her vision cleared.

When she could see again, she looked up at her rescuer in total incomprehension.

"Who are you?" she called out.

70

Hudson Perry had two phone lines wired to his house, one for police business, one for everything else. At 2:22 A.M. the latter was flashing brightly on the night table. His wife opened one eye, and he picked up the receiver on the second ring.

"Yeah," he growled into the mouthpiece.

"Sorry to wake you," Patrolman Roland said.

"What?"

"We got a call from Central Monitoring. Someone put in an alarm at the middle school. From inside."

Struggling to rouse himself, Perry had trouble understanding why that merited a wake-up call to him. No one was in the middle school at that time of night, not even janitors. Obviously, something had gone wrong with the circuitry, a false alarm, like more than half the reports to the fire department. "What about it?" he mumbled. "The fire crew on the way?"

"Yeah, Central dispatched them before they got in touch with us. That's not it."

The haze began to clear from Perry's mind. "Who the hell would be inside the school at this time of night?"

"Catallo is in the area and says there are two cars in the lot. One of them looks like Jarrett's."

Perry's invocation of the Lord's name woke his wife for a second time. He swung his legs over the edge of the bed and started to unbutton his nightshirt. His wife put a warm hand on his shoulder and wanted to know what was going on.

"Who's the other one belong to?" Perry barked into the phone. He cradled the receiver in the crook of his neck so he could start to get dressed.

"Dunno. Maybe Gomes," Roland said. "We don't know what he's driving yet."

Perry bolted from the bed, telling his wife not to worry, that it wasn't anything serious and that he'd be back within the hour. She knew from his voice that he was lying about all of it.

He was. If the second car belonged to Gomes, and Gomes had the woman, he had just bought into the beginning of a very nasty hostage situation.

Actually, that was the best-case scenario. If Jarrett had already tried to get to Gomes, he could be dealing with another homicide.

Or two.

71

Nearing the office, Jarrett brooded about the lunacy that had become his normal life. Two weeks earlier, on the other side of the country, he'd beaten senseless the animal who'd killed his partner. Now he was in a suburban New Jersey school, trying to do the same to a kid and cop killer. In his ability to find cataclysm, he was proving to be bicoastal.

Jarrett's gait quickened when he heard Meg's muffled cries not far ahead. The next thirty seconds felt like half his life. The gym bag felt leaden with a million in paper. He slowed to a crawl and inched forward a step at a time so as not to make a sound. He listened intently for a trigger being cocked, someone breathing, the squeak of a shoe.

Melacore's office was on the left side, past several classrooms that made up the science wing. Jarrett felt his way along the wall and covered the distance in the pitch darkness without losing contact with it. Eventually his hand moved to an open space where there should have been a door. He thrust his hand into the opening and waved it to the right. When he lowered it he found part of the door, the bottom, guarded by a jagged perimeter of glass.

Where are you, Meg? Where, Gomes?

He squatted, and the joints in his knees cracked like

small rounds of ammunition going off in the stillness. He duck-walked ahead into the dark room. The space sounded as a school should in the early hours of morning, eerily quiet. A faint smell of ozone filled his nostrils. Farther in the smell became more pungent.

On the next step his foot contacted something on the floor that felt soft, not furniture. The object was covered with fabric, and he recoiled at its warmth.

Please not her.

His hand moved over the cloth one way, then the other, until he identified the limb as a leg. There was no evidence of movement in it. Despite its warmth, he sensed it would never move again. Starting from the knee he traced the tibia down to the ankle and touched the stiff edge of a man's leather shoe.

Not Meg, he assured himself gratefully. *A dead man.*

He reached higher on the cadaver and located the face. The hairline was high up, the hair itself wispy and straight. There was a thin strip of metal wrapped around one ear that ended in small round glasses hanging from it.

The scream came from behind him, beyond the offices, and it was bloodcurdling. Jarrett bolted to his feet, needing light. He felt for the wall and ran his hand up and down until he found a switch. On and off, like a flashbulb.

The flash lasted long enough to make out the body. One side of its head had two wires embedded in it. A compact taser lay next to it on the floor, the source of the ozone smell. The corpse's hands were two tight fists, the mouth distorted and clamped shut in a parody of pain, eyes wide open. The tortured face of Wesley Gomes.

Which didn't explain the scream.

72

What in holy hell is going on?

The sound of glass shattering forced Jarrett's attention outside the administrative offices. Dropping McVicker's money bag on the floor, he sprang into the corridor and followed the sound. An ear-splitting scream tightened the muscles in his legs and made them work harder. The glass he'd heard breaking probably came from one of the science labs, he surmised as he ran.

There was now some light coming from the lab. It had been dark when he passed it before. He was maddeningly ignorant of who was in there, some new player who'd executed Gomes and now had Meg. Maybe Gomes had a partner he didn't know about. Or someone hated Gomes for another unknown reason. After all Gomes had done he was easy to hate.

Meg called out twice more before Jarrett got to the lab and halted at the doorway. End of the line. Every part of him tingled and was ready to work.

Steeling himself against a surprise that could cost him and Meg their lives, Jarrett jerked his weapon from his belt and held it near his ear. He peered around the open door and took a quick mental snapshot, then ducked back outside. The fluorescent overheads were on, and he'd seen a litter of broken glass on the floor. But he'd only seen the left side of the large room.

In another moment he tightened his stance and launched himself into the lab, gun first. When he saw the two of them, he let up on the trigger and went slowly numb.

73

Meg was a statue, her face ashen and bruised. A gaunt man with coal-black hair stood behind her, with only part of his face visible behind her head.

Something familiar about him.

The man had Meg in a chokehold, the kind police use. Her head was wrenched back at an unnatural angle, and it looked as if one quick move by the man could snap it off her torso. Her captor's other arm was around her chest, his hand holding a lit Bunsen burner a few inches from her wary, terror-stricken eyes.

The deadly flame made a steady hissing sound. A raised welt puffed up Meg's cheek under her left eye where the blue and yellow fangs had already come too close. Her attacker probably had a gun, but it wasn't visible.

Jarrett froze in place. He cocked his weapon, and pointed it at the visible part of the head. He searched for the best target, instinctively holding his breath for accuracy.

Where had he seen him before?

"Put it on the floor or she's dead," the man ordered. To demonstrate, he tightened his grip on Meg's neck and closed off her airway. She choked as he nearly snapped her neck.

Jarrett took in more of the room. The couple was facing

him from behind a low lab table fifteen feet away. One side of the table was flanked by a row of other work stations, smaller ones for students. The other end was near a set of shelves that reached up the wall. The shelves contained bottles of chemicals behind what was once a glass door. The door was shattered, explaining the litter on the floor. It occurred to Jarrett that he was standing in Errol Volpe's old laboratory.

Jarrett narrowed his focus to a small portion of the assailant's skull to the left of Meg's eyebrow. He just might be able to do it, he estimated. He'd taken the same shot before, but only once. A post office clerk in Pico had gunned down two fellow workers and was even money to execute a young woman he held in a death grip in front of him. That man had offered only a momentary glimpse of a sideburn, and Jarrett put a bullet up his ear before he could pull his own trigger.

But the post office clerk hadn't been holding Meg.

The time spent debating cost him his chance. Gomes's killer sensed his search for a target and dropped lower behind Meg. He'd made it an incredibly lousy bet.

"Put it down and kick it to me," the man commanded.

"First we talk," Jarrett tried.

The man tightened the vise around Meg's neck and brought the tip of the burner to her hair. A small patch ignited and shriveled. "I'll kill her right now. It makes no difference to me."

"Okay, no problem," Jarrett said. "No problem at all." He stooped and placed the gun on the floor, then gave it a shove with his foot. It slid for most of the distance between them, too far to get to it even if he dove. He wished he'd taken the shot when he could have.

"What do you want?" Jarrett said when the killer had the gun and Meg.

"I want you dead," the man spit back.

Jarrett stood too close for him to miss. He felt impotent. There was nothing he could do to save either of them.

"Just for the hell of it," Jarrett said with a studied casualness that appeared to unnerve the unknown man. "Who are you?"

74

The killer moved to his right, revealing all of his face, which contained a victorious and malevolent grin. "See if you can guess."

Jarrett studied the unappealing combination of features. An asymmetrical set of planes contained a deep scar that crossed the mouth and had healed white. The eyes were sensual, but in an indolent way. There was something all too familiar about him, but he couldn't get to it. "Doesn't ring a bell," Jarrett answered coolly.

"The name is Vasquez, Domingo Vasquez."

Meg stiffened in recognition, at the same instant Jarrett did. The night at the warehouse, when Frank had been murdered, flashed back into Jarrett's mind. Julio was the brother, the one who'd reached out of the shadows and cut Frank's throat, the one Jarrett finally caught at the studio. Domingo was the leader, the one they'd come for, and his reputation for cruelty made his brother's seem trivial, he remembered from his rap sheet. He'd once eviscerated a rival while the young man's family was forced to watch. Domingo was out there somewhere beyond sociopathic, a genre all his own. He'd have no problem torturing and killing Meg and him. He'd prefer that to a simple and unsatisfying double execution.

Frank's dying words, *Look after my daughter,* and this was how well he'd done it.

"I'll give you a million in cash if you let her go. No questions asked. I swear I won't follow."

Vasquez looked at him studiously for a second, then was amused. "What do you ·think, I got here by accident? That I haven't been watching you and that other crazy fucker for days? I already know about the money." He spit on the floor, as if to seal his decree with his saliva. "Why do you think you're still alive after what you did to my brother?"

"You killed the man in the state park?" Jarrett asked, already knowing the answer. All at once the grisly way Haucklin had been murdered was easier to understand.

"I thought it was you. But now I got the real thing."

Without warning, Meg bucked in Vasquez's hold and let out an outraged cry. She twisted in his grasp and was able to get an elbow up into his face. Vasquez winced at the feeble blow, and for a moment his gun hand arched up into the air. Jarrett started for him, but checked up quickly when he saw how fast Vasquez recovered.

"I don't need this shit," the killer shouted. He lifted Meg effortlessly off the ground and sent her flying into the glass shelves. Her forehead struck part of the frame and rocked the entire unit. She went down with a gash over one eye. When she hit the floor she tried to roll over onto her back but couldn't.

Vasquez trained the pistol on Jarrett and raised the torch in his direction. "Give me your face, or she says hello to her father."

"I don't think you want to—" Jarrett started to say, but the gun barked once before he could finish, and a white hot spear sliced in and out of the fleshy part of his thigh. Jarrett clutched it and fell forward.

"Get up," Vasquez said. "You're not dead yet."

Jarrett held his leg as tightly as he could, trying to stop the blood that washed over his hands. The limb felt numb, but the other one was still operational, maybe enough for a last leap forward. He'd have to risk another bullet on the way.

Face down, Meg blinked and sighted along the plane of the floor. She saw Vasquez's feet pivot away from her under the table. She rolled her head around and could see the shelves above her. On the bottom one a number of bottles of chemicals were still intact. She remembered one of the labels from high school chemistry. It had been hard to spell. Naphtha. Then, too, it had been locked up, because it was so volatile.

Jarrett was still down on one knee when Vasquez commanded him to come forward. He had a partial view of Meg through an open slot between tables, and out of the corner of his eye he could see her hand suddenly come off the floor and inch toward one of the bottles on the lower shelf. There was no way to signal for her not to try it. He had to keep Vasquez distracted.

"You kill us, you kill yourself," Jarrett shouted, and waited for the gun to go off again.

Vasquez pointed the gun at his good leg, but hesitated the instant he sensed something move to his left. He turned to face the shelves, but was a second too late. The bottle came up at him from below and struck the tip of the burner with force before he could move it out of the way. Instantly, the glass shattered, and the liquid inside ignited in a flash of dazzling light. The blazing chemical drenched his hands and splattered onto one side of his face, spreading the fire to whatever flesh it touched.

Vasquez screamed as a large portion of his upper body was swiftly engulfed in flame. Reeling backward, he aimed his gun blindly, and it went off three times in rapid succession, wild shots that shattered plaster on the wall behind Jarrett. In agony, he dropped the gun to try to tear the fire off his skin, at the same time bolting toward the door, howling and clawing at his eyes.

Jarrett reached up and hooked one of Vasquez's legs as he passed by, taking it out from under him. He threw a punch at his groin and connected, but Vasquez's momentum carried him forward and out of reach. He lunged forward blindly out of the lab. Still trying to beat out the flames, he stumbled into the hall.

Jarrett watched Vasquez race away and tried to stand. Together, his legs held his weight. One of them hurt like almighty hell.

Meg reached for the top of the table and hauled herself up. Her forehead was covered with blood.

"You all right?" Jarrett said when he saw her stand.

She moved her head up and down without conviction.

He scraped the Medusa off the floor and offered it to her. "If he comes back, use it."

She took it with both hands and didn't need convincing.

75

Vasquez sprinted ahead of him by a dozen yards in the corridor; amazing that he could run at all, Jarrett thought. The sickening smell of burned flesh filled Jarrett's nostrils as he watched him turn at the T in the corridor. Jarrett forgot about the fire in his own body and raced after him as fast as he could move, fueled by adrenaline.

He closed the distance between them by the time Vasquez reached the second stairway landing and launched himself up it. Stealing a fleeting glance at his pursuer, Vasquez tripped, then scrambled up faster when he saw how near Jarrett was.

With a sustained burst of speed, Jarrett climbed close enough to make a dive for Vasquez's ankles, which were just above him on the stairs. He caught hold of one and pulled it back sharply, collapsing Vasquez's body. Vasquez slid back down toward him, spewing curses and clawing at the stairs for a purchase.

Jarrett hauled him in with both hands, but Vasquez twisted onto his back and sent the heel of his free foot flying. The kick struck the side of Jarrett's head and he let go, tumbling back down. Vasquez got to his feet and literally crawled up the rest of the staircase. He was out of view by the time Jarrett started for him again. The clamor of Vasquez's feet on the upper staircases told him he was headed to the top of the building.

The pain in his wounded leg lit up his whole body by the time Jarrett reached the landing at the fourth level. He leaned against the wall for support and sucked in huge gulps of air. In the scant light the hall ahead was empty. It was half the length of the ones on the lower floors, and all the rooms were built on the interior side. Cartons were stacked up on that side next to an old-fashioned fire cabinet, the kind that had a coiled fabric hose built into the wall. This level had no sprinklers.

The opposite wall was unbroken except for windows that overlooked the parking lot four stories below. The only illumination came from street lamps, but it was enough to show that there was no exit except for where he was standing. Vasquez had to be up there with him.

Except it was deathly still.

Jarrett clamped a hand on his thigh. His jeans were soaked through with blood. He should have tied a tourniquet, but there hadn't been time. He limped down the hall as noiselessly as he could, thinking about the empty holster under his arm.

The first room was padlocked, so he kept going. The second had no door and nothing inside when he peered in. The third one was a few feet past the fire cabinet, and the door opened when he pushed on it. Inside was a large space that contained music stands and folding chairs. It was logical that band rehearsals would be conducted in a place isolated from the rest of the building.

Before he turned completely away, his ears pricked up at the sound of short bursts of breathing, and he went electric. With the rest of the room open to his view, there was only one other place it could be coming from.

Jarrett sucked in a breath and pulled on the knob as if to shut it. Then he abruptly reversed direction and slammed it all the way back to the wall. He could hear and feel the sound of bone splintering when it went as far as it could.

Vasquez bellowed in pain and bolted out from behind the door. He threw himself on Jarrett, and his superior weight knocked them both out into the hall. Vasquez landed on top, and tried to pin the lighter man.

Jarrett worked an arm free and sank his fingernails deep into the place where Vasquez's skin was burned raw. Vasquez howled and spun away. Jarrett made another grab for him, but Vasquez reached down the length of his leg, and his hand came into view holding a jagged-edged blade.

He slashed wildly at Jarrett, but the swipe went wide. A second one came too fast and cut a long gash into Jarrett's upper arm. Vasquez stood and leaned forward with his head down, circling, his knife probing the air. *"Por mi hermano,"* he shouted in an echo of what Jarrett had shouted on the television when he beat Julio.

"Your brother was a coward," Jarrett yelled back, calculating the effect. "The scum killed from behind."

The taunt had the hoped-for response. In a rage, Vasquez sprang forward again, but Jarrett had already focused on one small part of him. He grabbed his wrist in mid-air and shunted the blade to one side, at the same time sending a fist into Vasquez's belly. The killer lost his air with an oafish groan and folded in two. Jarrett hoisted him up by his shirt and slammed him at the wall and the fire cabinet, which was directly behind him. The back of Vasquez's head crashed through the glass, and Jarrett hung on. Vasquez's scalp was bleeding everywhere. This close, his skin smelled like charred meat.

Before Jarrett could strike again, Vasquez suddenly stopped struggling and went limp. He drew his head higher and looked at Jarrett oddly. A self-righteous sneer spread across his face and he said, "You still don't know, do you?" His breathing was labored, and he had trouble forming his words. "That cop . . . deserved to die. He sold you out."

The accusation took Jarrett off guard. For a moment he loosened his grip on Vasquez.

"The fuck he did," Jarrett responded, and shook the lying face hard with his hand.

Vasquez gathered himself. "Your partner . . . he took our money, then tried to take us down. He wanted it . . . both ways."

Jarrett's instant reaction was denial. One time, one time only, Frank Foley had been caught with his hand out, when he'd had a daughter to support, alimony, other bills he couldn't manage on cop's pay. But after that he'd changed. Jarrett had helped him.

"I gave him money myself. You were too stupid to know," Vasquez cried with delight, his head still wedged into the fire cabinet.

Not on the take, Jarrett tried to convince himself. Not his partner, not Meg's father. But for a fleeting instant, he'd felt a small shred of doubt.

Vasquez used his momentary distraction to act. With unexpected strength he wrenched his wrist free and drove his blade deep into Jarrett's thigh near the first wound. Jarrett roared and reached for the knife, but Vasquez twisted the handle and pushed it in even deeper with a vengeful cry.

Jarrett screamed again. At the same time he planted his good leg behind him. He let go of the knife and drove Vasquez back into the cabinet. Vasquez bucked wildly, but it was no longer an even match. Holding him there with one hand, Jarrett yanked the nozzle of the fire hose free and loosened a section of hose. With lightning-fast speed he wrapped it around Vasquez's neck and he slipped the brass nozzle inside the loop. When it was in place he pulled on it with all his might, and Vasquez choked.

Keeping tension on the hose, Jarrett watched without pity as Haucklin's killer struggled for air. Those soulless eyes had a tormented look, but his baseness could never be touched. If he went to jail, he'd be out again someday, to take other victims. Maybe he'd come back for Meg in revenge, as he had for Jarrett. He was crazy enough. Vasquez was beyond redemption. He deserved to die.

Out of oxygen, Vasquez's body slumped. Jarrett felt the pressure on the knife ease, then go slack as his adversary's hand came off it. Inexplicably at first, he drew back and looked down at his own fists. He studied them the way a prizefighter might, knowing them.

The greater realization came slowly at first, but when it arrived it struck with the force of truth. His fists were doing what he'd always asked of them, to become the messengers of his personal outrage, the swift solution to a justice that took too long and that he could no longer count on. A few weeks ago he'd used them in an unrestrained act of retribution for Frank; before that, more times than he could remember. He suddenly wondered if this was what it had come to, if this was how it was always going to be with him.

His consciousness left the moment and filled with a vision of his father. Thomas Jarrett's eyes were bright with his own truth and his unflagging respect for the system he lived to protect. Part of that system, the foundation of it all, was the law that he saw only as written. Jarrett now saw condemnation in those eyes, for what his son had become, for what he was about to do, and for the first time, the violent line between justice and vengeance blurred.

With the sound of Vasquez wheezing for air, Jarrett came back to the present and stared at a killer who lay limp in his hands. Tentatively, he opened his fists and took the pressure off the noose, then let go of him completely. Vasquez slumped to the floor along the back wall with the hose still encircling his neck.

Jarrett took a step back and waited until he was satisfied that Vasquez was unconscious. Filling his hand with the handle of the knife, he yanked it out with a contained cry, and dropped it on the floor. He turned and staggered another few steps across the hall to the window, where he bent down to catch his breath.

Jarrett didn't see Vasquez when he came to life, opened his eyes, and reached for the knife. He never noticed him get into a crouch after he held it again. Only when Vasquez sprang at Jarrett with a piercing cry of revenge did he react.

The second of warning was just enough. With Vasquez

almost on him, Jarrett lurched to his right as the blade came down at his back. At the last moment Vasquez saw him move and tried to shift his direction, but his body was already committed to its original path. Unable to stop, his momentum carried him straight ahead at the window.

His hands were up in front of his face when he burst through the glass. His body followed, trailing the hose that was still attached to his neck. When his legs disappeared, the rest of the hose unspooled rapidly and went taut an instant later with a sharp whiplike sound. Outside, at the second-story level, the noose jerked tight and Vasquez's neck snapped back at an unnatural angle. His legs and arms kicked the air violently, lessened their frantic movements, and then quieted. In a brief time, Vasquez hung lifelessly in the hangman's noose less than a story from the ground.

In time, Jarrett crept back to the shattered window and looked down. He heard the wail of sirens and looked past the killer's dangling body. In the entrance to the school's parking lot a police car came to a screeching stop, followed by two more with their lights flashing. All the doors of the first one opened just before the car stopped. Three of the officers left and scampered toward the front of the building, gawking at the human scarecrow above them.

The one Jarrett recognized as Chief Perry remained at the car and raised his sight higher than the dead man, all the way to the fourth floor. There, he was able to make out a man who leaned against the wall for a few more seconds, then turned away and was gone.

Jarrett limped down the three flights and made his way back to the science lab. From the door he could see the place where he'd lain after being shot and where his blood had pooled on the linoleum floor. Meg was sitting up on the ground, her back supported by shelves. She had the pistol pointed at the door, unaware of what had happened.

"Where is he?" she said with a shaky voice. Her hands were trembling when she lowered the gun.

"Nowhere," Jarrett said in a whisper. "It's over."

He went to the one knee he could still feel and pried the weapon from her. She didn't let go of it easily. Jarrett put the weapon in his holster and reached around her to stop her from shaking.

In a little while he felt her letting go against him.

EPILOGUE

Five days later they stood in a waiting area across from a packed Continental Airlines gate at Newark Airport. The previous morning Jarrett had announced that he was returning home to face a grand jury about the death of Julio Vasquez.

Stryker had actually been upbeat about the outcome. At the height of the clamor for justice, the local news media had dredged up old accounts of the murder of Frank Foley and quieted the loudest voices that tried to turn the death of a lowlife into a social cause. The oddsmakers were betting on Jarrett getting off with a censure, perhaps another loss of rank. But you never knew with grand juries. In any case, it was time to face the music.

The departure time of the last flight to Los Angeles had remained unchanged since they arrived, keeping the difficult wait to a minimum. There was still too much to say for either of them to start. In a while, the news that the jet was boarding was the final pronouncement of a decree that seemed preordained from the beginning.

Meg turned from the runway with moistened eyes. "It was always going to come to this, wasn't it?" she said as evenly as she could manage.

Jarrett reached for a loose strand of her hair, but his hand returned to his side without touching her. He felt he no longer had the right.

"Sorry," she said. "I promised myself not to do that."

"Go ahead, make me feel worse. Actually, I couldn't feel any worse."

"Once a cop, and all that, I guess."

"Yeah, a man's gotta do, and all that."

She took his hand and pulled him toward the gate. He let her lead him, battered by conflicting tides of emotion. It was one of those times, something wondrous and eternal, ending before it was over.

"This thing you have, to get the bad guys? Is this an incurable flaw, or something the DNA people can work on?"

Jarrett smiled a fateful smile. "It's in the genes, I guess. My father had it, and his father. If I had a son, probably him, too."

Meg stopped and turned to face him. "Have you ever thought about having that son? Or a daughter? That a time might come when that could become the most important thing?"

"The thought had occurred to me. Right now, I think I'd have a tough time sitting through Little League, as long as I knew what was out there somewhere, beyond the fence."

"Maybe someone could distract you from that thought," Meg returned.

Jarrett tried to answer, but all he came up with was a longing gaze.

"Yeah, I knew that," Meg said.

In another moment he surprised her and reached into his pocket. "I have something for you."

Clumsily, he fished out a shiny object and offered it. Meg took the smooth piece of silver metal and turned it over. There was an engraving of the Los Angeles City Hall on the other side. Under it was a serial number and the inscription "LAPD." Her eyes brimmed with tears.

"I thought you'd like to have it," Jarrett said. "It meant more to him than anything, anything but you."

"You saved it all this time?"

Jarrett nodded. He was fighting himself, trying not to hear the last thing Vasquez had said before he died, about Frank, about the money. The past was the past, whatever it was. The accusation would be buried with her father's killers.

Meg pressed the badge to her heart and a tear traveled down her cheek to her mouth. Jarrett cupped the sides of her head with his rough hands and tasted salt.

When their lips separated, she let go of his hand. "Gypped again," she said, and turned away too fast for him to see her valiant expression fail.

It was going to be a long ride home.